I0762154

# NATIONAL SECURITY

## Other Kate Killoy Mysteries

Fashion Goes to the Dogs

Puppy Pursuit

## Other Books by Peggy Gaffney

The Crafty Samoyed Knits

The Crafty Labrador Retriever Knits

The Crafty Golden Retriever Knits

The Crafty Bernese Mt. Dog Knits

The Crafty Newfoundland Knits

The Crafty Welsh Corgi Knits

The Crafty Poodle Knits

The Crafty Cat Knits

The Crafty Llama and Alpaca Knits

Knit a Kitten, Purl a Puppy

Do It Yourself Publishing Nonfiction in Your Spare Time

# NATIONAL SECURITY

## a Kate Killoy mystery

*Suspense for the Dog Lover*

PEGGY GAFFNEY

KANINE BOOKS

Kanine Books is a division of Kanine Knits Books & Patterns
877 Marion Rd., Cheshire, CT 06410



http://www.peggygaffney.com

Cover design by the author.

ISBN 978-0-9964531-8-9

# ACKNOWLEDGMENTS

I would like to express my thanks to my friends in the world of Samoyed dogs who have made my life full and happy. I would like to thank my editors from Wizards in Publishing, Kate, Kathleen, Kathy and Nan who made sure my book was the best it could be.

I want to thank Lisa Perterson and Cheri Hollenback who thanks to their wonderful Pele and Kehei, made it possible for me to have my wonderful Dillon.

I want to thank my son Sean for his support and encouragement and for making me laugh when I need it most.

# DEDICATION

To Dillon and all of my Samoyeds of Westernesse down through the years. You have brought happiness into my life, along with a *lot* of hair.

# CHAPTER ONE
## *Thursday, afternoon*

"Kate, did you get an email from Krystyn Machnicki this morning?" Kate's phone had interrupted her work. Since it was not quite eight o'clock eastern time, the call meant Cathy Harrison in Idaho was up early. Kate hooked the handle of the pressure hose she'd been using to clean the runs in her boarding kennel on the chain-link fencing and headed for her office.

"I haven't checked my emails yet. Give me a moment to boot up my computer. Not to get off topic, but what are you doing up so early?"

"I'm bathing puppies. I've got new owners coming to pick up their puppies from my litter today."

Kate opened her emails. "Here it is, just let me read it." She began to skim the email, stopped, and then began again, reading more carefully.

*Dear Fellow Members,*

*It is with regret, but I feel it is necessary to state the following members must not be elected to responsible positions on*

*the board of directors of the club due to their unethical breeding practices. They are not worthy of holding positions where they might influence important decisions. They are Natacha Grunsfeldt, Tracy Nikas, Cathy Harrison, and Sherman Wiel.*
*Krystyn Machnicki*

"Is she nuts? What the hell is this? How could Krystyn accuse any of you of being unethical? This is ridiculous. Have you called her?"

"I did. She says she didn't send the email. Kate, she was crying. Apparently her phone has been ringing off the hook with people yelling at her. The email must have gone to the entire membership. Since this is the first year the club has used online voting as well as mail-in ballots, many people have left it to the last minute. This email could affect the final vote. I don't understand how someone else could send an email from Krystyn, but she swears on the lives of all her puppies she didn't send it."

"Unfortunately it's not hard for a hacker with talent to do this, and it can often be difficult to trace them. Let me talk to Harry and my brothers, and I'll call you back."

Kate finished her morning routine in the boarding kennel, checked on her dogs who were playing or sleeping out in the exercise yard then headed across the lawn to her grandparents' home, also housing the offices of Killoy and Killoy Forensic Accountants. Her older brother, Tom, had moved into the house with Grandma Grace after their grandfather's death from cancer. When their father died of a brain aneurysm several months later, Tom was left with the responsibility of running the company.

# NATIONAL SECURITY

She ran up the steps onto the porch but, instead of heading for the door to the house, she turned right toward the entrance to K&K. There was nobody at the reception desk yet, but Tom would already be hard at work in his office. The door was open, so she strolled right in and sat in one of the wing chairs facing his desk.

"Kate, what's up? Nothing wrong with Harry, is there? You're still getting married?"

"Everything is fine with us, and the wedding is still on. I got a call from Cathy this morning about something more in your or Harry's skill set than in mine. A nasty email was sent to the membership of the Samoyed club casting aspersions on the ethics of four people running for board positions in the current election. The problem is the person who supposedly sent the email swears she didn't do it. How hard is it to steal someone's email identity this way?"

"Not hard at all, if you have some talent as a hacker. The problem lies in tracing it back to find out who the hacker is. Sometimes it's impossible. It could be someone in another part of the country, or it could be her best friend who visits her home on a regular basis. I take it you haven't asked Harry about it yet."

"No, he's in the air, flying back from Germany. He's due to land at Logan in a few hours then he's probably going to want to sleep for a while."

"After what he did on the case, not only trapping the guy online but then chasing him across Europe, I'd say Harry deserves some sleep before you get him involved with this. Will can't help you since he's knee-deep in classes, trying to finish his degree while taking advanced work toward his PhD. Tim is spending every spare minute at basketball practice. Why don't you ask Seamus if he'll check on it? I'd do it, but I'm leaving in three hours for four days in Austin with a new client. Seamus might find it fun to do some searching for you. He's toying with the idea of working for Harry after college, and this might be good practice."

Kate thanked him and wished him a safe trip then went to visit her grandmother. Seamus wouldn't be home until later since he, along with his twin brother, Tim, was in his senior year in high school.

Though Kate had loved her father and grandfather dearly, it was Grandma Grace whom she considered God's gift to her sanity. Grace would sit and listen but never judge. She allowed her to talk out any problem without trying to tell her how to think. But she was also a marvelous cook, so these discussion sessions were always accompanied by something delicious. This morning, a plate of sweet bread sat next to Kate's cup of tea. She loved these long buns made from the same recipe Grace used for hot cross buns at Easter time, only without the dried fruit.

Kate asked Grace about all her activities, including teaching knitting and crochet at the senior center. Then they discussed the wedding and the invitations. Grace had taken charge of those.

Grace, in her early seventies, appeared much younger and often seemed to have more energy than her grandchildren. She expressed horror on hearing what had happened with the email, especially since Cathy had been her guest earlier this month. She warned Kate not to let Seamus get so caught up in her investigation he neglected his own life. They knew he wouldn't shirk his studies; it wasn't his style. However, he didn't have an active social life. He swore his twin had gotten all the social genes of the pair when they were born. Kate knew better than to let him use working with her as an excuse to miss out on the many of the activities of senior year. She had avoided all the high school activities in favor of showing dogs, and it had left her completely unprepared when confronting life and love. Luckily, she fell for Harry, who understood and cherished her anyway.

On her way back to the kennel, Kate texted Cathy, telling her she'd have more information for her by the end of the day. Then she took Shelagh, Dillon's half-sister, a Liam daughter out of Kelly, from the exercise yard and, slipping a show collar on her, she headed toward the barn to practice gaiting, stacking, waiting patiently, and coming to perfect four-square finishes when they moved. Next came their favorite part of the work session—the games. Shelagh was lightning fast and deadly in all the games of catch and fetch. Her leaps to catch the toy before it hit the floor were even higher than Dillon's. Ten minutes of one-on-one jumping, and racing around with toys to shake and throw up in the air had her happy as a lark. So it was a smug bitch Kate let back into the exercise yard to brag to the others about how she had been spoiled.

Dillon and Quinn managed to take advantage of Shelagh's exit to slip through the door into the kennel. They followed Kate into her office where she had been working on the schedule for the fall search-and-rescue training dates. She decided she'd skip lunch since she was full of Grandma

Grace's treats. Wrestling her chair from Hecate, her twenty-five-pound Maine Coon cat, she opened her laptop.

But when she clicked on email, a flood of more than a hundred messages appeared. There was a firestorm of protest against the email from this morning. She started reading the angry replies and realized Krystyn had a serious problem. About thirty minutes into reading the mountain of outraged responses, Kate scrolled down the list of emails until she came to some from her cousin Agnes.

As a former supermodel who had become a bank president, the assumption might be made she would have become more staid and sober-minded. Not Agnes. She was still a lady on a mission, and her latest mission, unfortunately, was Kate's wedding. When Harry and Kate announced they were getting married on the Saturday after Thanksgiving, Agnes freaked. She screamed there wasn't enough time to plan the catering, much less a whole wedding.

Kate and Harry disagreed. Working around their schedule, they got organized. They sat down that night and made a spreadsheet of those whom they'd invite to the wedding. Then they chose a design for the invitation, ordered rolls of stamps and, at her request, placed the invitation and reply job in the willing hands of Grandma Grace.

Kate's brother Will had claimed the job of catering. He knew what they liked and was a top chef—though his career focus was on math. His contacts in food services would make everything work smoothly.

One of the dogs Kate had trained last year belonged to the owner of the town's only florist. When Dina heard about the wedding, she insisted on doing the flowers. In five minutes, she'd discovered what Kate liked, and all the floral plans were complete.

Attendants weren't a problem. Agnes would be her maid of honor. Cathy as well as Harry's sister Sarah would be bridesmaids. Rufus, Harry's best friend, would be best man, the twins, Seamus and Tim, would be groomsmen, and Tom would give her away. Kate insisted Agnes, Cathy, and Sarah work together choosing what to wear in the way of bridesmaid dresses. She'd only be looking at Harry.

That left the bridal gown. Today's six emails from Agnes, aka "Her Highness," would all contain photos of gowns from the top designers in the world, all of whom Agnes modeled for over the years. She could have her choice of any one of them. The dresses were all gorgeous, but Kate had been resisting the suggestions and so far was putting her off.

Unsure what she wanted, she but thought it should be something reflecting who she was. An idea had been flitting around in her brain for the last couple of days. Since she didn't have anything pressing at the moment, she decided to steal some time and play with it. She pulled up her design program, chose her measurements from the files, and began to fiddle with a possible design for a wedding dress.

Since the weather would be colder by Thanksgiving, the dress should have long sleeves tapering to a point at the wrist. The fitted bodice would extend up from a natural waistline to just below the bust. There it would join a yoke of knitted lace. The front of the dress itself would have a scooped neck, while the lace overlay would continue up the neck to just below the chin. In the back, the dress and the lace yoke would descend in a V to mid-back where a knitted lace rose would mark the attachment of a short train of the same knitted lace. The skirt would flow from the natural waist straight to the floor in front. However, in the back, it would divide into six gores, allowing fullness for dancing. Harry was a wonderful dancer.

As she tweaked the design of the hemline, her phone buzzing in her pocket jerked her attention from the fantasy creation. It was Harry. Quickly, she saved the design and answered the call.

"Hi, love. How's my bride-to-be?"

"She's probably a lot less tired than her groom-to-be. How was your flight? Did you get everything finished up in Munich?"

"It's all done. The police have the man in jail, and the client is delighted. I'm in a taxi on my way home from the airport. I'll do laundry, take a nap, and pack for next week. I should be on your doorstep by eight thirty or nine."

"It sounds wonderful if you're not too tired to drive here. In fact, I have some questions about hacking I need to ask when you get here. A problem has come up involving one of my friends. You go get some rest, and I'll see you later. I love you."

"Love you more," he said.

The connection ended, and Kate checked her incoming emails again only to find a posting from the Samoyed club president.

*Notice to all members.*

*It has come to our attention an email was sent to the membership, supposedly from Krystyn Machnicki. It was not from Krystyn. This is a case of identity theft. Someone, purporting to be Krystyn, sent out the email without her knowledge. We will be setting up an investigation. In the meantime, please do not encourage this malicious act by believing the contents or source of the email.*

*Robert Bicknell, President*

Kate's phone rang again. It was Cathy.

"Hey there. Did you see Bob's email calling off the dogs, so to speak?"

"Well, hopefully it will work. Krystyn is a basket case. She called to say she was taking her phone off the hook, turning off her computer, and locking herself and her dogs in the house. Her husband is away on business, so she's alone. I've got my kennel help coming here in an hour. A couple of us from the local club are going over to her place to give her some support. I texted her so she'll know we're coming."

"Harry will get here later this evening. I'll tell him the problem. Maybe he'll know how to find this person and stop him or her."

She hung up and was just about to take a tea break, when the intercom buzzed. Ellen wanted her in the design studio, immediately. Kate headed to the barn and jogged up the stairs to her studio on the second floor. Ellen Martin wasn't in her manager's office but rather sitting at the computer Kate used, on the work floor. Nobody was knitting. All the women were gathered around Ellen, talking in hushed tones. As Kate walked in, they all stopped and stared at her. Startled, she asked, "What's up. Is there a problem?"

"Everything is fine. In fact, everything is perfect," Ellen said as the women all smiled.

Kate walked around so she could see what had everyone's attention and there, on the oversized monitor, was the dress she'd been playing with earlier. She'd been so distracted when the phone rang, she'd saved it automatically to her design files. Ellen must have thought it was something new for the upcoming fashion show and opened it to begin planning what the design would need in yardage per size and color.

"Oh," Kate said. "I was just playing around with an idea. I didn't mean to send it over here. I was just rebelling against Agnes sending me so many pictures of these over-the-top dresses. I was fiddling around trying to come up with an idea of what was more my style."

"Oh my God, it's perfect," Ellen whispered. "We have to make it. I can have the yarn here by Monday, and Anna has just passed her test on the new lace machine. I think an ultrafine merino on the fine gauge machine make a fabric supple enough to flow. You will be the most beautiful bride in the world."

"But I leave on Saturday for the National. In only two days,"

"No problem. You'll be gone a week. We can fit it to you when you get back. This is our chance to be part of the wedding like everyone else. Please, Kate. Let us do this for you."

Tears filled her eyes. She was so choked up, she couldn't say anything, just hugged each of them, nodded at Ellen, and, before she started crying, quickly headed out and back to the dogs.

On the way into the kennel, she scooped up a stack of mail from the basket by the door. Leafing through the stack, she saw a letter from Krystyn dated three days ago. Curious, she tore it open, hoping for some insight on what was going on.

*Kate,*

*This is just a quick note. Something of vital importance has come up, and only you can help me. We will discuss the details at the National, but though I know this might put you in a tenuous position, I must ask for your help. Your being at the National is essential. I will meet you on Monday afternoon in the hotel lobby and fill you in. Don't tell anyone about this meeting. It could be risky.*

*Krystyn*

She read the letter again. What was vitally important? What did Krystyn want? How could meeting her at the National be risky? Why was it essential she be there? Kate was reading the letter for the third time, feeling no less confused, when her phone buzzed. Relieved, she saw it was Cathy again.

"Hi, Cathy," she said. "How's Krystyn?"

"Krystyn's dead."

# Chapter Two
*Thursday, evening*

Opening Kate's door at nine o'clock, Harry found her sitting at the kitchen table with all the other lights in the house off and a cold, half-empty cup of tea in front of her. She was staring at her computer with pages of notes on cybercrimes surrounding her, buried in research, the only oddity, a pile of used tissues beside her laptop and the sigh she emitted.

"Kate, what's the matter?"

Startled, she leapt from the chair and shot forward into his arms. "Harry, it's Krystyn Machnicki. She's dead. Murdered, and probably because of that hateful email."

"What email? Why are you sitting in a dark house, surrounded by printouts on hacking?"

Kate shivered and, drawing in a deep breath, slowly slipped out of his arms. Harry picked up her chair that had fallen over, and she sat. "An email was sent out early this morning, supposedly from Krystyn to all the members of the Samoyed Club. It claimed four people who are running for the board of directors have questionable ethics in breeding. One of those was Cathy Harrison. When people got it, they went ballistic. Cathy called to tell me Krystyn swore she didn't send the email. Tom said it wasn't hard for a good hacker to steal someone's email identity.

"Krystyn was so harassed by the responses, she called Cathy to tell her she was locking herself in the house, taking her phone off the hook, and bringing in all her dogs. Cathy texted her that she and another member of the local Sammy club would be at Krystyn's in an hour. When they arrived, the police were already there. They'd gotten an anonymous tip a shot had been fired at Krystyn's address. When the cops showed up, the place was locked. When they looked in the windows, they saw her body lying on the floor, broke in, and found her shot in the head with a gun lying by her body. They're calling it a suicide. It's impossible. I've known Krystyn since I was seven years old. Harry, she was murdered." Sobs racked her body. Harry lifted her into his arms and carried her to the living room where he sat on the sofa with her snuggled in his lap.

"We'll figure it out. We'll find out what really happened." He stroked her hair until the tears stopped. Then he pulled out his phone and hit speed dial for his assistant. "Sadie, sorry to call so late but a friend of Kate's died today. The woman, Krystyn Machnicki, was from...Kate?"

"Coeur d' Alene, Idaho."

"She lived in Coeur d' Alene, Idaho, and the police are calling it a suicide. Kate has known the woman for almost twenty years. She says it's impossible. Check into it and get back to me. Yeah, we're still leaving on Saturday. Tomorrow, we have to meet with Fr. Joe and get some of the wedding stuff done, and then we'll be on the road early

Saturday morning. Thanks, Sadie. Get some rest. Yes, I'll tell her." He put the phone aside and studied Kate's face, so pale and drawn. He lifted her and set her on her feet. Then, taking her hand, he led her into the kitchen and pushed her into a chair.

The dog dishes drained by the sink. Good, they'd been fed, so the chores were done. He opened the freezer and took out a bag filled with pancakes ready to be heated up then put some bacon into the microwave and started it going while he arranged the pancakes on a plate. He filled the kettle and put it on to heat, got down some mugs, and laid them out on the table along with butter, syrup, milk, sugar, plates, and silverware.

"I'm not hungry." Kate slumped in her chair.

"Well, I am. I didn't stop for supper, so the last food I had today was the meal on the plane." The microwave beeped, and Harry quickly moved the food to the table, poured the tea, and filled the plates. After taking a couple of bites and urging her to as well, he picked up her phone from the table and dialed Cathy.

"Kate?" Cathy said.

He hit speaker. "Hi, Cathy, it's Harry. I'm here with Kate, and you're on speaker. Have you heard anything more about Krystyn Machnicki's death? Kate is really upset."

"Yes. I asked one of the policemen where her dogs were. It turns out all of them had been locked in the mudroom, and her body was found in the den. Kate would know how impossible it was. She would never have her dogs away from her, especially if she were upset. Plus, I can't think of any time when Pavlik has been more than ten feet from her over the years. She doesn't even go to the banquet at the National because the dogs can't go. He has been her shadow for twelve years. Two are entered in the National: Yerik as an open dog, and Pavlik in Veteran Sweepstakes and as a special. I sent them to Karen for preliminary grooming so they will be ready to take to the show so I'll bring them along with my bitch special, Bliss. We'll show them for Krystyn. The police also said there was a handgun found beside her body, but as far as I know, Krystyn didn't own a gun. She worked for the NSA. They don't carry guns. None of this adds up."

Kate broke in. "Who's taking care of Krystyn's Sams?"

"Allison was with me. Since she's not going to the National, she told the police she'd be responsible for the dogs. I think they were relieved. Luckily, we had come in the van, so we could just load the six of them in. However, Pavlik wouldn't leave until they took her body away. When freed from the mudroom, he bolted through the house and jumped at the door to the den, barking and howling. It would have broken your heart. And the mudroom was torn apart, as though the dogs were clawing at the door to get out. The police were worried the dogs were dangerous, the way they were barking and carrying on, but we managed to convince the officer in charge they would be fine with Allison."

"Kate said the house was locked when the police arrived. Is it an older home or a modern one with all the bells and whistles of electronic gadgets?" Harry asked.

"Modern. I was traveling to a show with her once

when she remembered she hadn't left a light and radio on for the dogs. She whipped out her phone and pressed some buttons, and it was done. The program was even fancier than what you installed in your kennel and studio. She could even push a button on the phone and get a live video of the dogs in the house. With so much security, I don't know how anyone could have gotten in. Oh, there's Allison. She needs my help with the dogs. I'll see you on Monday, Kate."

"Thanks, Cathy. We'll see you as soon as we get to the National. Dillon and I have all-breed agility on Monday. Call if you find out anything else." Harry ended the call. He noticed Kate reach for her teacup and realize she'd cleaned her plate and finished her cup of tea. The pot was still hot, so he poured her another.

Harry held his phone, texting. When he lifted his head, she nodded toward the phone.

"I'm asking Sadie to find what company Krystyn used for her home security and if they still have the streaming video from earlier today. Some companies keep the video for twenty-four hours."

"What about her phone? If she could do all this from her phone, did they find the phone?"

"Good question."

A knock sounded on the front door, and Seamus let himself in. "What's wrong, Kate? Gram said you need my help to find a hacker using one of your friend's accounts."

"Oh, I'm sorry, Seamus. I forgot all about it. With what's happened, it just went out of my mind."

"What happened?"

# 24

# NATIONAL SECURITY

Harry placed a hand on her shoulder. "Your sister's friend, Krystyn Machnicki—"

"The lady who came to visit Dad? The one who bred her bitch to Liam's dad? She is great. She brought us all things from Denmark and Belgium."

Harry explained. Kate is upset about what's happened."

"Her dogs weren't with her? She was frightened and didn't have one at her side? I'm not even a dog nut, but growing up in this house, you learn things. If Kate were frightened, would she go somewhere in the house where there weren't any dogs? Hell no. My dad and granddad each had one at his side twenty-four seven till the day they died."

Harry counted a dozen dogs if you counted those in the kitchen and living room. Quiet and sleeping, each in his own spot, but they were there. Kate's mom, Claire, had gotten upset when a kidnapper had taken Rufus's son when he was with Liam. She'd accused Kate of being at fault because the dogs were supposed to keep them all safe. If Claire, the least dog-oriented person in the family, thought that, it seemed reasonable to agree Krystyn might have been murdered.

"Sweetheart, you're exhausted. We've got a lot to do tomorrow. Why don't you go to bed, and I'll get Seamus up to speed on this. Maybe he can track the hacker or find some pattern we can use. What was the name of the dog you said would never leave her side?"

"Pavlik."

"Right. Okay, off you go. We'll find out what happened, but I need your good, well-rested brain to do it." He opened the bedroom door and walked her to the bed, made her sit, let the dogs out in the small yard for the last time then took off her shoes and tucked her under the covers. Letting the dogs back in, he closed the bedroom door and sat down at the table, picking up Kate's phone again. He called Cathy.

"Kate?"

"Cathy, it's Harry again. I've just gotten Kate to go to bed. She's taking this very hard."

"I would think so. Kate has been part of the Samoyed scene for almost twenty years. She was very close with her since Krystyn used Liam's father to reestablish her line when it needed an influx of new genetics. Krystyn's top winners in the last few years are all down from Shannon Samoyeds."

"We've been discussing the fact her dogs weren't with her as being extremely odd. I wonder if it's because they would have stopped the person who killed her."

"Probably."

"I wonder if they would recognize the person if they saw them again?"

"Absolutely."

"Did you say you were going to bring Pavlik with you to the National? If the person who did this is there, it might help to have a witness, even one who can't testify in court."

"I'll be bringing both Pavlik and Yerik. Count on me. Let me know what else I can do. I leave early tomorrow morning."

"I will. Seamus is going to begin checking on the email. He can work while we're on the road. We'll see you on Monday." He disconnected the call.

"I've forwarded the email and all the responses and relevant texts to my computer," Seamus said. "I'll start first thing tomorrow."

"Here is my number and Sadie's. If you have any questions, just call. And, Seamus, thanks. This is important to Kate, and she's important to me."

"Me, too." When Seamus left, Harry locked up and went into Kate's room to get her out of most of her clothes. Then he undressed himself and crawled in next to her. It was hard waiting until the wedding to have sex. But Kate was a virgin and, as her grandmother had pointed out to him late one night, waiting was nothing compared to the family tradition of honoring their wedding day. Her happiness was too important to him to push her, especially since she'd agreed to move the date of the wedding up to less than six weeks from now. He settled in to hold her as she slept and saw Dillon's head appear on the edge of the bed. Harry leaned over the edge of the bed, reached out his hand, and scratched his friend's ears. The dog sighed and, lying down, went back to sleep. Seamus was right. Dillon would never allow something to happen to Kate. He'd never been a fan of locked-room mysteries, but there was no doubt. This was murder.

# CHAPTER THREE
## *Friday, morning*

As Kate came out of the shower the next morning, she spotted a folded piece of paper sticking out from under the corner of her nightstand. How had it gotten there? It was the letter from Krystyn. Sitting on the bed, she scanned the letter again. The words jeopardy and risky jumped out at her. If she showed this to Harry, he would try to stop her from going to the National. The fact her life had been threatened, they'd been shot at, and Harry had taken a bullet during each of two separate attacks this year would be reason enough to stay home. She wouldn't be able to fault his reasoning, but hiding in Connecticut wouldn't help her find Krystyn's killer. After folding and unfolding the letter as she thought, she refolded it and tucked it into the zippered pocket in her purse. Decision made, she went to get some breakfast.

They spent most of the day taking care of last-minute errands before the trip then headed to the rectory where Fr. Joe talked them through the Pre-Cana instruction, asking the personal but important questions required prior to a wedding. The priest had known Kate most of her life and Harry since February. He'd talked to Harry's priest and seemed happy with what he'd told him about how he'd grown up. They answered all his questions. He told them he was surprised they were waiting until marriage for intimacy, calling it unusual in the extreme these days. Once they'd gone over all the details of the Mass, arranged for the music to be performed by her cousin Darcia who'd trained at Hartt School of Music and sang in concerts with a number of orchestras around the country, and discussed the vows, they stood to leave. Kate asked Fr. Joe to have a Mass for the dead said for Krystyn.

"Was your friend Catholic?"

"I never asked her. But I've known her since I was a child, and yesterday she was murdered. I would like a Mass to be said for her." Kate kept a tight control on the tears that would spill if she let them.

"Then, absolutely. I'll let you know when the Mass is scheduled.

Harry put in, "We'll be away for a week, beginning tomorrow. Perhaps it could be scheduled soon after we return."

"I'll see to it," Fr. Joe told them, giving Kate his sympathy. He escorted them out of the rectory, saying he'd see them for their final Pre-Cana session on the Saturday before Thanksgiving. They walked to Harry's car and drove without talking the ten minutes home. Finally, Harry broke the silence asking what vehicle they'd be taking to the National.

"Oh, we'll be going in Charlie. I had him tuned up last week, so we're good to go. He doesn't have all the bells and whistles this car has, but Dad and Gramps swore by him. I just need to vacuum him out and make sure everything gets loaded. We can leave early in the morning and be on I-84 into New York State before rush hour."

"Charlie, huh? Okay, I'll change out of this suit. Then we can eat an early supper and load up."

"I have a question," Kate said as they walked through the front doorway. "I don't remember getting undressed last night. I remember talking to Seamus and then waking up this morning with you telling me it was time for breakfast." Harry smiled and ducked into his room without answering. As she pulled on a T-shirt and jeans, she thought about his smile and sighed. Less than six weeks to go, thank goodness because, if Harry was going to sleep with her, she sure as hell wanted to be awake to enjoy it.

He and Seamus were at the table when she came in from checking the kennel and sat down to the spaghetti and meatballs plus a big salad waiting at her place. She took a bite, closed her eyes, and sighed. Smiling into the green eyes of the man beside her, she murmured, "Yum. You realize I'm marrying you for your magic touch in the kitchen."

"In six weeks, you'll find out about some of my other magical touches," he whispered back.

"Yuck, impressionable minor in the room." Seamus laughed at them. "Well, Krystyn definitely didn't send the email. Whoever did, he didn't bother keeping his fingerprints off the style of the hack. However, he was smart enough to route the message through a bunch of servers both in the US and in Eastern Europe, making finding the gold at the end of the rainbow more difficult. I got the feeling the person who actually sent the message was not the one who wrote it. The message was first posted as a Twitter link from Krystyn's account. Less than a minute later, it was retweeted. Three minutes later, the message itself was broadcast and routed through the Samoyed club's server using their mailing list. I think it had to be approved by someone first. I'm checking on the retweets, but so far they're anonymous."

"Did you get any sleep last night?" Kate stared up at her younger brother who, like Harry, was tall, but also seemed to grow daily, going through the beanpole stage.

"Sure." I set the search going before I went to bed, and, when I woke up, the trace was there. All I needed was to sort the steps. It took about thirty minutes, but I'm getting faster."

"Don't give up your studying or social life, but if you could keep an eye on the hacker to see if he gets active again, it would help." Harry smiled at him.

"No problem. Thanks for the grub." Seamus helped load the dishwasher and left. They headed out so Harry could meet Charlie.

Kate saw his jaw drop when he sighted Charlie, a classic Class C Winnebago in beautiful condition with the words Shannon Samoyeds painted on the side along with a head study of a beautiful Samoyed very much like Dillon. She opened the door and stood for a minute, struggling to catch her breath as memories swamped her. She reached out and stroked her dad's hat that still hung on a hook by the door where he'd last left it. It was a baseball cap with Shannon Samoyeds embroidered on the brim and their logo above. Harry reached out and gathered her into his arms. "Have you been in here since they died?"

Kate shook her head. After a minute she said, "Sal took it in for a tune-up last week and to make sure everything was good to go. He fell in love with it and wants to borrow it to go fishing with his pals later this fall."

"How many miles does it have on it?"

"About four hundred thousand. We've crossed the country a few times, even though we only used it for dog shows. It can comfortably carry four people and six dogs. We won't be camping in it once we're at the show. However, it's the easiest way to travel since we can pull off and sleep anywhere along the way or stop for a snack, a meal, or to give the dogs a chance to exercise with ease. Gramps and Dad bought it when I started showing because it was easier for two men and a little girl to travel this way than to book hotel rooms. All the equipment we need for showing is here, from leads and collars to dog baths and dryers." She blinked back unshed tears. "So now you've met 'Charlie.'"

"Who was the Steinbeck lover?"

"Gramps. He'd like that you recognized the connection right off."

Harry sat in the driver's seat and checked out the few bells and whistles in the motor home. There was a TomTom GPS plugged into the cigarette lighter and an add-on backup camera covering the area not shown in the huge mirrors. "How does it drive?"

"You'll love it. It's like driving a big Ford truck hauling a load. It has lots of power, though you won't break any speed records. Charlie's a workhorse. He'll get us to the

National and back, in style and comfort."

"Great," Harry said. "Where do we begin? Do we hang our clothes in the closets so they don't wrinkle?

Kate opened the cupboard door nearest the front and showed him the typed lists of food, clothing, dog supplies, water, books, and cleaning supplies. She showed him where things like Kindles, tablets, and laptops, and chargers had been added by hand then took a deep breath, sat down in the passenger seat, held out a key to him, and asked, "Want to take him for a spin?"

He had the engine on, seat belt attached, and was shifting gears before she could blink. They pulled out from behind the barn, drove past the kennel and Kate's house, up the drive past the main house, and out onto Route 6. He drove around, practicing turns, parking, backing up, and getting used to the feel of it. Twenty minutes later, they pulled back into the driveway, swinging around in the parking lot in front of the barn and pulling up right next to Kate's house. Harry grinned like a kid at Christmas. He opened the driver's door and walked slowly around, running his hand lovingly over the big engine, until he reached the passenger door. He opened it and reached up to lift Kate down. Not letting go, he pulled her into a deep kiss. "That was amazing." He stroked her cheek and held her head still. "Thanks for sharing a bit of your childhood with me."

Overwhelmed, Kate stared into his eyes for a minute then whispered, "Welcome to the family."

# Chapter Four
*Friday, evening*

It took them two hours to load everything and check out the equipment. The side awning worked smoothly. The custom exercise pen Gramps had designed and built to provide a safe place for the dogs to play and take care of necessities was still in great shape. It only had to be pulled out from the under carriage storage, tipped vertically, and then opened. Reversing the process got it back into storage. Kate had been doing it on her own since she was seven, so she could attest to its ease. The extra crates for the show site had their own storage on the back along with compartments for the grooming table and arm and grooming box. By seven thirty, Charlie was packed, the list had been checked, and all the dogs were ready to go. Shelagh was coming back into her full coat and looking beautiful.

Since Kate spent most of her time showing Dillon, Shelagh didn't have a vast amount of ring experience, but Kate had confidence she'd show beautifully. Dillon, who never appeared out of coat, was groomed and ready to go. He was doing a performance competition of agility before showing in breed, so he'd need another bath later. Liam was going to show as a veteran. The final addition was sentimental. Ever since Quinn arrived, Liam had seemed to grow younger. Where he had been dignified, he was now full of beans. He played with the puppy constantly. Because of this, Kate decided Quinn would come, too. He was much too young to show, but his father and grandfather loved having him with them, and Shelagh treated him as her own puppy, something she'd yet to have. They would occupy the four crates built to fit in the cab-over space above the driver and passenger seats.

Earlier in the day, Kate had spent an hour with Sal, going over all the details of classes and boarding dogs. All but the beginners were given the week off. With careful scheduling, this meant the classes would end prior to the wedding, a necessity since she'd be on her honeymoon the following week. Ellen came into the kennel office to wish her well and inform Kate in no uncertain terms she was banned from her studio until further notice. The knitters were nervous to be making the wedding gown and didn't need the extra pressure of a visiting bride-to-be. She wished them good luck at the show and then returned to work.

While the men talked about traveling with Charlie, Kate checked her emails. The firestorm that had raged when the bogus email first appeared had turned into an equally large response to the news of Krystyn's death. Her husband had returned from his business trip to the Hague and had gone through all the official steps of identifying the body. He told the police Krystyn didn't have a gun in the house, but the police pointed out an online purchase for a gun made in his wife's name and shipped to their address three weeks ago. Her husband pointed out they had been away at Krystyn's niece's wedding at the time. So, the police were finally investigating it as a murder.

Kate's phone buzzed with Grace telling her dessert would be ready in thirty minutes. She closed out the computer and gave Sal a hug. Harry rose out of the wing chair in her office, and Sal told them to stay out of trouble as much as they could. She heard him mumble something about their track record but chose to ignore it. He mentioned the new security system he'd recommended meant he could see the whole property at any given minute and could keep track of everything from his laptop and phone. "Technology is great!" he declared. With what she'd learned about Krystyn's death, she wasn't so sure.

Blueberry pie added flavor to their talk about the wedding. Grace said she'd heard back from all but five people so far, and everyone was coming. She had been sending them recommendation lists for places to stay in the area, and it seemed as though most people had already booked their rooms. They wanted to be sure they could find something nearby on the holiday weekend. She walked them into her spare room where gifts were displayed on tables. Each was labeled so Kate could send thank-you notes. She'd also, with Seamus' help, made a spreadsheet with the information about the giver and a photo of the gift. Harry chuckled, "I bow to the organizational gene of the Killoy family, but where are we going to put all this stuff?"

Grace laughed. "You'll have to do what the rest of us did, Harry. Build yourself a big house."

As they were leaving, he asked Grace about the

Samoyed whose picture was on the side of Charlie.

"Ah yes Rory. He was our first home-bred champion," she told him. "Tom handled him to his championship in four shows. He was a fantastic dog."

"He looks just like Dillon."

"He's Dillon's great-great-great-grandfather. Tom would have told you their similarities are the result of good breeding and genetics."

Grace wished them a safe trip then handed Harry a cardboard box filled with snacks and meals, frozen for the trip. He raised an eyebrow. "They'll fit," she said. "I've had lots of practice." She gave them each a hug as they left. They headed back to Kate's house, hand in hand, not talking but enjoying a few minutes of peace and happiness. All at once Harry pulled them to a stop. He gazed around taking in the early evening half-light and asked, "Where should we put it?"

"Put what?"

"Our home." Their hands entwined, they strolled down the hill. Suddenly the door to Kate's house opened, and Seamus's twin brother, Tim, strolled out and toward them.

"All set for your trip? The mailman put your mail in our box again. I meant to bring it over yesterday but forgot. It's on the table. There's even a real card in there. Who sends cards anymore? Well, have a great time. Sal's already got a list of stuff for Seamus and me to do while you're away. He's the man who can't stand idle hands." Tim walked by them up the hill, laughing.

Harry put the food in Charlie as Kate went inside

and picked up the pile of mostly bills and checks. Sal could handle those. But, at the bottom of the pile, she found the card and checked the postmark, Coeur d' Alene, three days ago. No return address. As she stared at the envelope, the room began to tilt, and she fought to get a deep breath. Arms clasped her from behind, and she found herself being lowered into her kitchen chair. A minute later, a cup of hot tea was placed in her hand. Harry pulled a chair tight beside hers and embraced her.

"Tell me, love, what's the matter?"

"It's a message from the dead. It's from Krystyn."

Harry took the card from her and opened it. The front showed a fancy illustration and the message Happy Engagement. Inside was written,

*Dear Kate,*

*I wanted to send this, even though I shall see you next Monday, to let you know how happy I am about your engagement and upcoming wedding. I'll give you and your Harry a hug at the National and the major, and I will be flying out for the wedding. I'm looking forward to chatting with you. I have some information I want to share, but I have to check with a third person first. I'll see you on Monday to talk.*

*Love,*

*Krystyn*

Kate just sat, her hand resting on the card, submerged in anguish over the fact she'd never see Krystyn nor talk to her again. Her mind wandered away from the shock to the words Happy Engagement worked in an ultra-modern script. The design was in black and white with swirls and dots reminiscent of an Albrecht Durer drawing, only this one had been worked as a wedding cake. She was pretty sure Durer never drew a wedding cake. Kate was jerked back to awareness when Harry lifted her hand that held the teacup she'd forgotten was there, and told her to drink. The hot tea forced her to focus on the room and what was happening. The clock showed twenty minutes had passed. Harry was saying goodbye to someone on his phone.

She watched as he locked up, let the dogs out for a minute, and brought them back in. Then he turned off the kitchen light and, in the dark, walked up, gathered her to him, and held her tightly against his chest.

"You need to rest. We'll talk about this in the morning. I promise you, we will find out who's behind killing Krystyn. We'll see they're punished. But we've got twelve hours of driving on the first leg of this trip." He opened her bedroom door and Dillon, Quinn, and Liam moved past them to find their favorite spots. "Do you need me to stay?"

Her mind screamed, Yes! but she shook her head. He'd been good enough to let her wait this long. She wouldn't make it harder for him to wait till the wedding.

She wanted to say something but was unable to speak. He bent down, kissed her, and said, "I love you, too." Then he closed the door. She heard the sound of the door to the guest room shutting. After shedding most of her clothes, she didn't bother with pajamas but just crawled into bed. She knew she wouldn't sleep.

# Chapter Five
*Saturday, early morning*

Harry shook Kate awake at four o'clock and handed her a cup of hot tea. He told her breakfast was cooking so she should get showered and dressed quickly. The dogs were out. She flopped back onto the bed only to have the covers pulled off her. Harry stared at her wearing only bra and panties.

"Out. I'll get into the shower," she shouted, though she couldn't help chuckling at his smile. She showered, dressed then went to the kitchen table. Picking up the card, she slid it back into its envelope and tucked it into her purse next to Krystyn's letter. It was a new day. She would put sadness aside for a few hours.

Just after five, Harry drove Charlie out of the driveway and headed for the interstate. Kate was munching on one of Will's scones Harry had fished out of the freezer to thaw and have warm for breakfast. Once they got on Interstate 84, she passed the other scone to him then settled with her tablet. An email from Sadie with the information attached had arrived last night. She had gotten access to the video feeds from Krystyn's home, which had been automatically uploaded to the company's cloud's security server.

Kate opened the first file dated five days ago, and saw Krystyn sitting on the floor in her den, grooming Yerik while she watched Masterpiece Mystery on PBS. The second file showed Krystyn cleaning the whelping room while puppies tugged at her pants leg. Chuckling, she scrolled through the list of files that seemed to include seven days' worth. She found the one for the morning she was killed.

The video opened showing Krystyn standing in an entryway, pushing at the screen of her phone. The sound came of a door locking and the alarm being engaged. Krystyn then moved into the den with six dogs at her heels and a second camera took over as her phone buzzed. She stared at it for a minute. Kate watched her shoulders relax. The text must have been the one Cathy sent telling her she and Allison would be coming over. The house phone rang but she didn't answer, and as soon as the ringing stopped, she took the phone off the hook and flopped into a wing chair by the fireplace. All was quiet for a few minutes, the only movement the younger dogs playing a quiet game of tug-of-war. Then the camera changed again and picked up the front door opening.

A figure wearing a hoodie, jeans, sneakers and an Anonymous mask, stepped in and moved quickly to the door of the den. The den camera caught Krystyn glancing up. Her face turned white, ashen, and she gasped. The man walked forward and pointed a gun at the nearest dog. In a mechanically distorted voice, he said he would kill them all if she didn't put them away. Krystyn called the dogs and walked to the laundry room, each camera following her actions. She told them to go in, gave pats and hugs to each as they went by, and then finally closed the door.

The gunman ordered her back to the den, pushing her forward. He told her to open a safe, pointing to the painting of her first champion hanging next to the fireplace. She touched a button by the fireplace and pulled the painting forward, exposing a safe. Keying in the combination, she opened it. He told her to take out all the papers and flash drives. She did what he asked and then started to take out a jewelry case, but he instructed her to put it back and to close the safe. She shut it and, as she turned to face him, he lifted the gun to the side of her head and shot her. As she fell, he caught her, and lowered her into the wing chair. Then, taking her hand, he pressed her fingers around the grip and on the trigger. Then he let the gun drop to the floor. The cameras then captured him moving to the desk, picking up the papers and flash drives, and putting them into a plastic bag as he left the room. The cameras followed his movement through the house and showed him exiting the front door, after checking to make sure it was locked.

Kate drew a long, painful breath, only to discover they'd left the highway and parked in a commuter lot. "You've stopped."

"Kate, you've been screaming hysterically for the last five minutes."

She stared at him and then swallowed painfully. "I'm sorry. I didn't realize." She tried to swallow again. "It was so horrible watching him murder my friend."

Harry stared at her. She felt wetness on her arm and realized she was crying. She fumbled for the box of tissues on the console between the seats and blew her nose. He reached over, unhitched her seat belt, and pulled her into his lap.

It took another five minutes before Kate was able to stand and reassure the very upset puppies above her head. She opened each crate and hugged each dog. While she did this, Harry took the tablet and watched the video. Then, once the pups were settled, she handed out treats and moved back into her seat. She accepted a fresh cup of tea from the thermos Harry held.

"Kate, I am so sorry. You should never have had to see that. Sadie must have downloaded everything and, with the early start, I put off checking the files." Harry took her face in his hands and stared into her eyes. She gave him a small smile to reassure him she was all right, and he kissed her gently, leaning his forehead against hers for a minute before he sat back, started the ignition, and got them back onto the highway.

"Harry, I don't think her death had anything to do with the Samoyed club. I think the email might have been used by someone who wanted to muddy the waters of the investigation. Suddenly having more than a thousand people upset with you makes for a large suspect pool. But, from the video, it's clear she was killed for whatever was on those papers and flash drives the killer took. The police need to review these files and to talk to her husband. I've never met him. He isn't a dog person. In fact, I have no idea what he does for a living. I'm not even sure of his first name. Krystyn always called him 'the major'."

"Why don't you try googling 'Major Machnicki' and see what you get?"

She entered the search parameters into her tablet. "Here it is, Major Wayne Machnicki. It seems he is some high ranking legal eagle for the State Department."

"Well, it would explain why he flew home from The Hague."

"Apparently he was a JAG lawyer with the rank of major when he shifted to working for the State Department because his best friend was made Secretary of State."

"If they were involved in that world, I wonder if your great-aunt Maeve could tell us anything. She must have known Krystyn since they were showing Samoyeds at the same time. I remember her saying she was also still working part-time for MI-5 in those days. She might know something about their background. You should call her later today."

Kate tipped her head back and closed her eyes. Though she had slept last night, the force of what she had just seen had left her mentally slogging through quicksand, every step seeming to pull her deeper into a depressing morass. They were transitioning from Connecticut into New York. They'd managed to avoid rush hour traffic in Danbury, and would only be in New York for about an hour and a half before transitioning into Pennsylvania, making good time. Harry rested one arm on the seat, the other relaxed on the steering wheel. She must have blanked out when screaming because only the pain in her throat spoke to the truth of it. Thank God Harry was a steady driver, getting them to safety in spite of her histrionics. Her body relaxed, slowly. After a few minutes, she loosened her seat belt and leaned back so she could see the crates on the platform over their heads. All four Sams slept.

She picked up her tablet again and this time googled Krystyn to see what was listed about her. Her name kicked up many pages of articles. The most recent talked about her dog show judging and breeding. Many articles related to charity work she'd done since she retired. Krystyn had been a lawyer as well when younger and had even worked in the White House for a while. She'd been involved in some spy trial about twenty years ago and even won a case before the Supreme Court. Her main job seemed to have been working for the NSA. Kate sat back and breathed out slowly. She'd had no idea her friend, this person who would visit and bring presents for her and her brothers, this person who would talk dogs with her by the hour was a woman of such substance and notoriety. Kate eventually came to the article about her retirement from her role as chief council with the National Security Agency following an injury incurred preventing an assassination attempt on the wife of the Secretary of State. No details were given other than the fact she'd retired to her home in Idaho.

A phone call to Maeve was definitely in order. Her great-aunt knew everyone who was anyone in government in the U.S, England, and many other foreign countries, including Russia. Kate often felt if Maeve and Sadie were in charge of the world, it would be a much safer place. Between them, they had enough dirt on people to blackmail everyone of note on two continents into behaving nicely.

It was nine forty-five when they spotted the golden arches and agreed they both craved decadent junk food.

They parked Charlie and walked the dogs. Since it wasn't too hot out, they left the roof vents open for the dogs' comfort and went inside. They were arguing over who would do the driving for the next bit as they walked in, Kate insisting she should so Harry could rest. When her phone buzzed, she didn't recognize the number.

"Hello," she answered tentatively, holding the phone so they could both hear.

"Is this Kate Killoy?" a cultured baritone voice asked.

"Yes, who is this?"

"My wife called me the major."

"Oh, Major Machnicki. I am so sorry for what happened to Krystyn. She was my good friend. I've known her for most of my life. The man who murdered her should rot in hell."

"If you know for sure she was murdered, then your information is further along than what has been given to me by the police here. I need to talk to you. I got a message from my wife mentioning you the day before she died. It was in code, which was strange since neither of us have used the old code in years. The e-mail said if something happened to her, I should talk to you. I cut my schedule short and was leaving to come home, when the police contacted me telling me my wife had committed suicide."

"She was murdered. I have proof, but the man was in disguise so I can't tell who did it."

"We need to talk face-to-face."

"We're on the road now, headed toward Kentucky

for the specialty. Oh, you should know Cathy Harrison is bringing some of Krystyn's dogs to be shown. Allison is caring for the rest. We also thought if her killer is at the National, at least Pavlik would recognize him."

"Pavlik loved my wife more than life itself," he said after a pause, with an ache in his voice. "I will be finished with the police tomorrow and head out to Louisville. You have my number from this call. Just phone me when you get there. You say my wife was murdered but it wasn't the only crime."

"You mean the papers and the flash drives?"

Kate heard the sharp intake of breath followed by a firm, "Tomorrow," ending the call.

Harry stared into her eyes. She didn't have to say it. It was happening again.

At the door of Charlie, he stopped and held her shoulders. "Are you sure you want to do this?"

"She was my friend. If we can find justice for her, how could I run away?"

He stared at her for a minute, searching her face then kissed her gently, opened her door, and helped her in. He climbed in and turned to her. "You're sure you want to do this?" he asked. Kate nodded, and he pulled out of the driveway and headed west.

She needed answers. Why did Krystyn mail her the letter asking her to meet at the National instead of emailing? She had no idea what she could tell the major. He could see the videos but she didn't know anything else.

# NATIONAL SECURITY

That left her with the most doubts and the biggest questions was "why her"?

# CHAPTER SIX
*Saturday, late morning*

Charlie easily handled the long grades as the highway ran west, over the Hudson River and on through Duchess County. Here, the scenery was open, rolling hills. Quickly they passed into Orange County. This whole area had been settled in the late sixteen hundreds and still had an air of age and permanence about it. They hadn't been driving long when a sign appeared announcing they were entering Pennsylvania. This would be the longest part of the day's drive since they would continue on I-84 until they reached Scranton then head south on I-81 until it met I-80 south of Wilkes-Barre. Once they were heading west again on I-80, they would be in the vast stretches of forest populating northern Pennsylvania.

Harry had settled in to listen to a concert of the Boston Pops a friend had given him he'd not yet had time to hear. Kate opened her tablet but avoided the files Sadie had sent. Instead, she pulled up a program Tom had downloaded for her. It allowed people to design their own home, furnish it, place it on their property, and landscape it. He suggested she complete filling in her choices and give the finished layout to an architect who could turn their dream home into reality.

The directions explained she must answer some basic questions first and then the program would give them the shapes with which to begin. She could then add, move, or eliminate rooms, add wings to the building, and more. She began thinking about the number of bedrooms they would need. This got her thinking about kids and how they came about. Harry peeked at the page and grinned. She gently punched his arm, and he laughed. Soon she joined in and, for the first time in days, felt lighthearted. She started filling in the numbers, and soon the blueprint of a house grew on the screen. Lost in moving rooms, resizing them, adjusting the size of windows, and adding fireplaces, she felt them slow. Harry was getting off the highway.

They parked in front of an old-fashioned diner. After exercising the dogs, they went inside to eat, thankful for the privacy of being the only ones in the place at this hour of the afternoon. Kate ordered a chicken salad sandwich and Harry a cheeseburger. They opted for iced tea and then relaxed. Kate took out the tablet she'd brought with her, and Harry reached for it and quickly found the program.

"Hmm, five bedrooms. Now, there is a goal I can get on board with right away."

"Have I mentioned, in my family, it is tradition to get pregnant on your wedding night?" Kate teased.

Harry leaned across the table till they were almost nose to nose. "A challenge. I've got four weeks to plan my strategy."

Kate fluttered her eyelashes and asked, "Why, sir,

whatever could you mean?"

"You'll find out, woman. You can count on it," he growled, but the moment was interrupted when his phone buzzed. He answered, clicking on speaker. "Seamus, what's up?"

"I thought I would update you on the activity of the hacker who sent the message. I thought he would have dumped the phone but, stupidly, he didn't. He's been using it quite a bit. I found him doing searches on both Krystyn and her husband. He also is communicating with someone on Tor, but tracking him there is beyond my skill set and technology at the moment. What concerns me most is, he also has been searching the Samoyed club specialty. I still doubt he is the brains behind the operation, but it is suspicious he's checking on these topics. Oh, and just to let you know, Katie, your name came up in one of his searches."

"Have you found a location on him?" asked Harry.

"Yeah. Louisville. You're heading right for him."

"I want you to contact Sadie and share with her what you've got. I'll have her give you some of the searches she's working on. This will free her up to try to track the killer."

"Great. I'll call her now. You can count on me."

"I know I can. And, Seamus, thanks." Harry ended the call.

"You know my brother idolizes you. He wants to work for you after college," Kate told him.

"If he stays this quick and on the mark, he can

work part-time all though college. Work ethics like his are hard to find in today's economy. I intend to encourage it."

"He is a Killoy. I think it's part of our DNA."

Laughing, he glanced down at the tablet in front of him. "You've placed our home right next to your little kennel house?"

"I thought we could attach them, turning mine into a wing of the new one and using it as a home office. The front room could be for you to talk with clients, and the spare room could act as your office. We could link it to the new place in such a way I could go from the new place to the kennel without disturbing you and without having to reconfigure the dog exercise yards."

"I like the idea of a kitchen there for me to make tea or a sandwich when I'm working late."

"'We've got all week to work on this," she added then she finished up her sandwich. As they walked toward the door, Kate spotted a display case full of freshly baked pies. She reached into her pocket for some cash and asked, "Peach or strawberry-rhubarb?"

"Love them both, but you don't often find strawberry-rhubarb, so let's go for that. It will make good dessert tonight."

When they got back to Charlie, Kate tucked the pie into the small refrigerator and then quickly exercised the dogs again before she slipped into her seat and got comfortable.

Back on the highway, she mulled over the information Seamus had given them. "If the person who sent the text is in Louisville, then the possibility exists they might be associated with the Samoyed club and are there early either because they have a dog competing in herding, they live in the area, they are an officer or member of the board, or they're a member of the show committee. We're dealing with a lot of possibilities at the moment."

Harry scowled.

"What's the matter?"

"I just don't like it. This guy has you on his radar. If he's searching for people who are well-known in the breed and who would make a noticeable target, you're right at the top with a bullet, if you'll pardon the expression." Concern had darkened his eyes, and her stomach sank. First New York then Lubbock. She didn't need anyone else trying to kill her. Her lunch felt like lead in her stomach. She closed the computer and fished around in her tote bag for something to take her mind off danger and killers. She jumped when her phone beeped with an e-mail. She pulled it from her pocket and stared at the subject.

"It's from Agnes, and says it's more choices of wedding dresses. That's odd. She knows I've got my dress, so why is she sending me photos of others?" Kate moved her thumb to open the email.

"No." Harry shouted, knocking the phone onto the floor as though it were a snake about to strike.

# Chapter Seven
## *Saturday, afternoon*

"Kate, do not, under any circumstances even think of opening that email. Take the battery out of your phone. Do the same with your tablet and your laptop. Do you have your Kindle?"

She nodded.

"Don't ask why. Just turn it off completely. Get them all disconnected now." His breath coming fast, he scanned the dashboard of the motor home. He grabbed the GPS and unplugged it from the cigarette lighter then turned it off. Then he exited the highway and drove a twisted route in silence through several tiny towns with him constantly checking the rearview mirrors. Finally, they came to a small city with a mall. He pulled into the parking lot, drove to an isolated area, and parked, facing the entrance.

"Harry, what the hell is going on?"

"Hacking, is what. Grabbing power and control. Making you helpless is what's wrong. Spying on your every breath, your every move, your every thought, is what's wrong."

Kate stared at him then reached over and pried his hands off the steering wheel. Taking a huge shuddering breath, he buried his face in her hands while struggling for control and then said, "Kate, love, you know I've just spent three weeks chasing someone across Europe. Someone who tried to take down not only my client's corporation but the branch of the Navy they work with. The company became vulnerable when someone in their human resources department opened an email from her mom. When she opened it, she released a virus into the company's system and it took control. I stopped them only after tracking them back through their hack. It was sheer luck. Eventually, I tracked them to Germany. I worked with every cybercrime department here in the U.S. and across the E.U. In the meantime, the hacker stole both money and intellectual property that he later tried to sell on the deep web. As it works out, that is how I got him."

Kate stared at her phone. "The email?"

"Sweetheart, I know you don't follow the latest in hacking, but it's what I work with every day. Take my word for this. If you had opened this email, the hacker would have owned you. He'd have all your browsing history, your emails, and your banking. He'd be able to turn on the microphone in your phone and listen to everything you say. He could turn on your camera and, if you were holding your phone, see where you were. I had you take the battery out because if he found a way to get any control, he could turn on your phone and not let you turn it off."

Kate paled. "I think I should be reading the hacker magazines Seamus leaves lying around. Are we safe, now?"

# NATIONAL SECURITY

"For the time being, we should be off their radar. But they're not going to stop. Sweetie, when they sent you the email, they pinned a target to your back. I know you're determined to find out who killed Krystyn, but I can tell you it's not, definitely not, going to be the enjoyable trip to the National you were planning."

They quickly walked the dogs and put them back inside Charlie. Harry fought the urge to turn around and head back to Connecticut. Instead, he had Kate lock herself in with the dogs and told her not to open any door until he got back. Then he headed inside the mall. Checking the list of stores, he sighed with relief when he saw the mall was big enough to have an electronics superstore. He bought four burner phones and several items he could jury-rig into bug detectors and signal jammers. It was a good thing he hadn't had time to unpack his tool kit from his suitcase. It still held the high-tech gadgets that had helped him in Europe. He bought each of them new tablets which he would set up with hidden identities tonight when they reached the place they were going to stay. He needed to talk to both Sadie and Seamus again, and he wanted Kate to call her Aunt Maeve. He had to get ahead of this mess to protect Kate. He crossed the parking lot, checking the area constantly as he went. His panic and anger were under control, for now, but if anyone even glanced cross-eyed at his bride-to-be, they were toast.

Using a map from her father's massive collection, they were able to avoid the highway for a while and, when they got back on, they didn't see any sign of anyone following them. Harry found a campground to stay at for the night then he and Kate set up the fancy exercise yard her grandfather had designed. In under three minutes, the dog yard was set up, a water bucket put in place, and Quinn got his second meal of the day while the others got their evening snacks.

"How often have you traveled alone in Charlie?" Harry asked as they sat at the table eating Grandma Anne's wonderful chicken casserole and a spinach, walnut, and cranberry salad.

"Actually, never. After Gramps died, Dad and I cut back on showing. Then, when Dad's aneurysm hit, killing him, I was destroyed and stopped."

Harry reached across the table for her hand.

"Before Agnes dragged me into New York and forced me to change my life, I was just hiding out, cleaning dog runs and exercise yards, my life on hold. Much as you think Agnes is a pain most of the time, and I'll agree she can be trying, she pulled me out of a depression that was ruining my life. She made me cut my hair, change my style, take on a fashion show, and start living. It was scary, but I owe her a lot."

As she got up to serve dessert, she peeked out at the dogs who were all sound asleep in the pen. Putting a piece of pie topped with ice cream at each place, she watched Harry empty the shopping bag he'd brought back from the mall onto the table. Then he pulled a small case from the overhead compartment holding his stuff and unzipped it. He reached in, pulled out two guns that he set aside, and then three phones. He set a phone in the green case on the table and replaced the other phones and the guns in the case and back in the overhead.

"So, Dirty Harry, I see you're back to carrying."

"Kate, there is no way I am going to let you be harmed. I am licensed to carry in all these states."

"Sweetheart, I'm not complaining. We would have been a lot safer in Texas if you'd had a weapon. But remember, I'm not defenseless. I'm carrying, too."

"Darlin', Mr. Dillon here will never let me forget he is locked and loaded."

He leaned in, licked a smear of ice cream from her lip, and kissed her. Breaking the kiss with a sigh, he shifted his attention to the table.

"Okay, let me get these phones set up on our server and then you can talk to Maeve."

Sadie's voice came from the phone Harry had gotten from his bag. "Katie, I will set your phone so it can't be hacked by any of these bastards. Did your family ever have a nickname for you?"

"Yeah, but they haven't used it in years, thank goodness."

Harry's eyebrow rose and he tilted his head.

"Rapunzel," she growled.

Both Harry and Sadie laughed. "Well, I know where that comes from," he said. When she frowned, he leaned over and kissed her then asked, "Do you miss your long braid?"

"You mean the one that took five hours to dry every time I washed my hair and, because of the curl, tangled unmercifully? That braid?"

He reached over to touch her hair, and Kate leaned into his hand. "I love your short curls."

Her smile soon faded. She asked, "Do you think it's going to be as bad as New York and Lubbock?"

"Sweetheart, I'll admit, this one feels funny. There is something very strange going on and, to tell the truth, it's got me worried. Maybe once we get to the National, we'll be able to get a better handle on what's going on."

"Okay, Katie," Sadie's voice came through. "You're all set. Harry, keep me posted." She disconnected.

Harry handed Kate a phone with a bright-green cover. "Say hello to Maeve for me."

Kate dialed Maeve and put her on speaker so they could both ask questions. "Hi, Maeve," she said.

Maeve answered, shouting, "Kathleen Killoy, by all that is holy, what in God's blue Earth have you gotten yourself into this time? Having thugs shooting at you is one thing but, national security? Katie, have you lost your mind?"

# Chapter Eight
*Saturday, evening*

Kate and Harry stared across the table at each other and then down at the phone. "Maeve, what are you talking about? What national security? The only national in my world right now is the Samoyed Club National Specialty. Where did you get the idea I have anything to do with national security?"

"Well, first I find Krystyn has been killed and then the major, Wayne Machnicki, calls to inform me my great-niece is involved in a national security crisis and has vital information necessary to the safety of our country. He said he talked to you. You told him about the stolen papers and flash drives. But the most important piece of information was a note left with their lawyer from his wife telling him if anything happens to her, he should contact Kate Killoy. The note said you would have the answer."

"Maeve, it's Harry. I am as much in the dark as Kate. Two days ago, a friend called Kate to tell her an email has been sent to all the Sam Club members telling them four people running for the board of directors were unethical and it's supposedly from Krystyn Machnicki."

"Yeah, I got it, too, but Krystyn didn't return my call."

"Well, a few hours later, Kate heard Krystyn had committed suicide. Later that same evening, Tim brought by a misdelivered letter from Krystyn saying she had a problem only Kate could help solve, and she would talk to Kate at the National. Kate got me involved. We found out Krystyn had security video in her house. My assistant, Sadie, downloaded it for us and as we started out this morning, Kate watched the videos and saw a masked man enter Krystyn's house, force her to lock up her dogs, open her safe, give him the papers and flash drives but showed no interest in the jewelry. Then he shot her in the head."

"Oh my God, Katie."

"Since then, Seamus has been tracking the hacker who sent out the original email and has found he was active again, is located in Louisville, and targeting Kate. We had gone dark with communication until I could get a couple of burner phones and some equipment to check for bugs, bombs, and boogies who might be following us. Luckily, we're in Charlie, and it is completely low tech and can't be hacked.

The phone went silent for a minute and then Maeve spoke again. "You know, Padraig and I haven't been to a National in years. Who are you bringing?"

"Dillon, Shelagh, Liam in veteran, and Quinn, Dillon's son, is along for the ride."

"You do realize you've set yourself up with three Sams who could possibly qualify to be in the specials ring at the same time? You definitely need another set of hands. We'll see you there tomorrow. In the meantime, please take care. I've got a wedding to attend."

The conversation ended, and both of them stared at the phone on the table between them as though it had grown fangs and hissed. Harry studied Kate's face and saw a vulnerability she had never shown before. He had to do something and do it fast. He picked up his phone and called Seamus. "Hey. Have you made any progress on tracking the bastard who's hunting your sister?"

"Almost. Sadie gave me a quick course in TOR 101, or how to follow someone through the deep web. What I've learned is, though it's hard to trace his emails, he isn't hiding his browser history. I've found a bunch of sites he's visited lately on the deep web. I get the feeling this guy is a spy wannabe from his shopping history. I'm just guessing, but I think he got paid for this job in Bitcoin because he's spending like a drunken sailor, buying everything from listening devices to drones. I've got a program going on him, so the next time he buys something, I can trace back and find where he's sending the stuff. We'll find him sooner or later."

"Thanks, Seamus. Oh, before I forget. There's a trade show of these kinds of toys tomorrow in Boston. If you can get off from school, I think you should attend and learn more about them. Oh, and do you know a smart girl? You do? Fine. Take her with you. I've found women spot things we overlook. Right. Since I'll be out here, and I've got complimentary tickets, you can use them and learn. I'll have Sadie send them to you. Be sure to take your smart girl with you. We did this in my FBI training." Harry hung up. "Kate, who's Satu Mizutani?"

Kate gaped at him for a second and then grinned. "Go Seamus! Satu is his competition for valedictorian, and she's also, according to the guys, a stone fox. You've just sent them on the perfect date in Boston. You are my hero. Recently, his social life has been as empty as mine was before I met you. Spending a day with Lady Cool, should not only make him very happy, but it will raise his social status into the stratosphere."

He took her hand and pulled her to her feet. "That's the first real smile I've gotten out of you in hours, sweetheart. You're beautiful when you smile. It lights up your face, and those radiant blue eyes sparkle like the sea in sunlight."

Kate stroked his cheek. "I love you, and I would really love to stand here and snuggle for the next five hours, but it's getting late, and we still have pups to walk and a pen to put away. If we're going to get an early start, we'd better get to bed." Harry raised his eyebrows but only collected a gentle sock in the arm.

After a quick walk, Kate folded up the ex-pen and stored it while Harry got the dogs settled in their crates with biscuits. He had just closed Quinn's crate when Kate slipped behind him, lowered the table and, with a few quick flip of cushions, was making her bed. Harry stepped forward to put a case on the pillow. "I can sleep here, and you can take the bed."

"Your offer is gracious, but this bed only fits people under six feet tall." She ducked under his arm and into the bathroom, emerging four minutes later, in pj's. She hopped into the made-up small bed and curled up under the blanket. Kate pulled out the printout of the National packet from her tote on the shelf behind the bed. Harry left her then came back a few minutes later, shirtless, wearing sweatpants and barefoot. She glanced up and stared.

"I think if we try to get on the road by five tomorrow we'll..." Harry stopped as he saw her face. Oxygen stopped flowing into his body. He wanted to gasp, but the raw longing in her eyes stole his ability to draw in even the smallest breath. He couldn't break eye contact. He couldn't move at all. Then she dropped her gaze. He heaved in a breath but at the same time felt ripped loose and dragged away from his journey's end, his destination. He shivered. The loss left him abandoned and craving.

Kate's eyes were focused on her fists, now crushing the blanket. "Right. Five o'clock. If we get up at four thirty, we should be able to get the dogs done and be on the road by then, and we can eat later. Night." She dove under the covers, turned away, and pulled the blanket over her head.

Damn. Four weeks. He was strong but... This was going to be a very difficult week, no, revise that, a very challenging month. She'd promised herself and her family she'd wait until they married. Loving her enough to agree would seem asinine by some, but his word was all he could hold onto as he struggled to stay sane. He was going to need a lot of long walks or cold showers this week.

His phone beeped with a text. Opening it he read,

*Sadie and I have been going over the patterns building in this guy's texts. Kate is his new target. Be careful.*
*Seamus*

Harry stared at his phone, this shock better than any cold shower to his system. This was going to be much worse than New York and Lubbock. She hadn't been the ultimate target in those cases, though it didn't keep her from becoming collateral damage. But someone, for some reason, had her in his sights, and this person, as he'd shown with Krystyn, wasn't averse to murder. His every instinct screamed for him to jump into the driver's seat and drive as fast as he could back to Connecticut. Only two things stopped him, well, three things. She had dogs to show, she was determined to find out who killed her friend and, probably most important, if this guy really wanted her dead, she most likely wouldn't be any less of a target back home.

He slept eventually and woke before dawn. Harry emerged fully dressed to see the door open, Kate's bed returned to a dinette, and Quinn and Dillon missing from their crates. He pressed the button on the kettle, grabbed leads for Liam and Shelagh, and followed Kate outside. She wasn't far away. Quinn was dragging a branch as big as he was with him as he tried to catch up with his father. Dillon was stretching his legs, running circles around them. Liam got right down to business, as did Shelagh, after a minute. It was a cool morning, and after checking the area for threats, Harry headed back inside, snatching biscuits out of the bin and doling them out as the Sams eagerly jumped into their crates, turning around ready for treats. He made a mug of tea for each of them and brewed a pot for the jumped in and into his crate in two bounds. Kate boosted

Quinn in and lifted him into his crate. Harry passed biscuits over her shoulder and into the waiting mouths. thermos. He was just putting the milk away when Dillon He twirled Kate around and lifted her against his chest, his hungry mouth on hers, teasing and coaxing until her legs gave way. When he set her down and stepped away, he whispered, "I love you, and it's thirty-four days." He placed a travel mug of tea in her hand as he brushed by then stowed the thermos, fastened his seat belt, and turned on the ignition. Kate took a long breath, slid into her seat, took a sip of tea, and fastened her seat belt. "Thirty-four days, five hours and fifty-six minutes," she said, turning to stare directly at him. "But who's counting?" Laughing, they headed out, Kate serving as navigator with her father's map in her lap.

She was taking them on a shortcut that would connect with the highway farther down but would also take them through two small towns. As they drove, she reached behind her seat for the bag where she'd tucked the printout of the National information. Most was very familiar to her after so many years of attending the events. What was new this year was the site, and apparently the fancy building where the judging would take place was worth taking up two pages in the brochure. Kate read the information aloud. "The National committee announces, the building will be ultra-secure. There will be cameras everywhere, and secure areas accessed only by specific codes so expensive equipment may be stored overnight. The lights, air condi tioning, heat, ventilation, Wi-Fi, and exits will all be controlled from a central server. This automation will allow the building to be run with a much smaller staff, lowering the cost for the club to use it." Kate wondered aloud. "I never thought we'd need such extra security." Shrugging, she continued, commenting on what she was reading. "We've got about six hundred and fifty Samoyed entries in classes from Futurity to Best of Breed, plus herding, agility, weight pull, obedience, and rally. Normally, the worst thing would be a dog gets sick or a person falls in the ring or some other medical emergency occurs. Nationals are like big family reunions with lots of relatives you love and a few crazy aunts and uncles. Having grown up in the breed, I know most of the people who will be there. I know their dogs and their dogs' parents, grandparents, and siblings. So, I don't feel as though I'll be among strangers. That being said, after what happened this week, having Big Brother keeping an eye on my back may not be a bad thing."

Harry was silent when she finished. He kept driving, facing straight ahead.

"What?" she asked after a few minutes of silence.

"If we're making Orwellian references, I'd say, it depends on who's Big Brother."

# Chapter Nine
*Sunday, early afternoon*

It was early afternoon after jumping on and off the highway and stopping only for quick breaks for the dogs and to grab food, before they arrived at the exit to the host hotel located across from the show site. Harry had checked the paperwork at their last stop and therefore knew where the motor home should be parked. They walked the dogs and got them settled then headed inside. Dillon came with them as they went to check in. Kate had booked the room last November when the short window of opportunity to reserve one had opened. Not being in the host hotel could be very inconvenient and would definitely keep a person away from most of the action.

As they approached the check-in desk, two men blocked the way. "Kate Killoy?" the younger looking man asked.

"Yes," Kate answered, stopping with Harry on one side and Dillon on the other.

"You must come with us." The young man's voice was cold and firm.

"No thank you. Excuse me." She neatly sidestepped the twosome and approached the desk. "Kate Killoy, room with two queen beds allowing dogs," she told the clerk as she handed over her confirmation and her credit card.

The two men didn't have long to wait because Kate turned back to them holding a key card and a bunch of brochures and paperwork. She slipped one of the keys into her pocket, pressed the other into Harry's hand along with the folder giving the room number, and then turned back to the men standing in the middle of the room.

"I assume, though you failed to follow procedure and introduce yourselves, you are the gentlemen from the National Security Agency or the FBI. I will be happy to speak with you once I get my dogs into the room. Believe me, I am just as anxious to find the murderer of Krystyn Machnicki as you are. This is my fiancé, Harry Foyle, who will be sitting in on any discussion I have with you. And, in the interest of full disclosure, you should be aware Harry is former FBI. Now, it should take us about twenty minutes to get the dogs walked and crated. At that time, gentlemen, I shall be at your disposal."

Kate turned and with a quick wave was out the door. The younger of the men started after her, but Harry stopped him. "I would wait if I were you. You definitely want her on your side." Harry addressed at the older man who, was probably in his sixties. "You're dealing with Maeve Killoy Donovan's great- niece. By the way, Mrs. Donovan will be joining us later, as will Mrs. Machnicki's husband. If I were you, I'd just rest up. You're going to need your energy."

"Maeve's coming?"

"Oh, yeah."

"Thanks for the warning," He nodded, went to the nearby sofa, and sat down.

The younger man stared at him for a second then at Harry and said, "Screw that. Who the hell does she think she is?"

He took two steps toward the front door before the man on the couch said, "Stop. If you don't want your superiors to have you on the road back to DC in the next two minutes, you will sit, you will be polite, you will listen and, if you are very lucky, you will learn." He reached into his pocket and drew out a set of car keys, jingling them. "Choose."

The man sat as Harry walked out the front door to go help Kate.

When he rounded the corner of the building, he saw Liam moving across the grassy area next to the motor homes with Maeve striding out as though she were twenty-five. She spotted him and waved. He walked over and hugged her. "You and Liam work well together."

"Two veterans working in lockstep. Liam's an old friend. He was John's best friend. You have to realize not only did Katie suffer massively when my brother and nephew died, but these dogs lost their alphas. For all Agnes screamed and yelled when Katie imploded and shut herself off from the world after the funerals, for these dogs, it was a time to adjust to the fact, though the people they most loved in the world were gone, their kid, the child these dogs had raised, was still here with them. Tim told me she use to sit in the middle of the exercise yard for hours at a time, just holding one dog after another, hugging them, crying with them, sharing their grief. He said he wanted to pull her out and make her smile again, but the dogs needed her too much."

"When Kate loves, she gives her heart 200 percent, something I thank God for every day."

"I can tell you if I didn't think you were the right man for her, Foyle, you wouldn't be within ten miles of my girl. I know you'll love her right."

"I will. Where is Kate?"

"She and Padraig are setting up crates in the hotel room and getting the crew relaxed. I was just playing with Liam before bringing him up. I've got to see if I can still move well enough to badger Kate into letting me show him."

"Well, if you ask me, you're ring-ready. Oh, by the way, two gentlemen from Washington are waiting not so patiently for Kate in the lobby. I warned them you and the major would also be attending their tea party. Why don't I take Liam up to the room and you go entertain what Kate calls 'The Long Arm of the Law Club.' The lead agent seems to know you well."

"Sounds lovely. It's always fun to chat with old friends."

Harry and Liam reached the second floor and found the room right away. He suspected Kate, after so many years of doing this, knew exactly what to ask for in the way of a room when booking. The door was open, and

Padraig sat on the floor, playing with Quinn.

"What do you think of Dillon's son?" Harry asked Padraig as he strolled in. He released the catch on Liam's lead and watched him move into his crate, after stopping at the basket of chew toys in the corner to pull out an old, well-worn Kong. Harry could have sworn he heard him sign as he walked into his home away from home with his toy.

"I see a lot of old Rory in him. The nice thing about Maeve's being in the breed since there was a class for dinosaurs, you get to see puppies many generations down from dogs you loved, and their special characteristics appear again."

Harry turned to Kate. "Sweetheart, if you're done here for a while, your audience awaits in the lobby. Maeve is entertaining them for now."

Kate tipped her head. "I really expected them to come chasing after me to drag me back inside."

"The young guy started to but got told to sit and play nice or he could take his marbles and head back to D.C."

"Which he did because…?"

"Well, I may have dropped a few names."

Kate grinned. "You're an evil man, Harry Foyle, and it's one of the reasons I love you. Let's go before they have second thoughts and I have to sic Quinn on them."

The three of them walked into the lobby to find Maeve holding court not only with the pair from Washington but with a distinguished gray-haired gentleman and about twenty Samoyed owners who treated her like a Hollywood star. Donovan walked over and kissed his wife's cheek, and she gently excused herself from her fan club. Their small group moved toward a room the agents had co-opted off the lobby.

Maeve took the seat at the head of the table, and they all arranged themselves around it. She began by introducing people to one another. "Kate, I'd like to present an old friend of mine, Wetherly Brownridge. We worked together on a case back during the Cold War when he was a young turk in the cyber division of the NSA and behaving like James Bond, though with fewer toys. This gentleman is Agent Deshi Xiang from the FBI. You have already spoken to the major, Wayne Machnicki. Gentlemen, this is my great-niece Kate Killoy and her fiancé, Harry Foyle. Harry is former FBI who has his own cybersecurity company. Some of you already know my husband, Padraig Donovan. But before we begin, I think we'd like to offer our sincere condolences to you, Major. Krystyn was a dear friend, and she will be sorely missed."

"Thank you, Maeve. I'll admit I didn't make the connection when I first called Miss Killoy."

"Understandable, since this isn't your world the way it was Krystyn's."

Wetherly Brownridge spoke up. "Miss Killoy, the major has told us you have some proof Mrs. Machnicki was murdered and documents were stolen. May I ask how you, who I am told have just driven here from your home in Connecticut, would know what happened in a house in Coeur d'Alene?"

Kate reached into her tote and pulled out her tablet. With two clicks, she had the video playing. She turned it for everyone at the table to see but herself. She couldn't watch it again so soon. Every eye was on the screen except hers and Harry's. She watched the men react and knew when the murderer had arrived. She would have shared this more gently with the major, if she could have, but she had no intention of being bullied by Washington's alphabet soup. Maeve gasped when the shot went off, and the men flinched, but none of them turned away until the end. Kate handed Harry her tablet then, and he quickly asked for transfer addresses from the agents, the major, and Maeve, and in under two minutes, he had sent the videos to their laptops or tablets or, in the case of Xiang, his phone.

Once the files were transferred, Kate began to speak in a gentle voice, knowing the shock her audience had just experienced. "Harry and I discovered the house in Coeur d'Alene was very modern and high tech. Since I put a security system in at my home and businesses this past summer, I know how they work. We were able to find the company that owned the server storing the data from Krystyn's house. They still had video from that day. We acquired it just as we were leaving for the National yesterday and only saw the video then. This was the reason I knew what had happened when you called, Major Machnicki. I'd seen the video and therefore knew the papers and flash drives had been taken and Krystyn had been murdered. Harry and I are still trying to identify the man in this video as well as the person behind the email who so inflamed the Samoyed owners. We will keep you informed of what we find as we make progress."

"Miss Killoy," Deshi Xiang spoke up. "Pardon me for saying so, but this is not the place for an amateur playing detective to get involved. I understand you are here to run around a ring with your dogs all week. This is what you should do, and leave the investigation to the professionals."

Kate sat with her hands folded, staring at the men in silence. Harry, on the other hand, scribbled a phone number on a piece of paper and passed it to Xiang. "Dial this number. When you are connected, ask for the director."

The agent picked up the paper and quickly dialed, using his thumbs. He glanced at Harry when the call was answered but quietly asked for the director. A moment later, he frowned at Harry. Then he introduced himself and asked if the name Kate Killoy meant anything to the person at the other end of the call. For the next several minutes, silence filled the room as everyone watched Agent Xiang listen, with only an occasional "Yes, sir." He ended the call, gently placing his phone on the table as though it had grown fangs. Then he raised his eyes and focused on Kate. "Thank you for finding this information, Miss Killoy. We will be grateful for any help you can give."

"You're welcome, Agent Xiang. I'm sure you'll want to review the video. You all should be aware Krystyn sent me a note saying she had something to discuss with me and would see me at the National. Major, she may have been planning to give me the information she mentioned to you then. However, since the meeting didn't take place, I'm afraid I am as much in the dark as the rest of you. We have been able to trace the location of the hacker who sent the email. It was sent from Louisville. He either lives here or is at the show. If we get any more information, we'll pass it on."

Agent Brownridge turned to Harry and said, "Maeve tells me you have Sadie working with you, which I think explains the videos. Great lady." He smiled fondly. Harry nodded and told Kate she should explain about the email.

"On Thursday," she began and went on to explain what happened. "If you were to question every person attending the National this week, you would get the answer Cathy gave the police. It couldn't be suicide because she wouldn't do it, if for no other reason than the dogs. When Cathy was told the dogs had been locked in another part of the house, she realized it was proof Krystyn's death must have been something other than suicide. Dog people who are at all upset keep their dogs by their sides. Cathy will be arriving at the show later today with her own dogs as well as two of Krystyn's. These Samoyeds of Krystyn's have seen and smelled the killer. If he's here, anywhere on the grounds of the show, they will find him. They are the best witnesses, never distracted or fooled by disguise. They will smell out the killer."

# CHAPTER TEN
## *Sunday, evening*

The meeting broke up, and Kate and Harry went with Maeve and Padraig to get some supper. After their food was served, Kate said, "Why were those agents here? They didn't know Krystyn was murdered. Plus, they were expecting me. Why am I of interest to the NSA and the FBI?"

Harry's gaze traveled from her to Maeve and Padrig. Then he pulled out his phone. "Sadie. Any idea why Kate would be of interest to the NSA and the FBI? Hmm. Krystyn? Hearings? Got it. Keep digging. Thanks, Luv."

"It seems Krystyn had some information she was going to share with the NSA in reference to an investigation they are doing. Apparently the information was timely and would be pertinent to a hearing scheduled for later this month in the senate. Brownridge was assigned here to meet her, and Xiang came because Agent Brownridge's boss thought this might relate to an old FBI cold case. Actually, since Brownridge was an old friend of Krystyn, and Xiang is beginning to climb the ladder of advancement at the bureau and has been working on this case, I think they didn't expect a problem. Because of the nature of Krystyn's evidence, it was felt sending people who were already involved in the ongoing case in Washington at the moment would make good sense."

"Well, it explains why they were here to meet with Krystyn, but how did they get my name?"

"Krystyn told them if for any reason she was kept from attending the meeting, they should talk to you."

"So she thought something might happen to her." Kate shivered at the thought. "The only problem is, I have no idea what information she was going to give to these agents. I was hoping to spend time with Krystyn. She said she had something she wanted to discuss with me. Since it can't happen, I have no clue what to say to these men. I'm sure they think I know more than I do. Did you get any more details out of them, Maeve?"

"Not much, sweetie. It has something to do with an old case Krystyn was involved with ten years ago," Maeve told her.

"You mean the one with the spy? They think I'm involved with spies?"

"No, they think there's a spy after you."

"Oh, for heaven's sake. James Bond, move over, Kate Killoy, secret agent, is in the room? No, I don't think so. Why are they really here?" Kate asked, laughing. The others at the table remained silent until she felt the humor drain from her.

"I'm sorry, Katie, my girl, but it was all I got out of Wetherly before you arrived. I warned him if he let anything happen to you, I'd destroy him, but his concern is there already. Apparently, whatever Krystyn was going to tell you when she met with you here, would have involved the specific case which was vital to these men. "

"Yes, I see. But I still want to know, why me? I'm not a secret agent. Why did she think I could help her?"

"I honestly don't know. She was supposed to be retired, though, as I can attest, you never completely retire from the game. The only thing I can suggest is you talk to the major tomorrow. Maybe he'll have a better idea of what was on her mind. We know she was upset enough to ask him to come home early, and that was before there was an email."

"Which is another thing. Why did they send out the email? It served no purpose. Was it only to upset her so she'd be locked in her home when they wanted to come after her?"

They all turned toward Kate, and Harry asked, "Would you say that again?"

"Say what?"

"About the email."

"I only said they might have tried to upset her so she'd be home locked in her house." She paused and stared at Harry. "I wonder where she was supposed to be, making it necessary to get her to change her plans."

Harry didn't waste time but whipped out his phone. "Cathy, it's Harry and Kate. Do you happen to know what Krystyn was supposed to be doing the day the email came out? Was she planning on being home? She wasn't? Spokane, evaluating a litter. Thanks, Cathy. We'll see you in the morning." Harry put his phone away and glanced around the table. "Well, now we know why the killer sent out the email. It put her exactly where he wanted her."

"Oh my God." Kate grabbed Maeve's hand, feeling suddenly sick. "You know what that means."

"Damn, I was so hoping it was a simple out-of-the-blue distraction," Maeve said, her shoulders slumping as she sank back into her chair.

"What?" Harry and Padraig asked at the same time.

"It means the killer has to be someone in the Samoyed Club or close to the members who would know she was supposed to be away that day. Such an email would have made her change her plans and cause her to lock herself in her own home along with the papers and flash drives he wanted."

"When did you last talk to Krystyn?" Maeve asked.

"She called about a month ago. She told me how much she missed being able to bounce ideas off Dad and Gramps. Then we talked for almost an hour about the dogs. When she finished, we agreed to meet at the National. Except for the note saying she'd see me tomorrow and a card from her and the major congratulating us on the upcoming wedding, I've heard nothing."

They finished their dinner in relative silence, each lost in their thoughts. Harry and Kate decided to split one of the restaurant's monstrous desserts, a combination of brownies, ice cream, whipped cream, chocolate sauce, and nuts, with two cherries on top. Padraig and Maeve said they were full. They all had tea. It was getting late by the time their dinner ended, and they went up to get the dogs.

Exhaustion was catching up with her as she walked

Dillon and Quinn. Harry had wandered off with Liam and Shelagh, so she headed back to the room. She thought with all that had happened the day before, she wouldn't be able to sleep, but she fell sound asleep waiting for Harry to return with Liam and Shelagh. She remembered putting on her pj's and sitting on the edge of the bed, but afterwards… nothing.

Harry had found her half lying, half sitting on the edge of the bed sound asleep when he got back. He put the dogs away and pulled down the sheet and blanket. Then he lifted her, put her on the bed, covered her up, and kissed her gently on the mouth. It didn't wake her, but he did get a positive noise coming from her throat. Chuckling, he changed into sweatpants and, picking up his tablet, crawled into the other bed with a sigh and, after glancing at Kate sleeping peacefully, he began to do research. It wasn't hard to locate the case of the captured spy via a site he and Sadie often accessed when dealing with bureaucratic nightmares. He found details not available to the public, including Krystyn's case notes.

The spy apparently had operated under the radar for many years, managing to get access to a number of secrets. Though Russian by birth, he'd lived in the U.S. most of his life. When he was in his late teens, his parents had returned to Russia, but he'd stayed with a family who had sympathetic leanings toward the former USSR. The man, whom Krystyn referred to as Coyote, got involved with Russian covert agents during college and become more active following his graduation. He turned up at random spots around the country, doing mostly industrial espionage of documents and then disappearing. He only turned up on weekends, and was gone without a trace by Monday.

Other agents had worked on the theory he held a perfectly normal job during the week, and then traveled to and from the area where he'd steal the documents only to blend back into his normal job. Krystyn had gotten assigned the case in her second year with the agency. Because of her background, she was uniquely qualified to see a flaw in the previous reasoning. Her investigation confirmed it. Working with two unnamed associates, she tracked and confirmed he had been in a specific location of each theft on those particular dates. Once she convinced the agency she was right, she and her associates were able to predict his next strike and she caught him. It turned out the spy was a professional show dog handler, the perfect cover to travel to an area for the weekend and then disappear. Apparently, he was most annoyed because he was caught before he could show his champion, that day.

The Coyote was imprisoned for one year then traded to the Russians for an American chemistry student the Russians had accused of spying. Following his return to Russia, he covertly changed his identity and his appearance then disappeared. There had been nothing heard about the man—until now. If Kate was right, as he'd learned more often than not, she was, the man was probably here at the National, planning on showing a dog and appearing perfectly normal.

He glanced across at the other bed, watching one of her curls move as she breathed in and out, her face serenely beautiful in sleep. Though she seemed relaxed, two to one, her mind was cranking away on the spy problem, and she'd wake with two to three possible approaches to catch the man.

He loved her, but she scared him to death with the chances she took. Her sense of right over wrong always trumped her sense of self-preservation. He'd have to work very hard and get as much help as possible to protect her this week. She would not be deterred from her determination to find Krystyn's killer. He put his tablet aside and placed his glasses on the nightstand. Settling more deeply under the blankets, he was determined to sleep. He couldn't afford to bring anything less than his A game to this and, therefore he needed rest. Kate would be up early to get Dillon ready for his agility competition. Harry had never seen them compete in agility, and he looked forward to it.

# CHAPTER ELEVEN
## *Monday, very early morning*

Just after daybreak, Kate took Dillon and Quinn out while Harry walked Liam and Shelagh. They'd finished the necessities quickly, but Quinn wanted to play. She snapped a fifteen-foot tracking lead on him and found a deserted area. Removing Dillon's lead, Kate let them race around, and Quinn thought this was fabulous. Streaking after his father, he'd go to the end of the lead and tumble over. Dillon would jump over him and race off in the other direction. The puppy would then bounce up and return to the chase. Kate heard a bark from behind her and turned to see Lily with Katja, Quinn's mother, approaching. Lily wasn't alone. A young woman with an Aussie, an older man with a Border Collie, and a woman with a German Shepherd accompanied her. The lack of the show coat revealed this was a working shepherd rather than a show dog. Quinn and Dillon made a mad dash over to Katja, and she romped with them for a minute while Lily introduced the others. They were friends who'd been in the herding trials. This had been Katja's first chance to get back into competitive herding since she'd had the puppies, and she had earned a good score and the final leg on her herding intermediate title. Lily had herding titles on both Katja's mother and grandmother as well. One of the benefits of living on a ranch where there were sheep and goats available for practice. Kate reached down to congratulate her.

John, the owner of the Border Collie, teased Lily, saying she qualified but didn't place in the ribbons. "Sams don't have the instinct for sheep the way my guy does."

"Or my Aussie," the younger woman said. She turned out to be his daughter Susan. She laughingly explained the family competition they had going on.

Kate laughed. "I wonder how your guys would do with a herd of a couple hundred reindeer. The Sam would have you there."

Lily said Margit had brought her German Shepherd from Germany where he had multiple European titles. They were working on collecting American titles and awards. Her dog, Royce, had won it all yesterday and was fantastic to watch.

Margit fussed over Quinn. Lily introduced Dillon as the sire of Katja's litter. Lily said though the beautiful little red-ribboned bitch she kept, Faith, was her pick, she had to agree Quinn had turned out to be very handsome and did have the prettiest head of the litter.

Harry walked over with Liam and Shelagh, greeting Lily and telling her how great Quinn was turning out, especially as a crime buster like his dad. Everyone laughed.

Lily's friends explained they had decided to spend an extra day at the National to watch the agility competition. A friend of theirs had a Sheltie entered who excelled at both herding and agility.

"Speaking of agility..." Harry said, reminding Kate she needed to get moving. They bid goodbye to everyone and headed for Charlie. They were almost to the motor home when a voice caused Kate to stop.

"Oh my God, where's your braid? I barely recognized you. My my, you've changed. Dressing like a grown-up I see, though you're still shaped like a child. You needn't have bothered to show up at the National, Kate. Since you've lost your 'let the kid win' edge, you should have stayed home and rested on your laurels." A woman about Kate's age with bleached-blonde hair, wearing tight jeans and a loose cream-colored blouse unbuttoned enough to show off her ample breasts had stopped by the motor home door.

Kate drew a breath, pasted on a smile, and turned. "Joceline Levasseur, I see you haven't changed at all. Is this your new bitch? Who's she out of?"

"Gregori. Some of us can afford to use the top producer and aren't dependent on making do with what's running around in our backyard."

"My backyard has done very well over the years so I'm not complaining. How is your family? Didn't I hear your father's name on the news recently?"

"You must mean his nomination to become Secretary of State. Service to the country has always been part of our family tradition. The Levasseur family has served five presidents down through the years."

"You must be very proud. When you see him, give

him my congratulations."

"You'll be seeing him yourself. He's here to see me take the points."

"Well, good luck to you. But I've got to go, Dillon is doing agility." Kate hopped up into the motor home.

Harry stepped around the woman as he urged the dogs to jump up the steps.

"Well, hello there," Joceline said, turning her smile on Harry and throwing her shoulders back, giving him a better view of her cleavage. She stepped close, saying, "You're new here. I see you've got one of Kate's puppies," she said, nodding at Quinn. "I suppose there isn't much choice where she lives. You'll see much better specimens here at the National. It's a shame you didn't wait to explore other choices instead of having to make do. But, if you're in the market for an outstanding show prospect instead of this pet, I'd be happy to show you what's available. In fact, we should get together." She laid her hand on his sleeve as Harry lifted Quinn up the steps. "Perhaps we could have dinner one evening… I didn't get your name."

Harry stepped back and dropped his arm so her hand fell free and answered, "Harry Foyle. I'm Kate's fiancé."

"So you're why she cut off her braid. It's hard to think of the child as being grown-up and, let's say, skilled enough to attract a man like you."

Harry pasted on a grin as he reached for the door. "Well, you see, I never knew her as a child, but Kate is definitely skilled"—he looked her in the eye—"in every way you could imagine. Nice meeting you." He jumped into the motor home, letting out a breath he didn't realize he'd been holding. He shut the door and asked, "Not a member of your fan club, Kate?"

"Hates my guts. Did I just hear you tell her I am a sexpot?"

"Absolutely." He leaned in, staring at her over the top of his glasses.

"Thanks," she said, smiling.

"I speak nothing but the truth," Harry said, leaning in for a quick kiss.

He had already moved their laptops and other necessities from the room to the motor home, so they decided to eat breakfast once they'd parked the motorhome at the venue. Harry pulled out of the parking lot and got on the road.

The venue was only a few minutes away, and Harry found a space near the entrance. After setting up the exercise pen, Harry fed Quinn and gave each of the others a biscuit while Kate reached for her paperwork and checked the schedule for the day.

They'd been notified the building wasn't air conditioned, so the dogs would probably be more comfortable staying in Charlie. The temperature was supposed to get up only to the mid-seventies today, so the dogs would be fine in the motor home with the top vents open and the fans turned on. Today was an all-breed agility competition, so the Sams would compete alongside Shelties, Aussies, Poodles, Jack Russell Terriers, and even a Pomeranian they had noticed. Tomorrow, it would be only Samoyeds.

Harry had set out several folding captain's chairs, when the major joined him. Since he was making tea, he offered the major some as well as the breakfast pastries he'd just thawed out and warmed up. The major accepted, taking a chair at the folding table. He added milk to his tea and bit into one of Grace's blueberry crumb cakes. The major signed. "I have not tasted anything nearly this good in ages."

"Kate's grandmother stocked our freezer before the trip with homemade goodies before we left. Grace is a wonderful cook who made sure all of her grandchildren learned the skill, though Kate's brother Will has raised it to a high art."

"Is he a chef?"

"No, he's a mathematician, like most of the Killoys. He'll be joining Killoy & Killoy next summer. However, he'll be catering our wedding next month. Will is versatile."

"My wife was always charmed by the Killoy family. I have chatted with both Kate's father and grandfather over the years and was very impressed by their professionalism. Apparently, she takes after them. I came here because I need to speak with her about my wife. Kate and Krystyn had a connection, a friendship going back to Kate's childhood. Krystyn had an unusual rapport with her. We couldn't have children, but I never thought Krystyn missed them, until I found out about the relationship she had with Kate."

"Knowing Kate, it might have been more about her as a person rather than as a child. She grew up unique, sophisticated in some ways and naive in others. She competed against adults and won, but did not experience the things common to little girls going from childhood to adulthood. She is a one of a kind."

"Yes, and apparently, from what I've heard, she has a talent for dealing with crime. I have friends in the FBI and both your names were known to them."

"I was with the Bureau for five years, but Kate is simply an amateur gifted with amazing insight. However, because she has no training, she tends to take more risks than I'm comfortable with and, more often than not, she scares me to death."

"I understand and sympathize, believe me. Krystyn was much the same. There was even a time…well, I shouldn't talk about that."

"You mean the Coyote," Harry said while watching the major.

"How did you…?"

"I have my sources. I'm also guessing, though I don't have any proof, the two unnamed people who assisted her to carry out his identification were Kate's father and grandfather."

The major stood. "Nobody knows…"

"No, I did not find it out from a source, but rather from knowing how Killoys work. Their names were never released, for their own safety, I assume. The NSA has not let us know there is a spy tracking Kate. This information I discovered from my own sources. I know the Coyote was traded in a prisoner exchange many years ago. He has been free to investigate those who were involved in his being tracked down and arrested. I suspect he has decided on revenge. Is there anyone else you can think of who might have wanted your wife dead?"

Collapsing into the chair, he lowered his head into his hands. "No, there is no one."

"Then we need to work on the supposition the person behind her murder was the Coyote. Do you know what was on those papers and flash drives taken from your safe?"

"Not specifically. It was hard for me to watch the video last night, but I did notice the papers taken from the safe were not the ones there when I left for the Hague. The original papers were legal files tied with red cords. The night before I left, Krystyn was working on something and had a bunch of flash drives in a stack by her laptop."

"Where did she keep her laptop?" Harry asked. "I don't remember seeing it in the video."

"That's another strange thing. It was always kept on the desk where the killer put the papers. But, in the video, it wasn't there. The police asked me about it, and I assumed the killer had taken it. But now we know it wasn't there when he arrived." Both men sat in silence.

The silence was broken a few minutes later when Kate returned with Cathy and Lily. They were about ten feet away when the Samoyed walking with Cathy let out a sharp bark, broke free, and dove at the major, screeching to a stop in front of him. Then, burying his massive white head in the major's lap, he howled such a mournful wail, everyone but the major froze. The major's arms wrapped around the dog and lifted him into his lap to hold him closer. Kate reached for Harry and buried her head in his chest, her tears flowing. Both Lily and Cathy were also cry ing. Finally, the major lifted his head from the big dog's ruff, pulled a large white handkerchief from his pocket, wiped his eyes, blew his nose, and muttered, "Pavlik, Pavlik, Pavlik."

# CHAPTER TWELVE
## *Monday, mid-morning*

Kate headed back into the building with Dillon, still choked up from the sight of the major and Pavlik. She worked to get herself under control. Stepping into a quiet corner, she slowed her breathing then recited to herself, "Focus, focus, focus." She needed to get her mind in the game. Her heart ached with familiar pain. The agony those two were suffering, she knew all too well. But it wouldn't help their pain at all for her to let grief interfere with her run. She wouldn't allow her feelings to cause a distraction and make her let Dillon down. There would be time enough to grieve later.

She moved to a spot where she could be out of the way and watch the runs of the other dogs while awaiting her second-to-last start time. She worked at calming her body. Dillon's head rested in her lap, and she petted his ruff as she focused her attention on the ring.

A dog at the starting line brought a smile to Kate's lips and lightened her heart. The Pomeranian probably weighed only about six pounds but was obviously an enthusiastic competitor. At his handler's signal, he was off and flying over jumps, burning up the course. Both Kate and Dillon followed his progress. The small dog raced through tunnels and weave poles but then ran into his big challenge. The tiny powerhouse hit the seesaw at top speed, running up to the end, but then everything stopped. Ever so slowly, the board descended until finally he could go on with the course. She watched his frustration. His feet beat against the board, trying to pound it down but not having the weight to drop the board faster. It had the Pom spinning as he waited. Once off, though, he was flying again, positively airborne when he finally sailed over the last two jumps. She watched him leap into his owner's arms, thrilled with himself. The audience cheered.

As Kate rubbed Dillon's ears, she focused on each piece of the course. Speed and accuracy were what was needed. A mug of tea appeared in her hand as Dillon's lead was taken from her. Harry's arrival changed the dog from calm to being on the jazz. He took Dillon outside for one more trip to the exercise pen to relieve himself while Kate sat and drank her tea. She watched Dillon switch his focus from her to Harry and back when he returned. Harry rubbed his hands all over Dillon's body as he did when they were playing together at Kate's. Dillon bumped Kate's shoulder and she, catching on, bumped him back.

"Kate, you'll be up in two," someone called to her, and Harry leaned in with a quick kiss and took the cup.

"That's for luck. But remember, just have fun."

Fun? Right, fun. "Hey, Dillon. Are you ready to run? Run time. Yeah, run time," Kate coaxed, standing.

Dillon bounced as he trotted toward the ring.

As they moved away, Harry stopped smiling. He turned his focus toward the crowd and went into protection mode. He may have spent most of his time with the Bureau crunching numbers, but he had kept his skills up and made sure to re-qualify on firearms every year. Harry had found several places other than Quantico to practice so he wouldn't get rusty.

Deshi Xiang appeared on the other side of the course wearing a ball cap and jeans and looking like an FBI agent wearing a ball cap and jeans. Harry sighed. Better than nothing, he supposed. Since none of them knew what the Coyote looked like, they were flying blind. Every white male over the age of thirty would be watched and for some reason, today, there seemed to be a lot of them.

He pulled out his phone and, using texts, checked with the others. He'd asked Lisa to record Kate's run since his attention would be elsewhere. Cathy had Yerik and was wandering, on patrol, through the stands. Maeve, though sitting with Padraig, was focused on another part of the bleachers. Padraig watched Kate as did Maeve's friend Brownridge from the opposite side of the ring.

Harry was pretty sure nothing would happen today. The Coyote must want something and, if he killed Kate, the likelihood he'd get it would be zero. But it never hurt to be careful, because the contrary was also true, and he might think if he took her out, he'd be completely out of danger.

Moving slowly through the crowd, Harry scanned

the arena for anything suspicious. Kate was next up. She stood beneath a dark, empty broadcast booth at the top of the bleachers. Cathy moved up the steps into the bleachers toward it, but in spite of the tension, everyone else seemed calm.

At a signal from the judge, Kate and Dillon stepped forward, heeling smoothly, and as Kate stopped, Dillon sat. Harry hoped the experience with the major and Pavlik this morning hadn't upset her to the point where she lost her focus.

Kate and Dillon stood still, behaving the opposite of the Border Collie and the Sheltie who'd finished before them. At the judge's signal, Kate flicked her hand, palm up, to have Dillon remain sitting while she continued out onto the course then paused by the dog walk, turning. Unlike those competing before them, neither Kate nor Dillon moved a muscle.

At the judge's nod, Kate flicked her hand and, like a bullet, Dillon sailed over two winged jumps, zoomed across the dog walk, and raced through the tunnel. He dove through the tire, shot over the seesaw, and then flew over the next three winged jumps arranged in a semicircle. He dove through the chute, sped out, and flew over a wingless jump, whipped through the weave poles, then, making a sharp one hundred and twenty-degree turn, seemingly in midair, leapt onto the pause table, and screeching to a halt in down position. At a flick of Kate's finger, he was off again, up and over the A-frame and flying over the final two winged jumps.

Harry blinked. The Dillon he knew was cool and

controlled. This Dillon was on fire.

As Kate ran with him across the finish line, Dillon suddenly whirled around behind her and jumped on her back, knocking her to the floor, his body covering her head. The dirt on the floor beside Kate's head rose up in a series of puffs. From off to his right came frantic, enraged barking. He glanced up in time to see a rifle disappear into the broadcast booth and hear a door slam. Cathy raced to catch up with Yerik who clawed at the broadcast booth door, snarling.

Kate rolled over and stood, hugging Dillon as applause sounded around them. She explained to the judge Dillon wasn't being aggressive just playful. She told her, when she tripped and fell, Dillon thought it was an invitation to get in on the game and snuggle. The judge laughed, patted Dillon's head, and went back into the ring. Harry brushed Kate off while he scanned the floor around them.

"I'm going to have to say a few 'Hail Marys' for that lie," she whispered. Then she stepped to one side, receiving hugs from her friends.

Harry bent to picked up several items from the floor near where she fell, slipping them into his pocket. He scanned the arena once more. Then he reached out, wrapped an arm around Kate's shoulder, and headed toward Maeve and Padraig. Cathy came down the stairs with Yerik who was stopping every other step. She had to tug on the lead, fighting him as he pulled back toward the booth. After a minute, Agent Xiang ran in from the side door, out of breath. He shook his head at Harry. A cheer went up with the finish of the last round.

"You okay?" Harry murmured.
"Thanks to Dillon."
"We need to get you back to Charlie."
"After I go back for the scores."

Kate started toward the ring with Dillon but stopped. She turned toward the booth, trying to see into the dark box. Harry stepped to her side, giving her a hug as he whispered, "The bad guy is gone. You're alive. You win."

She grinned at him. Throwing back her shoulders and with her hand resting on Dillon's head, she moved to join the others. Kate realized the danger was truly gone when Dillon switched into "off duty" mode. He dropped his front and lowered his head till he was nose to nose with his new best friend, the Pomeranian.

The judge gave a speech about the quality of the runs, thanking the Samoyed Club for the assignment. She announced the scores. Kate had no idea of how well they'd done. Dillon had been fast, but what happened at the end had erased all memory of the run. Therefore, she was astounded when the judge announced Dillon had taken third place and was the only Sam in the ribbons. They'd lost second place to a Border Collie by less than two seconds. She hugged Dillon, thanked the judge, and then smiled for the photographer. Finally, after clipping Dillon's rosette to his collar, she cast one more glance at the broadcast booth, a cold chill running through her, and joined Harry.

# CHAPTER THIRTEEN
*Monday, late morning*

On the way back to Charlie, Kate told Dillon what a good boy he was, giving him one of his special treats. Then, removing his rosette, she put him in the pen to brag to the others and roughhouse with his son. She and Harry went inside to find Wetherly Brownridge sitting at the table with the major, Pavlik at their feet. Kate reached for the kettle only to have it rattle against the spigot. Maeve took it from her shaking hand.as Harry sat down on the floor and pulled her into his lap. He pulled her back tight against his chest and wrapped both arms around her. Cathy and Xiang pushed in, joining them on the floor.

Lily arrived last, out of breath. "Kate, what was going on with Dillon at the end? You were lucky the judge didn't disqualify you for having an aggressive dog."

"I told her I tripped and Dillon thought it was playtime since we often wrestle when he's done a good job."

"Squeaky-clean Kate Killoy lied to a judge. Now I've heard everything." Cathy laughed.

"I could have told her my protection dog had just kept me from being shot in the head." Shocked silence filled the motor home. Padraig asked Lily if she'd filmed the whole run, including the end. Nodding, she pulled the camera out of her tote and handed it to him as he found a cable in one of the drawers by the door. He had taken camping trips with her father and grandfather in Charlie, so Padraig probably knew where everything was as well as she did. He plugged the camera into the television and pushed play. As Dillon flew around the course, Kate focused on his movement, searching for ways to trim a few seconds off his run.

"There," Harry shouted. Padraig pushed the pause button. The screen showed Kate bending to pick up Dillon's lead as a puff of dirt blew into the air beyond her. Hitting the play button again, they saw Dillon launch himself at Kate's back, knocking her to the floor and covering her as two more puffs appeared, the last one barely visible above her body. Screeching howls and barks blasted from the television as Yerik went ballistic in the stands, and the crowd turned toward the broadcast booth. The video played out with Harry approaching her, helping her up while keeping his body between Kate and the shooter. Brushing her off, he bent down and picked a couple of items from the floor.

Silence filled the motor home. Everyone looked toward Harry as he opened his hand to show three slightly misshapen spent bullets then cleared his throat. "I think we can assume the Coyote has decided not to wait to get the information from Kate before trying to kill her."

Kate sat still and silent for a few seconds before adding, "We don't know the shooter was the Coyote. However, one thing we do know, thanks to Yerik, is the shooter today is the same one who murdered Krystyn."

Silence grew as the major's face contorted in rage. "If I had known he was so near—he'd be dead."

A knock came at the door and Padraig, who was closest, opened it. "Excuse me, but is Cathy Harrison in there?"

"Rufus," Cathy, Kate, and Harry shouted together.

"What are you doing here?" Cathy asked.

"I've got a conference in Lexington and knowing all of you were here, I took some time from the dull lectures and drove over. Since Cathy had said you were entered in agility, Kate, I asked at the hotel how to get here, and arrived just in time to see Dillon's run and the show in the stands." He stared at Cathy. "What was with your dog, anyway?"

"It wasn't my dog, and someone was shooting at Kate."

"Again?"

Kate groaned, and Harry opened his mouth as though to argue with his friend who continued. "I wondered why Dillon knocked you flat. I may have filmed it when I was shooting the run. I came in late and was across the building from where Lisa was filming. I thought you'd like two angles, which is why I saw Cathy's dog dash for the booth and try to get inside."

Padraig held out his hand. "Give me your phone." Rufus started but complied, and soon every eye was following the run from the opposite side. As Dillon flew up and over the A-frame, there was movement in the upper right corner of the screen. As he cleared the last winged jump, what appeared to be a pipe with something on the end slid out the window of the booth. There was a flash. Yerik yanked Cathy forward, forcing her to let go of the lead as he bolted to the door of the booth and jumped on it. Two more flashes came as Yerik went ballistic, trying to get into the booth. Then there was the sound of a door slamming, and the camera veered back to Kate being approached by the judge. Everyone began talking at once.

Kate kissed Harry on the cheek and stood. Taking the phone from Padraig, she grabbed her tablet from the pocket of her tote, inserted the USB cable, and copied Rufus's files. Then she copied the recording Lily had made. She leaned across Maeve and asked Agent Brownridge for his phone. He stared at her for a second and then nodded. Kate quickly transferred a copy of the folder to his phone. "Xiang, did you see anyone leave the building down the fire escape?" she asked as she handed Brownridge back his phone. Brownridge stood and nodded at Xiang to follow. "Let's all get together in the same meeting room of the hotel at two o'clock to finish this."

Kate was glad when the subject of lunch replaced talk of the shooting, and they agreed to get together at the hotel restaurant in half an hour.

Harry and Padraig followed the men out and began sending in dogs while Kate and Maeve lifted the dogs into their crates. The major had his car and took Pavlik with him. Cathy had come with Lily but returned with Rufus, and Lily took Yerik, followed out by Maeve and Padraig.

Kate stared into space for a minute. Then, focusing, she stepped forward into Harry's embrace. Her body was stiff but, as minutes passed, Harry began poking his fingers around on the back of her neck. She chuckled. He continued the search for pressure points until a laugh burst from her, and she grabbed his hand and placed it on the right spot at the base of her neck. As he slowly began a rhythmic massage, she dropped her head on his chest and, letting out a slow breath, relaxed.

"I'm thinking of getting a T-shirt with a target on it," Kate grumbled.

"Actually, I was thinking you should knit yourself an outfit the color of a Chartreux."

"Like my cat?"

"Well, remember her nickname is 'Invisacat' since in a dimly lit room she is invisible. You could be the 'Invisible Woman.'"

Kate, not letting go of the cat references, said, "I could knit myself a cat suit, complete with perky little ears."

"All sexy and clinging. I would definitely sign on for that, provided I'm the only one who gets to see it."

"With the right encouragement, it could be arranged." Kate kissed him and, still giggling, fell into her seat and attached the seat belt.

"Be careful I don't start calling you Kat instead of Kate."

"All my brothers and my dad and granddad beat you to it. Eventually, I got them to stop, so please don't get them started again."

Harry chuckled. "Hmm, you'll have to make it worth my while if you want complete cooperation, sweetheart."

"Or, I could just sic a dog on you the next time you try it."

"Good try, but your dogs love me."

As Harry maneuvered Charlie into his spot by the hotel, Kate said, "Maeve and Padraig seem to be waiting for us."

When Kate opened the door and stepped out, Maeve said, "New plan. We're to be in the meeting room in five minutes. Lunch will be catered by a local sandwich shop I'm told has great food. The police are being brought into the mix since there is a question of jurisdictions and who has the final say. The dogs have been outside all morning, so they won't need walking. We'll just help you move them to your room, and then we'll join Wetherly."

Harry nodded and handed her the lead attached to Shelagh. He took Dillon, Padraig took Quinn, and Maeve took Liam. Harry watched, a worried expression on his face, as she and Kate gaited the dogs up and down the parking lot before heading inside.

As expected, the walk to the meeting room off the lobby was a slow-moving meet and greet as more and more of their friends arrived at the show.

Xiang slid by them, carrying a huge tray of sandwiches, followed by a policeman with containers of salad plus bags of chips. Coffee, tea, and soft drinks had already been set out on the table, and it seemed as though everyone had arrived. The hotel had provided plates, cups, and silverware, so everybody just dug in. Kate took a corned beef sandwich, several types of salad, and some chips. Harry handed her a cup of tea then, putting his tablet on the seat next to hers, went to grab a plate and fill it. Once they all had arrived, Lily broke the ice.

"I couldn't believe Dillon's speed on the run this morning. He was so calm before it began, and then it was zero to sixty out of the box. He was amazing."

"Well, truth be told, this is his idea of playtime," Kate said. "Since I teach all the different activities simultaneously—be it conformation, search and rescue, or police work—he has to be focused on me for nuances. Agility, where he can do his thing providing he's heading where I point, is his idea of heaven. At the end of any hard training session, or a search without a good outcome, I'll use agility as a way to get him to shake off any melancholy and back to being Dillon."

"Well, it certainly paid off and, tomorrow, he'll get to do it all over again," Lily said.

Everyone stopped talking and stared at her.

"What?" Lily asked, glancing around the table. "Tomorrow is the Samoyed-only agility trial, and Kate and Dillon are entered to run."

"Absolutely not! You're not doing it," Wetherly Brownridge bellowed from the end of the table.

Every head turned toward Kate who finished chewing, cleared her throat, and said, "Yes, I am."

# Chapter Fourteen
*Monday, lunch time*

The arguing bounced from one end of the table to the other. As Kate sat eating her sandwich and salads, Harry stood and got her a second cup of tea and an oatmeal raisin cookie. She smiled up at him and got to work enjoying the end of her lunch and let them yell themselves out.

Finally, things calmed down. "Miss Killoy, Kate, you haven't been saying anything," Agent Brownridge commented.

"I'm sorry," she said. "I was hungry. Running around the ring and getting shot at burns a lot of energy. I was also taking time to think while I was waiting for your attention. I would like to make a point then ask for people's opinions when I'm done. Hypothetically, I'm a murderer who, for some reason defying all good sense, climbs up into a broadcast booth at a public event to use a rifle with a silencer to eliminate a victim. However, my victim does not stand still but runs hither and yon at high speed.

"Wanting a good shot, I wait until she finishes, and then I aim and take my shot. However, she bends over and I miss. Not to worry, I'm using a silencer and no one notices, so I try again, only to have her dog flatten her and cover her body. I shoot one more time, and suddenly, the Hounds of Hell are at the door of the booth, trying to attack me. I run out the back way, glad to escape unharmed. But I'm unsuccessful.

"Now, on the plus side, I find out my potential victim is going to be doing the same thing, in the same place, the following day. Terrific. However, I've also found out the police, the FBI, and the NSA are here on deck to catch me, not so good," Kate continued. "He's a murderer, but he's not an idiot. This guy is not going to climb up into the same booth to give a repeat performance. It is a good bet the law will have stolen his bird's-eye view. Gentlemen, maybe I'm optimistic, but it's my opinion, the safest place for me to be, tomorrow, will be running around the agility arena. Oh, and I highly recommend the oatmeal raisin cookies. They're delicious."

"She's right." The policeman whose name Kate hadn't been told spoke up. "He knows we'll be hunting him there tomorrow. But you referred to him as a murderer. Was it because he shot at you?"

"No. I called him a murderer because he has murdered before. He was identified by an eye witness about an hour ago as the man who murdered former agent Krystyn."

"Where is this witness? We want to talk to him."

"The witness is hopefully asleep upstairs in Cathy Harrison's hotel room and, no, you can't talk to him. You can only observe his actions. In this case, they speak much, much louder than words. Krystyn's dogs witnessed her murder. They may not have seen her shot, but they saw and smelled her killer, felt her fear, heard the shot, and smelled her death. Two of them are here. As we saw today, they know who the shooter is and, if given the chance, will happily rip his throat out with my blessings.

"Gentlemen, there are going to be six hundred and fifty Samoyeds here this week. Two of them can spot your killer no matter how he is disguised. They can literally walk through a crowd and smell him out. You have at this table some of the best talents in the dog world who know how to use this resource. They are available to help you. The choice is yours."

The policeman who'd spoken earlier answered, "She's right. Let me introduce myself, ladies and gentlemen. I'm Captain Bernard Glasmann of the Louisville Police Department, and I have been assigned to keep any and all murders, from happening here in Louisville during this event. You seem amazingly calm, Miss Killoy, for someone who was shot at an hour ago, if I might say so." There was a spate of coughs and throat clearing around the table, and Kate shrugged.

"It's not my first ride in that rodeo, Captain, so to speak." He glanced around the table only to encounter nods from almost everyone.

"Glasmann"—Brownridge leaned over and tapped his shoulder— "perhaps we should go over the combined resources we have in this room and then make a plan. I'll start the introductions. I'm Agent Wetherly Brownridge from the NSA, with me is Agent Deshi Xiang of the FBI. We were brought here by a written invitation from former agent Krystyn Machnicki. The letter came by the U.S. mail.

It stated she would have information vital to the country's national security and connected with the arrest ten years ago of a former Russian spy. We did not find out about her death until we got here. She also mentioned in her letter if something happened to her, Kate Killoy would have the information we need." He stared hard at Kate and then nodded to Maeve.

"I am Maeve Killoy Donovan, former MI-5 agent who has in the past, encountered the spy in question. I am also a longtime Samoyed breeder/handler and Kate's great-aunt. This is my husband Padraig Donovan who, is always handy in a pinch and because of me, has close to fifty years' experience with this breed."

"Cathy Harrison. I am by trade a surgical nurse, and I am also a Samoyed breeder/owner/handler, and judge. I was the one working the crowd with Yerik, the Samoyed mentioned, today, when he spotted our murderer. I was a close friend of Krystyn Machnicki, the murder victim."

"Rufus Blackburn. Math professor at UC Denver and friend with many of those here."

"Harry Foyle. Former FBI, now owner of Foyle's Private Corporate Security. I'm Kate's fiancé."

"Kate Killoy. Fashion designer, breeder/owner/handler of Samoyeds, and trainer of dogs for everything from the breed ring to police work."

"Lily Peters, County District Attorney from Texas, and I'm a breeder/owner/handler of Samoyeds. I was filming the run this morning and got the assault on video."

"Major Wayne Machnicki, legal counsel to the Secretary of State, presently assigned to the U.S. Mission at

The Hague, and on leave due to the death of my wife."

Everyone sat a little straighter when the major spoke. His soft tone belied the vast amount of authority his voice compelled. Kate suspected this mild-looking man could move mountains, which must be why Krystyn respected him so. Could this mismatched group work together to catch both a murderer and a spy while, at the same time, keep a low enough profile so they would be the only ones knowing what is going on? To add a degree of difficulty, some of them would be showing dogs in the year's most important competition for the breed.

At a knock on the door, Brownridge, who was closest, stood and opened it to find the desk clerk standing there, holding a white envelope.

"Excuse me, sir, but this envelope was left for Miss Killoy at the desk, and since it's marked urgent, I thought it should be delivered quickly. I was told she was here." The desk clerk looked nervously from one to another and fidgeted with the note he carried. He happily turned away as soon as the envelope was taken from him, but an arm shot out, stopping him.

"Who gave this to you?" the agent asked.

"Ah, nobody. Angie, she's one of the desk clerks, noticed it just sitting on the desk. She checked and saw Miss Killoy was registered. She was searching for the room number when one of the dog owners said if we wanted Kate Killoy, she'd gone into this room earlier, and they hadn't seen her leave."

"So, you have no idea of the source of the note."

"No, sir, we don't."

"Thank you." Wetherly Brownridge turned and placed the note on the table. Agent Xiang instantly had gloves on, pulling a Plexiglass box from his briefcase. He took the envelope and placed it in the box then sealed it. Inserting his hands into gloved openings that reminded Kate of an incubator, he gently opened the envelope and removed the note inside. He slid his finger into the fold of the paper and smoothed it so they could read it. Kate stood and walked to where he was working. She peeked over his shoulder, gasped, and read it aloud.

*"Dear Kate,*

*You don't remember me, but I remember you running around the ring with your long braid flying out behind. You are a good handler. I do not know who is trying to kill you, but I'm not a killer. I do not kill my friends or enemies. Krystyn was the friend who caught me, but it was business. She, I, we respected each other. Krystyn had something of mine I need to find. She was hiding it for me until I returned. She said if she died, ask you. So you know I would never harm you. I need your help to find what I'm looking for. I will watch for this killer and try to stop him.*

*Coyote"*

Kate returned to her seat and watched the conversation going on at the other end of the room. Turning to the major, she asked quietly, "Did Krystyn respect him?"

"Yes. I think she was sad when he had to be caught, and especially when he was returned to the USSR."

"Do you know who he was?"

"No. But I was told he had plastic surgery after he returned to Russia, so his appearance won't be the same."

"Do you think he shot Krystyn?"

"No. But he may have been the reason she was murdered. Whoever had her shot may have wanted to stop them getting together. I've had time to think, and I suspect she knew someone was after her and why. The more I learn, the more I agree the person has something to do with the Samoyed world of showing. I am also sure you have something that holds a clue. You may not know what it is, but Krystyn wouldn't have told me, nor Brownridge, what she did in her letter if it weren't already in play."

Kate's phone buzzed with a text from Seamus. *Will call 6p.m. Must talk u & H. fyeo, S.*

"Is it the Coyote?" Brownridge asked.

"No, it's my brother Seamus wanting to know how we did today."

"What does this brother do for a living?"

"He's still in high school," Kate replied, smiling.

Maeve added, "He's one of twin Killoys. Hold onto your hats when they grow up." The agent glanced at her and chuckled.

Maeve organized coverage for her and a search for the killer and for the Coyote. "With this crew of both professionals and nonprofessionals, there will be someone with her at all times. As for finding the killer, the two witnesses, Pavlik and Yerik, will be wandering around the show alongside experienced dog handlers. Those handling the two witnesses should notify Captain Glasmann's people where they will be at all times. If those people are armed, it wouldn't hurt. Major, even though these are your dogs, I think, unless they are in the ring, they should be with others to preserve their anonymity."

"What they can't do, gentlemen, is where your professional experience comes in. I will see you get a schedule telling you where Kate will be at all times. You can figure the best way to have eyes on the target and be able to check the crowd for suspicious action," added Harry.

"Now, this is a social event," Maeve continued, "with more than a thousand people. We don't want to panic anyone unnecessarily. The surveillance should be low-key as should our meetings. Cathy and Lily could make sure everyone knows this meeting is planning a memorial service for Krystyn in coordination with her former colleagues from DC. People have seen us here and will be curious.

"There will be official photographers and videographers working the event. Captain, you might have someone sitting in with them. Your officers, instead of shooting video of the dogs, will be shooting video of the crowd, to try spotting any suspicious activity. After tomorrow's agility run, the rest of the show will be in the exhibition hall. It is a smart building where everything is controlled from a computer base of operations. Captain Glasmann, your people might be able to use the setup to have eyes on the rings, meeting rooms, hallways, etc."

"Good idea. I have some people who've done similar work for political gatherings in the past and who are familiar with the setup. I would also like Kate to wear a vest when in an exposed situation."

Kate knew from her police classes the vests were heavy enough to slow her down, about twenty pounds. She'd have to think about that. But she wanted to go rest and be able to talk to Harry and Maeve. Her attention wandered as she picked up her tablet and watched her run again. Dillon was amazing. She was so proud of him and the joy in his flight around the course. With all the controlled activities they did together, it was so good to let him run flat out at the speed he chose. She watched it again, ignoring the talk flowing around her, only this time she watched the crowd, first from Lily's point of view and then from Rufus's camera. In the crowd opposite Rufus, there was a man holding his phone to record the run. She would have to play with the recording later and see if she could get the focus better. Could it be Coyote?

"Do you agree, Kate?" Brownridge asked.

"I'm sorry, wool gathering. What did you ask?"

"Mr. Foyle can fill you in on the details, but the gist is you do not wander off without protection of some sort. Of course, when you're competing, you'll be surrounded by crowds who will be watched, but no walking your dogs by yourself in dark parking lots at three in the morning."

"Agreed."

"Then we're done here."

Kate swept her tablet into her bag and stood to leave. When she reached the door, she asked Brownridge, "What were you working on where you needed Krystyn's information?" He frowned at her and mumbled he couldn't discuss an ongoing investigation. She nodded and followed Harry out into the lobby. Maeve was talking with the men from the NSA, so Kate stepped over to Padraig to give him a hug and quietly told him they were having a family meeting at six in their room. He hugged her back, agreed, and then kissed her cheek, shook hands with Harry, and turned back to meet Maeve.

Kate joined Harry, Rufus, and Cathy as they headed toward the elevators. The door opened, and they all entered. Kate pushed the button for the second floor but, as the door started to close, a man stepped in and, at the last second, a woman also entered with two beautiful Sams. Cathy greeted her. “Ruthi, I’d like you to meet my friends Harry and Rufus. Oh, and this is Kate Killoy who has been showing since she was a kid. Everyone, this is Ruthi Stern with Zhivago and Ziva. They’re both top winners and will be giving everyone stiff competition this week.”

Ruthi smiled, saying, “I’ve heard of you, Kate. I’m glad to meet you at last. I’d like to find time to talk to you later.”

“I’d enjoy chatting with you. Your dogs are lovely.” Kate leaned against Harry as exhaustion took over her body. When the door opened, they had to jockey around people and pups to get out. They turned right and, at the door, Harry fished his key out and opened it. Crowding in behind him, Kate gazed lovingly at the bed, but instead, turned to the bureau and began grabbing leads.

“No.” Harry took the leads from her hands. “You and Cathy stay here. Do not open this door for anyone, not even the pope. I’ve got my key. Rufus and I will take care of the dogs and be back in a few minutes.”

Kate started to object but at his grim stare, agreed. They left, and Kate toed off her shoes and fell back onto the bed, eyes shut. Cathy went to the desk and sat.

"So, Rufus is taking time away from work to follow you to the Nationals?" Kate murmured, rolling on her side so she could see Cathy whose color had turned very pink. "Is this getting serious?"

"We've been talking about how we can combine households. He's got his dad and Jordy, and I've got eight Samoyeds including one pregnant bitch. The house in Denver belongs to Ewen, so making structural changes to it might not work. But, at the same time, it is convenient to the university. Everything is up in the air. The big decisions don't seem to be ours. Then there's the problem with Antonia. I've already told Rufus she's a deal breaker. Ewen is brushing off the fact her daughter tried to murder both you and Harry, and she attempted to get you arrested. The only thing seeming to bother him is your mom called and read him the riot act about endangering her daughter while she was a guest in his home. I think he feels she could hurt his reputation in the math world."

"She could and would if he didn't apologize abjectly enough."

"So, how are the plans for the wedding coming?"

"Beautifully. Everybody else is taking care of the details, and I'm left to do my thing."

"Has Agnes talked you into a dress?"

"Actually, before I left, I was doodling on the computer, fooling with my design program and accidentally sent Ellen a wedding dress design I was playing with. I got distracted by a call from Harry. Ellen and the knitters loved the dress and they are making it for the wedding. Apparently they had felt left out and are delighted to be part of this grand plan. This wedding is a totally cooperative effort. Agnes is still muttering gloom and doom, but nobody's listening." Kate propped herself up on the bed and pulled her tablet from her bag.

"When I wasn't paying attention in the meeting, I was re-watching the videos. There's one Rufus shot showing a group of people standing together where there is one man on the end who is filming the action. Here it is." She slowed the playback down until it showed the man. For several frames, the cell phone blocks his face, but he moved it as the second half of the run transitioned to the far side of the ring. She froze the image as the door unlocked and the men and dogs entered.

Harry moved to her other side so she could see the screen. He reached over and hit some keys, and the image became larger and clear. They all stared at the screen and then at each other. The face on the screen belonged to the man in the elevator.

# CHAPTER SIXTEEN
## *Monday, late afternoon*

"Could we have just met the Coyote?" Kate asked.

"It's possible. We know he's here." Harry moved to prop himself up against the pillows and lifted Kate to rest against his chest, taking the tablet from her hands. After clicking a few times, he said, "I just copied the head shot and sent it to your phones. It will give us a face to keep track of when we're out there. He said he needed to keep Kate safe. I, for one, believe him. Spies are rarely killers, in spite of the body count in Bond movies."

Cathy studied the photo of the man on her phone. "Well, it's good to have this because he looks so ordinary. If we hadn't seen him literally minutes ago, I doubt I'd remember him at all."

"It's what makes him a successful spy. He blends with the setting, passing unnoticed." Harry glanced at his watch. The afternoon was rapidly disappearing. "We should decide where to eat supper."

"We have another meeting first. Seamus will be calling at six with news, and I've invited Maeve and Padraig to join us." Kate reached for the menu. "Since it is going to be well after six before we eat, why don't we call room service and see if we can get a snack to tide us over? Hmm, how does tea for six and an appetizer tray sound? It should hold us until we eat a full meal."

"I could definitely eat something," Rufus said.

Both Harry and Cathy agreed. Kate made the call.

Getting up, she took her ribbon and score card out of her tote bag and put them into the album she kept just for specialties. The album was then passed around, showing previous Samoyed specialties and Kate's wins going back to her first at age seven.

"You were so young when you started showing." Cathy turned to the front to study the early years. "Who is this you're showing? It's too long ago to be Liam."

"It's Liam's grandfather, Kegan. He was a good dog who liked the ring the way Dillon does. He was a high-scoring obedience dog as well."

Rufus peered over Cathy's shoulder. "How can you tell them apart? They all seem pretty much the same to me."

"You'll learn, Rufus, if you hang around Cathy much more. Harry and I have only been together since February, and he can tell all my dogs apart."

Harry piped up. "Actually, they each really do look different, and if you see two similar, you just wait a second till they move, and you'll know which is which."

A knock on the door was followed by a voice calling, "Room service."

Kate scrambled to put the album away and clear space on the top of the desk as Harry opened the door.

A waiter wheeled a cart over to the desk. Hot water carafes were unloaded onto the blotter and then the teapot, cups, and saucers. Next the waiter reached underneath and removed a large covered platter placing it alongside small plates, forks, knives, and napkins. Standing, he handed the bill to Harry to initial, but Kate took it. "The room is in my name, remember?" Smiling, she handed it back to the waiter and asked, "Would you like to join us and chat? I assume you have many questions, and there will be few opportunities to have any privacy at all in the next few days?"

He froze, his hand resting on the doorknob. He sighed, smiled, and nodded. "I like the short hair. You've grown up to be a very beautiful woman, my young Kate. How did you know who I was?"

Kate smiled at the compliment. "It was your movements. You can change your appearance, but I remember the way you'd give a little shake to your hand prior to setting up your dog for the judge. I studied you in the ring and, for a while, imitated it, but the gesture wasn't natural for me. For you, though, it's as spontaneous as breathing."

"Krystyn said you were very bright."

"When did you two last speak?"

"A month ago."

"By then, her phone was already being tapped. It's probably when the plot was cooked up, eventually leading to her death. And no, I don't think you killed her. For one, you're not anything like the man who did it, and I think she was more important to you alive."

"You are right. She was. How do you know I don't look like the killer?"

Kate reached across the bed, and Harry handed her the tablet. She pulled up the video of Krystyn's murder and handed it to the man. Four sets of eyes watched his reaction. He smiled at the beginning. "Pavlik, what a wonderful dog." His body stiffened and, when the shot came, his face went white, and the pain in his eyes could not be faked. He muttered for a few minutes in Russian then focused back on Kate. "Where…?"

"We have tracked him here. He is either at the show or nearby. We are working on finding him. Yerik let us know the shooter at the agility trial today was Krystyn's murderer."

"I must see the video again so I study his gestures, stance, and movement."

Harry asked for his phone and quickly sent him the file. He then glanced at his watch and asked, "What name are you using?"

"Roger Krylov."

"Well, Roger," Harry said, "we will be at the agility venue again tomorrow afternoon. An extra set of eyes would be welcome. However, it's five forty, and Maeve Donovan will be here soon."

"Ah, the beautiful Maeve. You are very much like her, Kate. I should go." He stood and moved to the door, made a quick check and, with the barest of nods, was gone.

"Well, we now know the man in the elevator is not the Coyote. He may have been an innocent bystander, but we should keep an eye out for him just in case. I need to talk to Roger longer, but, we should eat. I don't know about the rest of you, but I need a cup of tea." Kate made tea in the pot and poured for those who wanted it. Then she took several cheese puffs and a shrimp roll and returned to the bed to think.

It took her a few minutes to recall everything about the man who called himself Roger Krylov. She remembered him in the ring. He spoke the truth about being friends with Krystyn. She remembered them chatting at shows over the years. They had a special bond. No wonder when the assignment to find the Coyote had come her way, she recognized him immediately. Kate wondered if she thought of it as just business when she had to arrest him as a spy. He had a secret he'd shared with Krystyn, according to the note they'd received during the meeting. A secret she supposedly had. He hadn't mentioned it, but there had been strangers present. She was sure he'd find a way to speak to her again. Whatever his secret was, she didn't think it was the reason behind Krystyn's murder.

Harry scooted in next to her holding a plate filled with goodies. Rufus and Cathy had moved to the far side of the room, pulling a couple of chairs together and spoke softly to each other. Kate guessed they weren't discussing spies. Harry leaned in to her and asked, "What is this meeting about? I know you want to talk to Maeve about the Coyote, but what else?"

"I wanted to…" Kate felt an icy chill, like a dead hand laid upon her. The room became a foggy gray then white and cold, so cold. Something whizzed by her head. She tasted dirt. Over and over she was falling, pushed, flattened, squashed down under a weight. Dillon was on her back. His paw pushed on her neck. She twisted her head.

The dirt danced, spurting up with each hit, again and again and again. Dillon was in danger. The noise, the barking, the fear, the cold, the weight, Dillon crawling up her. His chest on her head, dirt flew, again and again and again. Bullets, dirt, dog, noise, pressure, mist, fear. All devouring fear dragged her into the black. She reached for help. She reached…

"Ouch!" Sharp puppy teeth bit through the cuff of her sleeve, drawing blood. Kate grabbed her wrist and gazed around. She was curled up in Harry's arms, surrounded by her dogs all pushing against her body. Quinn had crawled in and grabbed the nearest thing—her hand. Kate surveyed the room. Cathy and Rufus stood at the foot of the bed next to Maeve and Padraig, all gaping at her. Harry turned her face toward him, concern in his eyes and warmth in his light kiss..

"Welcome back," he said. "You'll be needing a fresh cup of tea."

Kate blinked, confused. "Yes, please. Sorry, everyone. Guess I was gone for a while."

"Katie, my sweet darlin', has this happened before?" Maeve moved to the side of the bed, pushing the dogs onto the floor and resting her hands on Kate's cheeks.

"Yes. I'm afraid my brain doesn't like it when people shoot at me. How long was I…"

Harry pulled her closer. "This time it was much longer than the last, about twenty minutes." He smiled at Quinn who was trying to jump back onto the bed. "Quinn is good at bringing you back, though. He's two for two, if you count Texas."

"I guess I should thank him, but those teeth hurt. I'd rather have people stop using me for target practice."

"Who's using you for target practice? Kate, are you okay?" Rufus spun around hearing a voice behind him speak. He saw a laptop computer on the desk and her brother Seamus staring out from the screen.

"I'm fine, Seamus, just taking a quick trip to Never Never Land. Ah, tea. Exactly what I need." Harry had boosted her half into his lap, and Cathy handed her a cup of tea.

"If people are shooting at you again, Sal's going to go ballistic," Seamus muttered but was forced to move aside as the person sitting next to him appeared on the screen.

"Kate, are you sure you are well? It sounded as though you were having an anxiety disorder episode, which can be very serious. Have you sought medical help for this condition? You must not neglect your health." Satu Mizutani's concerned face filled the screen.

"I'm okay, Satu. Did you two find any information that could help with the problem we have here?"

Seamus nodded at Satu. She gathered up some papers, tapped them to align the edges and, with a small smile, cleared her throat to begin. Kate waited, feeling as if she was about to hear the report of a Fortune 500 company.

"We did find information, and Seamus and I chose up for the opportunity to give the report." Her grin made Kate chuckle. "To begin with, the conference in Boston was exceptionally enlightening—"

"She means mind-blowing," Seamus interrupted.

The quelling look Satu aimed at her brother had

Kate covering her mouth to avoid laughter.

"As I was saying, the levels of hacking are far above those used by the person behind your friend's attack. The programs and equipment available to track these hackers are growing at an equally accelerated speed. Seamus and I were able to locate the vendor, a Mr. Casey, who supplied the man behind your friend's hacks. He didn't want to talk with us until Seamus flashed his badge showing his relationship to Mr. Foyle's company, and then he was extremely cooperative."

"He thought it was very clever of Mr. Foyle to have two operatives resembling high school students," Seamus said with a snort earning him another scowl from Satu.

"He informed us of the man's name, but, unfortunately, we're sure it is an alias since it is the name of a character in an early version of an online game we use to play. However, when he had his records open, Seamus distracted him for ten seconds with a question about something in his catalog, and I was able to memorize the credit card information on the man. It seems his Bitcoin account had gotten low, and he had to make a purchase the old-fashioned way. This information, including a list of purchases, is in your inbox."

She regarded Kate's brother with pride. "Seamus was able to place some code in the hacker's phone since the vendor contacted him right after we left the booth. Mrs. Sadie okayed the purchase of some equipment we found at the convention that allowed us to do this, as well as two other items that will eventually let us trace this person to within fifty feet. Seamus mentioned there are over a thousand people at the dog show, but this may help. We will keep working on finding him."

Harry had opened his tablet and was skimming the information the kids had sent. He glanced over at the laptop. "This is good data, you two. Thanks for all your help. You make a great team. Stay in touch." They signed off, and Rufus closed down the laptop.

Harry studied the tablet. "The name of the buyer/hacker may be false, but I'm wondering about the listing here for the person who responded to the tweet seeming to okay the hit on Krystyn. Does the name Sheiling Horne mean anything to you?"

The room was silent except for gasps from the three women. No one spoke. The three stared at one another. Maeve was the first to recover. She turned to Harry. "In answer to your question, Harry, Sheiling Horne is president and CEO of the JRA Financial Corporation. He's one of the top charitable donors in the country through his family foundation and is a long time breeder of Samoyeds with an impeccable record. I also must tell you Sheiling Horne is the judge for all the bitch classes here at the National on Friday."

# Chapter Seventeen
*Monday, evening*

The phone rang, breaking the silence that had taken over the room. Harry answered, spoke quietly for a minute, and then said, "We'll see you there."

Disconnecting, he addressed the others. "The major has made reservations for dinner at a restaurant he and Krystyn enjoyed when they came for the Kentucky Derby several years ago. He's invited us to join him at seven. It's probably not a blue jeans and T-shirt kind of place. If you want to go change, we can meet in the lobby in fifteen minutes. Oh, and I don't think it needs saying but, it would probably be good if we do not mention Sheiling Horne's name at dinner tonight. We still have a lot to investigate concerning him. Remember, he could also be a victim of someone hacking into his account to hide his identity. Until we have proof, this stays among us, understand?"

It took a few seconds before the nods came, but they did. The others left, and Kate pulled a clean blouse and pair of slacks out of her suitcase and headed for the bathroom. Harry tugged the T-shirt he was wearing over his head and reached for one of his dress shirts still in the wrapping from the cleaners. He turned when he didn't hear Kate close the bathroom door. She was staring at him, her eyes wide and her breathing irregular. "Kate, go get dressed. If you keep looking at me like that, I won't be marrying a virgin next month, and we probably won't even make it to dinner."

Heat traveled from her cheeks, a blush spreading. She ran into the bathroom and covered her face as Harry's chuckles sounded through the door. She dampened a washcloth and patted cold water on her face and neck, cooling herself. It wasn't as though she hadn't seen Harry without his shirt before. Maybe stress had her hypersensitive, but she would have thrown all her resolve out the window if Harry had even cocked an eyebrow at her. She was such an idiot. To have a panic attack in front of everybody and then want to jump Harry's bones half an hour later meant sensible, calm, take charge Kate Killoy had left the building.

Harry quickly finished dressing. Grabbing leads, he gathered the dogs and made a quick exit. He was still breathing hard from the look Kate had given him. She'd come to him in an instant and then beaten herself up over it for years. In this day and age, her resolve to remain a virgin till she married had even Father Joe raising an eyebrow. However, it was the way she'd been raised, and he wasn't going to destroy her beliefs. She had him in a twist, waiting. It would only be a few more weeks, if he could keep her alive that long.

Damn, what was it with people wanting to shoot

her, first in New York then Texas and now here. The flashback this afternoon was the worst she'd experienced, and it tore him apart. He'd been through PTSD episodes after being shot and almost dying right before leaving the Bureau. Sal had saved his life, and the man responsible was in prison, thanks to Kate. But the dark times he'd gone through following those surgeries were brutal. The fact this woman who was so precious to him was having to deal with something even a fraction as bad wreaked havoc on him. Quinn having done his business, the last of the four, Harry quickly cleaned up and headed back. He didn't want Kate to be alone any longer than necessary.

Kate managed to change her clothes, brush her hair and even put on some lipstick and blush so she looked human on the outside even if the person inside was an emotional tsunami. She emerged to an empty room, no Harry, no dogs. Heading for the door, she spotted a Post-it note at eye level above the knob. Dogs peeing, etc. be right back. F. Oh, great. She'd even forgotten her dogs. She was the one who needed a collar and lead. She smiled at Harry's use of F for fiancé.

She started to throw together the meals for the four Sams, letting her mind wander. What was it with Sheiling Horne? She'd known the man since she was ten years old. He'd always reminded her of the old actor, Monty Woolley from the black-and-white film she liked to watch with Gram, The Man Who Came to Dinner. He had the same appearance as the actor with his white hair and mustache and rotund figure. But he was a gentle man. He couldn't have any part in Krystyn's death. A tap sounded on the door, and Kate realized she was standing, staring into space, with a scoop full of kibble and an empty bowl. After dumping the kibble into the bowl, she opened the door.

As if conjured by her thoughts, the man who appeared before her was exactly as she remembered from his white suit to his equally white shoes.

"Kate Killoy. I need to talk to you." Sheiling Horne reached for her arm, backed her into the room, and, after checking the hall, shut the door.

"Sheiling, I shouldn't be talking to you. I've got a bitch entered. It is unethical."

"Don't worry. I've arranged for someone to cover my judging assignment. I need to leave at once. I came early to find the man who my son tells me, has routed messages through our business server and sent them out as though from me. I heard about what happened to Mrs. Machnicki and had Brian check, in case anyone else associated with this show had been affected. My son found an original email that had been converted to appear to be coming from me. I understand the helpless feeling Krystyn must have had. He tracked the name and address of the person making the change."

He handed her a slip of paper. "It was here, in Louisville. I went there. It was an old house. Nobody was home. However, I peeked in a window. The room was filled with guns and computers and who knows what else. This person has already dragged me into this by using my server. My son, his family, and I are leaving on a short vacation where nobody knows us until the show has ended and whoever did this is found."

"Sheiling, why you? I don't understand. Why would these people involve you? Krystyn was formerly involved in intelligence and national security..."

"She was not the only one. It is not known by many people, but for many years I was an undercover operative. I left the service years ago, but we all have our secrets. Krystyn called me a month ago to warn me there might be trouble. She didn't say what or why but only wanted to give me a heads-up I might be at risk. I told her not to worry, since we'd left that life behind years ago. But Krystyn is dead and I'm terrified. I followed you here and waited until your young man left. I am frightened, but because I have known you so long and respect you, I had to give you a warning. Krystyn told me if anything happened to her, you'd have the answers. Be careful, Kate. I've got to go." He turned and almost ran to the door leading to the stairs.

Perplexed, Kate had barely crossed the room to pick up the food bowls when the door burst open and she was surrounded by an acre of white hair and smiling dog faces. Snapping out of her stupor, she finished putting in all the ingredients for the meals and, with the command, "Kennel," all the dogs dashed into crates to wait for their dinners. It only took a second to convince Quinn he had to get into his own crate and couldn't stay next to his dad. Harry had run into the bathroom and in what seemed like only a minute, emerged shaved, hands scrubbed, and ready to go with two minutes to spare.

On the way to the lobby, Harry leaned in to ask, "Are you okay?"

"Yes, I'm fine though my brain seems to be operating on overload. We have to talk about something that occurred while you had the fuzzballs outside, but there's isn't time now. Sorry about the meltdown."

"Hey, you wouldn't be human if this morning's shock didn't give you flashbacks. At least tomorrow, the building will have been swept by the police prior to the event. I'm also glad your old friend is going to be providing an additional pair of eyes. Are you going to tell Maeve about him?"

"I'll play it by ear. You know, Maeve was still doing undercover stuff after she married Padraig and moved to New York." Kate offered him a wry smile. "Of course, she was a trained British agent, and I design sweaters for dog lovers."

"To say nothing about the fact she worked during the Cold War in the last century. Today, as we learned with Krystyn's killing, it takes a lot less work to do a lot more damage." Harry grew quiet as they walked into the lobby where the others waited with the major.

Rufus drove, following the major's car, while Cathy, Kate, and Harry discussed planned activities during the week. There seemed to be an unspoken decision to avoid talk of the shooting. By the time they got to the restaurant, the discussion focused on methods of weave pole training using wire fencing for the best speed in agility. They joined the others as they reached the restaurant. The place was charming with tables both inside and out. Since it wasn't that chilly, they decided they'd eat their dinner outside. A quiet settled over the group as they scanned the menu, checking out page after page of what seemed like delicious food. Kate decided on the stuffed filet of sole, Harry chose the pork chops, and the rest selected various cuts of steak. Finally the conversation got around to security for tomorrow. The major had spoken to Wetherly Brownridge as well as Captain Glasmann about security plans for the week.

"It will be easier once the show moves into the building where most of the judging will be held," the major continued. "It's a smart building. Access to and operation of the building is handled from a central control room, and the police will be working with the building security personnel. They were talking about it after you left this afternoon, and it takes a load off my mind. I don't want Kate put in danger again."

"I would certainly hope not," Maeve put in, reaching across the table to grab Kate's hand. "I wish we had a clue about the shooter. After Yerik's reaction this morning, there's no doubt it's the same person who murdered Krystyn. I'm sorry, Major, to speak of this, but there will be time to mourn once this bastard is behind bars along with anyone who's in it with him."

Harry had become quiet while the major spoke. Kate leaned over to ask if something was wrong, he just shook his head and muttered, "Later."

Dinner talk moved to the show and reminiscences between the major and Maeve of the old days within the security community. Then the conversation went on to changes in tracking spies and dealing with them due to the growing use of hacking and other cybercrime.

Cathy and Rufus told people about the cybercriminal Kate had fought the month before. The case had most everyone talking, but Kate and Harry were both sitting quietly, the memory still raw from the fright they'd had and from Harry being shot. Rufus quickly changed the subject to Jordy, Rufus's son, who, at the age of twelve, seemingly going on thirty-five, was a student in a special accelerated program at MIT. Then Rufus entertained them with stories of Harry who at an even younger age had been a student at Caltech. By the time the group reached dessert, everyone seemed relaxed.

As they stood to leave the restaurant, Harry pulled Kate into an embrace. She slipped her free arm around him and laid her head against his chest. Tilting her head up so she could see him, she sighed. "It's only Monday, and already I feel like Alice after a session with the White Rabbit—curiouser and curiouser!"

"We should get back to the hotel. The dogs will need walking, and we've got a lot to talk about before bed."

Kate remembered the fear she'd seen in Sheiling's face and hoped he and his family would be safe. She'd tell Harry about the visit tonight.

As they entered the hotel and headed for their room, Lily approached with her bitches heading out to relieve themselves. "Hey, Kate. I just heard there's a judging change. Sheiling Horne had some family emergency and had to bow out. I haven't heard who will be judging Friday, but thought you'd like to know." She called the last over her shoulder as her bitches pulled her toward the door.

Harry glanced down at her and said, "You don't look surprised."

"I'm not. Let's go walk the dogs. Then we can talk."

They headed to the room, got the dogs, and were down to the lobby in just a few minutes. As they passed through the doors leading out, Kate spotted the man from the elevator getting up from a chair and turning toward the door. The dogs pulled toward the grassy area, but Kate, after a few steps, turned back to check the door. The man emerged, stood looking their way, and then went in the other direction and disappeared around the end of the building. They walked the dogs across the parking lot to a larger grassy area and watched Quinn romp with Shelagh, both glad to be out of their crates. When they finished, Harry disposed of the poop bags in the trash can. As they headed back across the parking lot, an engine revved up behind them. A screech of tires had her tensing, and Kate had barely time to scoop up a lagging Quinn as an SUV swept around the end of the row of parked cars and headed at them at top speed. Harry grabbed her shoulders, thrusting Kate and the dogs into a space between two cars as the black SUV sped by. The only thing left in its wake was a roar of an engine, a gust of wind, and a smell of rubber.

# CHAPTER EIGHTEEN

## *Monday, night into Tuesday, morning very early*

Harry had his phone to his ear as he went through the lobby calling Wetherly Brownridge, who said not to bother calling the police because Glasmann was with him. By the time they reached their room, he heard the other elevator coming up. They moved quickly to get the dogs crated before things got too interesting. Biscuits were given out. Kate put away the leads, and Harry opened the door to the men before they even had a chance to knock. It seemed they'd been meeting in the hotel restaurant.

Filling them in on all the details they could remember about the car took a while. Kate told them she'd noticed a man taking special interest in her at the competition. She mentioned he'd accompanied their group into the elevator. When she saw he was following them out of the hotel, she'd turned to look back at him, but he ducked his head turning away from them, heading around the building. She couldn't guarantee he was the man in the car because she was too busy dragging Quinn out of the way, but she was able to send them the head shot they'd taken off the video.

Kate had been pacing the room as she talked, the

dogs watching her steps moving back and forth. Suddenly, she stopped and recited four numbers and two letters. "The license number. I just remembered the license number of the SUV. But I don't know what state it's from."

Deshi Xiang grabbed his tablet and as he began typing asked, "How were you able to get the number if you were ducking behind cars with dogs?"

"I just remember numbers. It's something I do without thinking," Kate told him. "I just had to calm down enough to remember it."

"I would love to have that talent," he chuckled.

Harry laughed as well. "It does seem to come in handy."

Kate stopped moving and yawned. Harry nodded to the men and hurried to finish filling in every detail possible of what had happened. They all agreed Kate shouldn't be left alone until they found the person behind this. It took five more minutes to complete the list of warnings and assurances, before the men finally left.

Harry had barely closed the door when he asked, "Kate, why weren't you surprised when Lily told you Horne wouldn't be judging? Kate?" His fiancée had flopped onto the bed as limp as though ready to sleep for a month.

This day had seemed a year long. Only this morning, he'd seen her shot at while exiting the agility ring. He'd seen her emotions pass from terrified through tense and angry. He watched her identify a former spy by the movement of his hand and then descend into the grip of a flashback, only to pull herself together enough to go to dinner. She had to deal with knowing, because Krystyn's messages were intercepted, someone assumed she was enough of a threat to need killing. It was hoped whatever information she had would die with her. This alone was more than enough to send any normal person into hiding under his bed. Then, tonight, to be chased down by someone in an SUV intent on killing her should have made Kate a basket case, curled up under the covers and howling at the moon. Instead, she sprawled on the bed, still fully dressed and sound asleep.

He removed Kate's shoes, socks, and jeans then, rolling her to one side, he pulled the covers out from under her and tucked her in. She never moved a muscle. Stepping into the bathroom, he stripped down to his boxers and, turning away from temptation, he crawled under the covers of the second bed. He reached for the light, stopping at the sight of her. She lay sound asleep, her curls mussed on the pillow, all the tension with her today gone, and a slight smile on her lips. Harry wondered if she was dreaming of him, and then snorted, shoving his ego aside. She was probably dreaming of cleaning the exercise yard in her kennel, surrounded by happy Samoyeds. As he watched, the urge to move the two feet separating the beds and hold her in his arms had his breath quicken and his body reacting. He turned out the light and rolled so his back was toward her. The stress of a shootout was nothing compared to that of lying here, inches from the woman he loved, and staying put. But stay put he would, dammit. He punched up his pillow, determined to sleep.

Later, a slight noise brought Harry awake. He listened. Nothing. He glanced toward the crates, faintly lit by the parking lot light seeping where the drapes didn't quite meet. None of the dogs were standing, but all were awake and staring at the door of the room. Then he heard the noise again, faint, a slight click of the door lock and the door handle being depressed. He didn't wait but leapt out of his bed, gun in hand. Releasing the latch on Dillon's crate then Liam's, he gave the dogs Kate's signal to drop and hold. As they crouched, he stepped toward the door and ducked inside the bathroom. The door opened. Slowly and silently, a figure moved past him, entered the room, and closed the door. But Harry didn't hear it latch. Harry didn't breathe until the shape moved and then he stepped between whoever it was and the door. Soundlessly, he latched the door, turned on the light, and stood pointing his gun at the young man who'd whirled, ready to fight.

"I wouldn't advise you to move. On the off chance I were to miss, though it would be almost impossible at this range, it would be the signal for plan B to go into effect. If you turn around, you'll see plan B."

The young man spun around and froze. "Do they bite?"

"Only if you give them a reason. Face the dogs and kneel." The trembling young man did as he asked, bringing his head closer to the level of the pair staring at him, daring him to move. Harry reached for a show lead hanging from the grooming arm of the table/crate, slipped the loop of the fine steel choker around the man's wrist then pulled his arm behind his back and tied his hands. He also slipped a heavier metal obedience choke chain over the man's foot and snapped on a six-foot leather lead. "Get up and sit on the edge of the bed."

"The police are on their way as well as the NSA and FBI," Kate said calmly, her phone in her hand. Harry reached into the bathroom for his jeans and shirt, pulling them on as a rapid knock sounded on the door.

"Foyle. Open up."

Harry tossed the lead to Kate then moved to open the door. As it opened, he heard a thud.

The police along with the two agents, pushed into the room, found a young man sprawled on the floor, one leg elevated where it was attached to a training lead held firmly by Kate. Looking down at the man, she said, "Stay."

Wetherly Brownridge pushed forward. "What's going on, Foyle? Who is this? What's your name?" he demanded as he lifted the man and sat him on the edge of Harry's bed. He was met with a glare and nothing more. Brownridge turned toward Harry. "What happened?"

"I woke hearing a faint sound. When I heard it a second time and realized someone was breaking in, I released Dillon and Liam to take care of Kate and moved so I could get behind him. When he came in, he left the door off the latch and moved past me. I simply waited and then slipped out, latched the door, and turned on the lights. Except for hog-tying him with dog leads, we haven't made any progress."

Xiang reached into the man's pocket, extracting his phone, a switchblade knife, and his wallet. Checking the man's other pocket, he found a handful of gadgets like computer components. Brownridge flipped open the wallet first. It displayed an impressive collection of credit cards in several names and a driver's license. Xiang pulled out the license and read, "His name is Jeffery Pulaski. His address is—"

Kate interrupted with the address and everyone stared at her. "When you check it out, be careful. You'll find arms and possible bomb-making equipment."

The young man along with everyone else in the room gawked at her. She shrugged. "I've got an anonymous source."

Glasmann pushed himself through the crowd, followed by several officers.

Harry stepped around the agents, took four biscuits from the bin on top of Quinn's crate and, signaling Dillon and Liam to return to their crates, rewarded all the Sams. He then sat next to Kate who was still tucked up under the covers, slipping his arm around her.

"Who can fill me in on what's happening here?" Glasmann asked.

Brownridge nodded at Harry then turned to Glasmann and repeated Harry's information. "He also mentioned Miss Killoy seems to know something about what has been going on but hadn't yet shared the information."

Glasmann turned his focus to the man slumped on the bed. "Mr. Pulaski, can you explain what you are doing in a locked hotel room without the guest's permission at two thirty in the morning?"

Pulaski glared at the men and then at Kate. "She could have broken my neck. I should sue."

"Mr. Pulaski, you haven't answered my question."

"I have nothing to say. I want a lawyer."

Glasmann sighed and began reciting Pulaski's Miranda rights. By the time he finished, the young man was smiling, a smug grin spreading across his face, happy to win the contest of wills with the authorities.

Harry stood as one of the officers removed the leads and chokers and replaced them with handcuffs. He handed the leads to Harry who glanced at the pile of computer chips and what appeared to be electronic bugs displayed on the desk as he replaced the leads. He turned to Pulaski. "Mr. Casey must have had a two-for-one special here."

The smile disappeared from the man's face, and Pulaski looked nervously from Harry to Kate.

Kate leaned back and smiled at him. "You're pretty much an open book, Argon. You're going to need a good lawyer when they charge you as an accessory to murder."

Pulaski lunged at her. "How did you find out—" Xiang grabbed him. He pulled himself up and declared, "I have nothing to say."

Ten minutes later, after an interrogation that gained them nothing more, and with a promise from Harry and Kate to give complete statements to the police and to meet the agents for breakfast, they once more had the room to themselves.

Harry turned out all but the bedside light, gave each dog a piece of ring bait, and then sat on Kate's bed staring at her for a minute. "Do you have anything you'd like to share with the class, Kate?"

She smiled. "As a matter of fact, I do. While you were walking the dogs, I had a visitor. Sheiling Horne had been waiting for me to be alone so he could talk to me about what happened to Krystyn. It seems his son is a techie, and when Sheiling heard about what happened to Krystyn, he got worried and had his son check his email files. They found the altered email along with the original. His son was able to track the alteration back to an address in Louisville. Sheiling came out here early to check out the address. When he found the place, he peeked in the window and saw what I told Glasmann to expect. He's convinced he'll be the next one killed, so he and his family have gone into hiding."

"Why would he assume he'd be killed just because she was?"

"It turns out my sweet old friend spent most of his life as an undercover agent. You know, at the rate this week is stacking up as an old spies conference, by Friday I'll be introducing you as 'Foyle, Harry Foyle.'" She teased. "But seriously, I wonder, how many retired, or semiretired, members of the Game are attending this National. It's becoming an old spies reunion. I need to talk to the Coyote and soon."

"I agree, but for now, we need to get some sleep. You've got another competition later today and Dillon will be pissed if you're off your game. He doesn't like to lose."

"You're right about that. I can't be napping in the ring."

Harry gave her a quick kiss, stroked her cheek, and said, "Sleep tight," then crawled into his own bed where, much to his surprise, he fell asleep with no trouble.

The dogs let them sleep until six thirty but then announced enough was enough. Since they hadn't been allowed to play with all the visitors last night, the pups declared they needed to go out and check if any new dogs had arrived. Kate and Harry threw on jeans and sweatshirts and made quick work of getting everyone out. The pups were focusing on business in short time.

Returning, they quickly showered and dressed for the breakfast meeting with the law. If Maeve spotted them, she would be guarding Kate's back against her fellow members of the Long Arm of the Law Club. After giving the dogs their morning biscuits, they headed for the restaurant. Maeve and Padraig were already seated in a booth along with the major and the agents.

As Kate slipped into the booth, she said, "I see we have alphabet soup on the menu this morning: MI-5, FBI, NSA, OLC, and BGU."

"BGU?" Brownridge asked.

"Best Great-Uncle," Kate replied, smiling and leaning over to give Padraig a kiss on the cheek.

Harry pulled up a chair next to Kate and they gave their order to the waiter. Kate's tea arrived immediately along with Harry's coffee. Kate surveyed the group. "At this rate, the only one who's missing is M arriving in Bond's Aston Martin. How is everyone this morning? Did you gentlemen get any sleep? Sorry I wasn't dressed for company when you called last night."

"Kathleen, this is no time for levity. You need to tell everyone what you know. You could have been killed yesterday. This is serious."

"Believe me, Maeve, I am extremely aware of the seriousness of the situation. However, since I seem to be the primary target, I would appreciate the courtesy of receiving information as well. One thing I'd like to know is, when the Coyote was arrested years ago, was it at a National?"

The major looked at Brownridge then shrugged and said, "Yes, but why does it matter?"

"It matters because of the sheer number of dogs with a similar appearance. The setting creates an assumption that any person on the human end of a lead belongs here. It renders any criminal, using a dog as a disguise, invisible. If someone walks around with a Samoyed at this show, provided it's groomed, nobody would question whether he or she was entered. In other words, the bad guy or guys will blend in.

"I assume because of his arrest ten years ago, the Coyote wasn't able to complete his mission. Do any of you know what the aim of the mission might have been?" Kate was met with blank faces and silence, so she continued, "Okay, could anyone give me a rough count of the number of agents were at the show, either from the U.S., an ally, or an enemy? I know the Coyote wasn't the only agent there. The reason I'm asking, gentlemen and Maeve, is I'm beginning to suspect for some reason, this National is being used as a reunion. A gathering of those same players who may also be behind Krystyn's murder."

Kate took in the group's tsunami of disbelief. "Or, I could have just gone completely nuts from being shot at and am just rambling without a clear thought in my head." The men's startled expressions changed to suspicious as they scrutinized each other. The silence following drove her to finish her food so she and Harry could leave because what she saw cross their faces wasn't doubt any more. It was fear.

# Chapter Nineteen

*Tuesday, early morning*

Kate nudged Harry, who stood. As one, they said goodbye, telling them she had dogs to bathe. Both moved quickly away from the table. As they headed for the doorway, she heard Brownridge spluttering. “Where are they going? They haven’t answered any questions. They can’t just stand up and walk away. Who do they think they are? Hey, you two, get back here. This is ridiculous. Maeve, do something.”

Kate glanced back and saw Padraig lean over and grab Brownridge’s attention. “Think what you are saying, man. This is Maeve’s great-niece. Of course she dares.”

They heard Brownridge tell Padraig. “God help us, we’re in trouble.”

Harry was chuckling when they reached the door from the restaurant. They had heard the whole thing, and both were fighting a losing battle to keep a straight face. “I don’t think Maeve’s ‘by the book’ friends are ready for a clone of your great-aunt.”

Kate’s laughter bubbled out. “Even at my best, I couldn’t be as kick-ass as she was in the day. Not only was she a good agent for MI-5, but she was a top-notch code breaker. You know, the more I think about it, the more weight I find in my theory about this being old spies week. The question is, why? Why are they here, and why do they want to kill me?"

Harry was reaching to open the door of the restaurant when a voice behind them caught her attention. "Miss, excuse me, but I think you dropped this." Kate turned and saw a waiter standing behind them. He held out a schedule of events for the week. Kate reached into her tote and then smiled.

"Thanks. It must have fallen out of my bag during breakfast. I'm glad I didn't lose it because it has my notes on who will be handling which dog. Thank you so much."

His quick grin flashed then instantly transformed itself into the bland face of a waiter just doing his job. He nodded and turned, disappearing into the back of the restaurant. Kate and Harry didn't speak until they reached the room.

As Kate let the dogs out of their crates, Harry walked to the bureau and held up a piece of paper. "Here's your schedule, on the bureau. You didn't drop it."

"I know."

"Then what was that all about in the restaurant."

"It's what we need to find out." Kate pulled out the schedule she had been handed, spread it on the desk, sat in the chair, and began her inspection of the paper, tilting it and holding it up to the light. Then she smiled at Harry. "If you give this a quick glance, it's like every other copy of the week's schedule. However, if you look closer, you'll notice faint pencil marks under certain letters. I feel like I'm a kid again, passing notes to Agnes so my brothers won't know what's going on. Here, you're faster at this than I am, so have my seat and read out the letters while I write them down."

Harry stared at her then moved into the chair. "You mean the waiter was your friend, the spy? He didn't look anything like the man who was here yesterday."

"That's why he makes such a good spy." She grinned, picking up a pad and pen. "Start with the heading."

They worked quickly, and the message was formed.

*X-pen 4 -9 & 45. K & S out 4 stand pat. Be wary of old enemies and new friends. Low tech.*

"I understand some of it, but what is X-pen 4 nine and forty-five?" Harry asked.

"He'll meet me at the exercise pen, by door four, at 9:45. X-pen is a euphemism for the pen where the dogs poop. He must have overheard my questions at breakfast because he's telling me since Krystyn and Sheiling are out of the picture, there are four people of interest left. He is warning me about breeders or handlers I might or might not know. I think he agrees with your suspicion they will try to use our devices to track us. I'm glad you got these special phones."

Kate turned at the sound of a squeal. Shelagh had Quinn pinned to the floor, his head in her mouth. "Quinn, what did you do?"

"Quinn?" Harry said. "Shelagh's the one biting his head."

"She's not biting his head. She's just holding him down until he gives up what he's stolen. Come on, Quinn, time to go." The puppy let out a noise that could have been a harrumph but then rolled to the side, revealing a pink stuffed pig under his belly. In less than a second, Shelagh had the pig in her mouth and was strutting around the room.

Kate laughed and scooped up the puppy who was getting heavy. "Lesson one, my young friend, is about teasing. You must learn the saying, bitches don't make threats, they make promises. If they say they're going to do something to you, believe it. So, if you're going to steal someone else's toy, make sure you don't take it from Shelagh. It's a game you won't win." Shelagh came over and leaned against Kate's leg, the pig still in her mouth, and accepted Kate's pats as congratulations.

"Let's go, we're on a tight schedule," Kate said. "If I'm going to meet the Coyote in an hour plus wash and dry two dogs first, we've got to get moving."

Today's Sweepstakes schedule had the puppies being judged in the morning and the veterans after lunch. This gave Kate time to do her agility run, but not unless they got a move on. The thought of Harry showing Quinn next year in Sweeps gave her the first reason to smile since the insanity in the wee hours of the morning.

Harry's phone rang. He listened, nodded, and said, "She won't object."

"'Won't object to what?" Kate moved closer, trying

to hear both ends of the conversation.

"No problem," Harry agreed, ending the call.

"Glasmann wanted to put in one of his cops undercover as an additional bodyguard. We'll meet him downstairs," he told her. "So let's go."

Since this cop would be working undercover, Kate figured she'd put him to work washing a dog.

A young man, dressed in a T-shirt and jeans, wearing running shoes, stepped forward as they headed across the lobby toward the door.

"Excuse me, are you Kate Killoy?"

"Yes." Kate stopped, wondering what was going on.

"My Uncle Bernie said that he'd talked to you about me learning the ropes from you about handling show dogs."

Kate thought for a second then smiled as it dawned on her Glasmann was providing extra security but in the form of a beginner dog handler. "Great. He said you wanted to learn from the ground up. Let's walk, and we can talk about what's involved. I hope you're ready for hard work because this isn't a job for the faint of heart. What's your name?"

"My name's Oscar, but people just call me G."

Kate laughed, and Harry looked confused.

As they headed toward Charlie, she leaned toward him and whispered, "Oscar the Grouch."

The drive to the venue, where the breed and obedience showing would be held, as well as the special events, only took only a couple of minutes.

Liam was a pro. As soon as he saw the bath, he jumped right in. Kate didn't bother securing his collar to the wall hook since she knew he wouldn't move. She tested the temperature of the water and then had G help her work the water into the heavy coat, making sure it was thoroughly wet. Then she squirted shampoo into her hand and began working it into the coat so every hair would be scrubbed. She was elbow-deep in suds when Harry arrived with Quinn in tow to let her know Maeve and Padraig had arrived. They and the major were holding court.

"Good, Maeve can dry and start combing out Liam while I wash Pavlik." She rinsed Liam then had G add a cup of white vinegar to the gallon container she had and fill it with water. She took the mixture and explained to G it was added after rinsing to make sure any soap escaping her notice and hiding in the coat would be neutralized and not cause skin problems. She rinsed him again with water and then used some extra-large chamois to draw off water. This started him drying. She got rid of the last of the dripping water with a large, fluffy bath towel. G stepped forward with the lead, hitched it to Liam's collar, and signaled him to jump out of the bath. Kate started to tell him to step back, but it was too late, and he got completely soaked by Liam's after-bath shake. G took a dry towel and got the water off his face then turned to the dog who was smiling brightly at him. "Just what I needed, Liam, a second shower this morning."

Maeve walked into the bathing area with Pavlik as G started out. Kate laughed. "Your timing is perfect, as usual. This is G. He's learning the ropes."

"I see you've had your first lesson in dog baths. They shake when they get out." She applauded and G smiled at her, utterly charmed.

They switched leads, and she headed out to dry a dog.

Kate reacted quickly as Pavlik prepared to jump into the bath and put out her arm blocking the move. Instead, she patted the edge of the bath, and he placed his front feet there. Without losing momentum, Kate swung her arm under him and lifted his rear end into the bath. She wasn't taking any chances with a dog his age injuring himself on the tub edge. She debated attaching his collar to the clip on the wall and opted not to in case the shooter showed up. She didn't want the dog hanging himself in an effort to get to the man. She had no doubt he'd be out of the bath and on the man before she could blink.

Harry moved to the front of the dog, scratching his ears and keeping him distracted while Kate wet him down and G rubbed soap in the coat. With all hands on deck, the job was done in record time. G clipped on the lead and, with a smile, handed it to Kate, inviting her to do the honors of holding onto him as he leapt out. She gave the dog the entire six feet before she stopped him, and he shook. She was far enough away to stay dry.

Harry laughed. "And that is how it's done. Lesson one, the dog bath, is complete."

Neither Cathy nor Joyce had sweepstakes entries, but they both came by to set up crates and grooming tables, staking claim to their preferred space early. Ruthi Stern waved as she headed toward her Ashley Craig Pet

Products booth. Beyond Cathy's setup, Kate's friends John and Kathy were setting up. Though they each had judged Nationals in the past they weren't this year. Instead, they would be competing with their dogs. Taz Gustafson was creating a series of kennel high-rises with her crates since she had whole a bunch of Sams in tow. She called over saying she had her VA Taz's Scrumptious Peanut Butter entered in puppy sweepstakes. G laughed at the name but was informed by Maeve that Taz had dogs named for all sorts of ideas, each meaning something to her. Often the registered name was only very loosely connected with the call name. She called the puppy Peanut. He nodded and moved the hose of the dryer to the angle she wanted as she worked on brushing the coat dry.

The major began brushing Pavlik as soon as Harry lifted him onto the table. Kate adjusted the dryer at an angle to blow warm air just where the brush was pulling the hair from under his hand. Kate toweled his feet and then used the blower on them prior to beginning trimming so they would appear neat in the ring. The hair covering the pads needed to be trimmed back to give him good traction moving. Harry picked up a comb and worked on getting every hair in place and neat on the back feet while Kate worked on the front. Then she moved to put the finishing touches on Liam's legs and feet as Maeve finished his back and chest. Kate combed out his ears and back-combed the backs of them so they would dry completely and made sure his ruff stood away from his body. Soon, both dogs were done, given treats, and resting in their crates.

Kate sat, taking a minute to get off her feet. She

watched the Futurity puppies competing in the ring. A cup of tea appeared in front of her. She looked up to see Padraig handing one to Maeve as well. He also had donuts from the concession stand in the lobby of the building. She felt Harry's hands massaging her neck and shoulders and had to fight to keep her eyes open. Tipping her head back, she smiled up at him and spoke softly, for his ears only.

"If we want to get settled in at the venue for the agility trial, we'd better get moving. I'll want time to play with Quinn and practice gaiting with Liam and Shelagh after I finish the agility and before going into the ring this afternoon. If I'm to meet up with the Coyote before Dillon and I have to do our run, we need to go. We can eat after I finish and before we come back here to show Liam, since we have plenty of food in Charlie." Kate put leads on Liam and Dillon then, snuggling Shelagh, attached hers as Harry took Quinn and clipped on his lead. With G at their side, Harry and Kate headed for Charlie and the ride to the agility venue.

Kate forced herself to move forward, a smile pasted on her face, but inside, she was scared. Surrounded by agents and cops, she should feel safe, but an unnerving feeling of being watched had followed her since she'd entered the building. Kate had been coming to the National for seventeen years, and this was the first time she hadn't felt safe. She needed to talk to the Coyote. She needed to discover what it was people thought she had. But, mostly, she needed to stay alive.

# CHAPTER TWENTY
*Tuesday, late morning*

"Kate, I'm not letting you meet the Coyote on your own. I know you trust him but I'm not taking a chance on being a widower before I've been a husband." Harry's hoarse whisper and scowl invited no arguments as they headed toward Charlie. G took one look at them and moved farther away to give them some privacy.

Kate stopped. Resting her arms on his shoulders she said, "You're really looking forward to your husband role."

"I wish we were already married. Then I'd refuse to let you run around using yourself as bait for spies."

Kate dropped her arms, staring into his eyes. "You'd refuse to let me? Refuse? I hope you're not expecting to find the word obey in our marriage vows. If you do, you're in for a big surprise."

"You know I'm only trying to keep you safe because I love you," Harry grumbled as he switched hands with Quinn's lead to wrap his arm around her shoulder.

Kate stood with the dogs milling around her legs. "Harry, we've been through this before. You've got a month left to back out of this wedding. I am who I am. I'm not going to suddenly change into some little wilting flower needing to be watched over every minute. Either we're a team on equal footing, or this marriage won't work. I want you with me in this. It's important. I'm not a stupid person who goes around making herself available for every yahoo who wants to use me for target practice. I am careful and choose my battles. That being said, you do not get to tell me what I can or cannot do just to keep me from what you see as danger. I respect you, your experience with the Bureau and what you do now. All I ask is for you to respect me, my instincts, and the training I've gotten. I don't have a death wish. I'm not about to take stupid chances. Plus, I'm not without resources," she said as she rubbed Dillon's ears.

"You still scare me to death when you get involved trying to stop criminals, and as much as I respect Dillon, he's no defense against a bullet," Harry whispered, placing his hand on her cheek.

Kate covered his hand, sighed, and with a small smile, reminded him, "The last one was your bad guy, and come to think of it, to a certain extent, so was the first."

"Well, this one isn't, and I have a feeling another death or ten wouldn't matter in the least to the people you're up against here."

"You're probably right, which is why it's so important I talk to the Coyote and find out what it is everyone thinks is worth killing for, and why they think I have it. I'm flying blind here, and the NSA and FBI, if they know anything, aren't inclined to share. If you really want to keep me safe, work with me to figure this out."

Harry leaned in and kissed her. "Okay, I will give you the independence you want. But I won't like it."

"No, Harry, it's not what I want." She let out an impatient breath. "I'm not asking for independence. I'm not asking for space. I'm asking for us to be a team with equal respect on both sides. I don't know if it's possible, but I need you to think about it. It's important."

"Kate, you don't mean—"

"Just think about it, please."

When they got to Charlie, they found Maeve, Wetherly, and the major had gotten there ahead of them and were waiting along with Pavlik and Yerik. Agent Brownridge started right in, grumbling about them walking out on the breakfast meeting, but Maeve cut off his rant. They loaded Kate's dogs into their crates. Then everyone got in. Harry drove to the agility venue while Wetherly Brownridge filled the major in on last night's break-in.

"Have the police been able to get anything out of Pulaski?" Harry asked. "Someone is financing his activities with a hefty chunk of Bitcoins so he can buy his high-tech toys. The tools he's been purchasing, according to my investigators, are some of the latest and best for hacking and causing trouble for his victim." Harry pulled into a spot by door three and parked.

"I'd like to talk to your people about what they found."

Seamus and Satu would love being called "your people" and considered undercover agents by the NSA. However, she didn't want their identities known because it might put them in danger.

"I'll print you a copy of their report. They're working undercover at the moment and aren't available for questioning." Harry rattled his reply off, not making eye contact with her. He'd pulled out the old printer her dad kept in the motor home and wired it to print from his phone. Kate lifted Quinn down and then stood aside as Dillon jumped to the floor and sat at her side. Maeve pulled leads off the hook by the door and released Shelagh and Liam then hooked on their leads. She followed Kate outside.

Harry shoved the report into the agent's hands as he rushed to the door, but Maeve stopped him.

"Harry, I can take care of Kate. Make yourself useful helping these Luddites understand what's in the report." She rested her hand on his arm. "She and I need to talk. Give us a few minutes."

Harry looked her in the eye then reluctantly nodded. "Guard her. She rushes into danger."

"I know. Don't worry." She pulled her jacket away from her body far enough to show the gun seated in a small holster at her waist. Then, after patting his arm, she led the dogs out to where Kate was standing, checking her pockets for poop bags.

Kate loved and respected Maeve but she'd give anything to be alone. She needed to think and not just about the killer who wanted her dead, but about what was going on between her and Harry. She had thought they'd worked out their relationship, which was why she'd agreed to marry him. Now he was going back to being all protective and treating her as though she were helpless. She hated it and she knew she could never be the type of sweet, helpless little woman he seemed to want. Pain welled up in her chest, and she fought tears.

They had only walked a short way when Maeve asked, "Kate, what do you know about the Illegals Program?"

Kate pulled her attention back to her surroundings and said, "You mean people who enter the country illegally?"

"No, this is different. It was a name given to an operation to identify and round up a number of operatives, or spies if you will, who had been living undercover here for many years. They were caught and traded to Russia by the Obama administration for four people we wanted to get out of Russian prisons. These people had come into the country by way of Canada. They found homes in various cities all over the East Coast and lived like normal, everyday Americans. What made the operation interesting and somewhat unique was the fact they were all caught before they could carry out their plans or cause damage. It became a high-profile case, and the media ran with it, unlike most operations of this kind."

"You mean unlike when the Coyote was caught and quietly sent back to Russia."

"Exactly. The major difference with him was the fact he never revealed the object of his final operation. There was enough of a record from his earlier activities to have cause to expel him. No one knew what his last assignment was, supposedly, or if he had completed it. However, I'm beginning to think Krystyn did. When she arrested him, he was on the show grounds, grooming a dog. Every agency involved went through his belongings with a fine-tooth comb but found nothing. He refused to talk. I suspect he and Krystyn had spoken, but she never came forward with any information. He was charged based on his earlier espionage activities and sent back to Russia. He never said what he was after. Nobody would have nailed him if it hadn't been for my brother Tom, your father, and Krystyn. I liked him. I was upset when I'd found out he was a spy. However, since we had spies in Russia at the time, I viewed it as a case of tit for tat. I knew Krystyn was his friend, and she even took the dog he'd been grooming at the time into the ring. She was good at her job and did what she had to." Maeve sighed, and Kate wondered if she suspected Kate was on her way to meet the Coyote.

They kept walking while Kate debated telling Maeve the Coyote was here but decided not to. She didn't want to put her great-aunt in a position of having to choose duty over friendship. Kate's mind wandered away from spies to the more pressing problem she was having with Harry's overprotective behavior.

"Maeve, after you married Padraig, you kept working for MI-5 on and off, didn't you?"

"Yes. Not full-time, but when they needed me."

"Were you ever in danger during these operations?"

"Yes. What is it you want to know?"

"How did Padraig react, and did he try to stop you?"

"Ah. Harry's trying to keep you safe, and you're

used to rushing into situations whenever you see a problem and trying to fix them. Lately, it has put your life in danger and led to Harry being shot. Remember, he is a trained professional. He may not be with the Bureau anymore, but he's not going to forget all that training.

"Did it cause problems between Padraig and me? I won't lie to you. Yes it did. We had some knock-down, drag-out rows over my putting myself in danger. He loves me, and it took a while for me to see how my work was hurting him. In our last fight, he asked me to think about what it would be like if he were the one constantly rushing into danger then he walked out the door not telling me where he was going, and he didn't come back." Maeve stopped walking and continued. "I was angry. It took me hours to calm down. Eventually, though, I remembered he wasn't trained the way I was. You see him as big and strong and smart. However, he's also a straight arrow who believes the best of his fellow man until proven wrong. I would move heaven and earth to stop him from doing anything that would put him in harm's way. I think you should talk to Padraig rather than me. You should ask how he dealt with it. I will talk with Harry, if you want. All I know is there had to be a lot of give-and-take on both sides. We worked to be sure we didn't lose each other's love. My advice to both of you is to thrash it out before the wedding."

Maeve's words sank in. The fact these two wonderful people whom she could not conceive of as being apart had almost lost each other, scared her. She loved Harry. Was her stubbornness going to cause her to lose him? Deep in reverie, she suddenly felt Dillon press against her leg.

Glancing down, she noticed he was alerting and looking past her off to the right. Turning, she spotted the man from the elevator, watching her as her great-aunt stopped to talk to a group of people. The man jogged over to join the group, not taking his eyes off Kate.

Maeve was chatting away with Taz Gustafson who was introducing the dogs she had with her, Jingle Bells, Jelly Bean, and Peanut, to those in the group. She mentioned the rest of her crew was up in her room. Taz had traveled from Virginia, so her trip had been relatively short.

As the pressure of Dillon's body pressing against her leg grew, Kate felt the hackles come up on his neck. Kate joined him in watching the man. He didn't fit. For one thing, it was obvious he wasn't a dog person. He listened to what was being said, paying close attention. He watched the behavior of those in the group, stroking the dog at his side just as the others were doing. But his attention was focused on her. He seemed confused when Taz talked about her dogs as though they were people. After a few minutes, he smiled, nodded to the group, and wandered toward the venue without having spoken. Kate watched him leave. She'd bet her favorite running shoes his face was in some file back in Washington. But was he someone she had to fear? He hadn't been aggressive. Kate didn't know. She mentally put him on the list for the others to keep an eye on.

Quinn was getting bored. He either wanted to be let loose to play or to continue their walk. Kate bent to give him some attention when she felt herself being bumped from behind. A middle-aged woman apologized, and Maeve introduced the woman as Mrs. Garner, whom Maeve and Padraig had met at breakfast. She explained it was her first National. She didn't talk much, but just stood with her puppy, watching Kate to the point where she began to feel uncomfortable. Twice, the woman reached out to take hold of Quinn's lead when Kate was distracted, but each time, Quinn backed away to sit at her side. After the second attempt, Kate noticed the woman had something concealed in her hand.

Taking advantage of Maeve's formal introduction, she stepped forward with a big smile pasted on her face and reached out, taking the woman's hand to shake, saying, "It's nice to meet someone who is just getting started in the breed. Maeve didn't say if you are entered in the show or—oh, I'm sorry. I didn't realize you had something in your hand." Kate lifted the woman's hand and checked out her palm before letting go. What Kate saw was almost an exact copy of the one of the gizmos Pulaski had brought to their room. Mrs. Garner pulled her hand back and stuffed it into her pocket. A minute later, the gathering moved on, and Mrs. Gardner broke off and met up with the man from the elevator.

Maeve turned to her as soon as they were alone and asked, "What was going on with you and Mrs. Garner?"

At Maeve's concerned question, Kate decided to share. "The thing that cut Mrs. Garner's hand when I shook it was a listening device. She was trying to bug my dog."

Maeve stopped and stared at her. "Bug your dog?"

Kate kept walking. She had to get Dillon to relieve himself before his run. She headed for her meeting with the Coyote. With Maeve on her tail, she wasn't going to be able to ask him what she needed to know. She'd better think fast because she had less than a minute to come up with a plan B.

# Chapter Twenty
*Tuesday, late morning*

Harry watched Maeve and Kate walk away. He forced himself to relax. Maeve was a trained professional. Granted, she hadn't been an active agent out in the field in a while, but if the stories Kate had told him about Maeve and the conversations he'd had with her himself were any test, Kate would be in safe hands.

Turning back to the NSA agent, he began explaining the first two pages of the report as he waited for the rest to print. On his way back to the printer, he reached into the cupboard over the sofa for a leather bag and pulled out a small black box. He flicked a switch, set it on the counter near them, and went to get the rest of the report. The major and Brownridge read the first pages together then Harry set the rest of it on the table for both men to see. Pulling out a folding stool from the cupboard, he sat at the end of the dinette and waited for their questions, though his attention was only half focused on the report.

"You've got good people working for you, Foyle. I wish half my agents were this thorough. However, you will need to explain to a non-geek what most of this is," Brownridge said after finishing the final page.

"In layman's terms, our hacker bought some very fancy toys allowing him to break into Krystyn's account and create an email, seemingly from her. This was sent to the entire Samoyed Club email list. Assuming he didn't get this list from her account tells me he hacked into the club's account as well. By sending out the email, he created a firestorm of activity, giving him much more data with which to work."

"I wonder if my account has been jeopardized as well." The major pulled his phone from his jacket pocket and stared at it.

Harry reached across the table for the phone and, opening the cupboard above the sofa, grabbed a second leather pouch. From this, he pulled a couple of small electronic gadgets and placed them on the table alongside a tiny screwdriver. First, he slipped off the case of the phone and then pried off the back. Gently lifting out the battery, he reached back into the bag for tweezers and used them to remove what resembled a small scrap of paper printed to imitate a chip. This was attached to several wires not much thicker than a human hair. He then pulled a small but weighty box out and secured the scrap inside. The silent attention of the two men continued as he checked the phone with two machines he had then replaced the battery and cover, handing it back to the now very pale major.

"This just gets worse by the minute. I've got to get Xiang over here. What is that thing?" Wetherly fished out his own phone and stared at it as though it would bite him any minute. Then he sent a text to his fellow agent.

"It's a very sophisticated bug that detects keystrokes. This part here," he said pointing to a small collection of squiggles on the tiny paper-like scrap, "is a listening device. It has not only very large range, but from what I've read in the report you're holding, is capable of having its signal picked up and broadcast just about anywhere on a narrow band. Essentially, Major, anything you said or typed into this phone could not only be heard or read but could be sent to a third party anywhere. Depending on when you last set it down and turned your back on it for a minute, which is all it would take to install, someone has been able to listen in on all of your conversations and read all your texts." Harry watched as the weight of what he said was absorbed. The major's skin turned gray. He dropped his head into his arms, and a shudder ran through him.

"Everything I said to Krystyn was heard? Everything I said to my staff, the Joint Chiefs, my God, everything I said to the President was heard? I'm going to be sick." He rose, pushed past Harry, and dove into the bathroom, slamming the door.

Agent Brownridge nodded to the front of the motor home, and they slid into those seats, giving the major some privacy. "I'm beginning to wonder just how powerful these people are. They've spent a ton of money on Krystyn's murder and the attempts on Kate. Who has that kind of money and power? What do they want? And the most puzzling part is, why here at a bloomin' dog show?" He sighed and picked up the stack of paper. "What does the rest of this report tell us, and keep it simple?"

A tap on the window made Harry and Brownridge

glance up. Captain Glasmann pointed toward the door, and Harry nodded.

"Gentlemen," Glasmann said as he entered, "my men are getting themselves into position. I thought I'd touch base with you and see if you had any updates. By the way, Miss Killoy was dead-on with her description of what we'd find at the house. It's a good thing we knew going in. If it had gone off, it would not only have taken the house, it would have put a large hole in the neighborhood and killed a lot of innocent people. Where is she, by the way?"

"She's out with her dogs, but her great-aunt is with her, so she's fine," Harry said. He checked his watch and realized if Kate were to meet the Coyote on time, she'd be doing it in the next few minutes. He fought the urge to run and be there to protect her. Kate was able to protect herself. It didn't stop him from being glad Maeve was armed. If she was going to keep throwing herself into dangerous situations, he'd talk to Sal about teaching Kate to shoot. Sal would be the first one to remind him, though, when he was set up in his final assignment for the Bureau, it was a dog that saved his life in the middle of the gun battle. His attention was jerked back to the problem at hand when Glasmann handed him a small black object appearing to Harry to be a transmitter but, he realized, was one he hadn't seen before. He took out his phone and took a photo then sent it to Seamus. "Where did you get this, and what is it?" he asked.

We found it at Pulaski's place along with some gizmos our bomb squad says are remote detonators. From the look of the place, he wasn't living there alone. We're not getting much out of him, and I've got a couple of my people watching him in case he conjures up a bomb from what he's got in his cell."

Harry's phone dinged, and he pulled it out to find a text from Seamus. It's a very powerful transmitter, just out in the last few months. Controls signals like ones sent to your car or your house. This transmitter can override your smart car's computer system. Could make you drive off a bridge. On Pulaski's purchase list. S.

"It's a transmitter, a powerful one." He turned his phone so the men could read it. "The question is why he would need it. This is a dog show. Everyone comes here and stays the week. I'm not sure why he bought it, unless it has nothing to do with what's going on and he just was into fancy toys."

"I think somebody has a plan for all this stuff, and we're standing on the edge of something very scary and dangerous," Glasmann said.

They all glanced up as the major appeared from the back of the motor home, followed quickly by a knock at the door. Harry stepped over to the door and opened it to see Joyce Marks and some other people staring back at him.

"Hope we're not interrupting, Harry, but we decided a few extra pairs of eyes can't hurt if Kate's out in the ring with Dillon and in danger of getting shot. Oh, hi there, Major, I'm so sorry about Krystyn."

"Hello, Joyce. It's been a few years since I've seen you. Gentlemen, this is Joyce Marks, a friend of Krystyn's who works for the Denver Sheriff's Department. This is Wetherly Brownridge from the NSA, Joyce, and this is

Captain Bernard Glasmann from Louisville Police. They're here both because of Krystyn and the fact someone shot at Kate yesterday."

"So I heard. Foyle, where's your fiancée? You didn't let her go wandering around by herself, did you?"

"No, she's with Maeve."

"Okay. Oh, speak of the devil. There she is."

Harry turned and saw Dillon and Liam in the lead with Quinn and Shelagh right behind and Kate and Maeve bringing up the rear. He didn't realize he was in motion until he found himself grabbing Kate and hugging her. After a quick kiss. he whispered, "Did you meet up with our friend?"

Kate nodded, but as she turned toward her those waiting by the motor home, she mumbled, "Later."

Joyce focused her attention on Quinn, talking about changes in him since she last saw him in Texas. "I think he's going to be as big as Dillon or maybe even Liam. The good bone is showing already, and the angulation is developing nicely. We'll talk later, Kate. You've got to get ready to compete, but I'll have you move him and your bitch after the agility competition finishes or tomorrow morning."

Harry scooped up Quinn and put him in his crate then held the doors open for Liam and Shelagh. He flipped on the generator switch and the fans and then he opened the roof vents fully. "Okay, gang. Get a good nap while Dillon goes and makes you proud. We'll be back before you know it." He turned to find Kate standing in the doorway, smiling at him. He cocked his head. "What?"

"You've become a real dog person," she said softly, and Harry felt her words hug him. From Kate, you couldn't get higher praise.

"Thanks." He pulled out his phone to check the time. "You're on in about twenty minutes, so we'd better get going." Then he contradicted himself by pulling her into a hug, holding her tight. "You scare me so much. I know I can't protect you from everything, but you've got to know when you take chances, you frighten me."

"Maeve thinks you should talk to Donnelly. He's had to put up with her derring-do for over fifty years. Maybe he could give you some hints on how he's stayed sane." Kate chuckled.

"Not a bad idea. At least I might get some sympathy." He kissed her quickly, and then they went down the steps and locked up Charlie. The dogs would be comfortable and sleep while Kate was in the ring. As they began to walk toward the building, Harry noted they had attracted a large group of friends and professionals with eyes on the crowd. Lily appeared on Kate's right. Without a word, Kate took out her phone, pulled up the icon for shooting video, and handed it to her.

"The crowd or the run?" she asked.

"The run," Kate said. "I know they're filming it officially, but I'd like to see how we do, and find if all these scares are throwing me off my game. I need to know I can still do my job in the ring because I've got a lot more events this week. At least, today, with enough protection to guard a small city watching over me here, I know I'll be safe in the ring.

"Got it." Lily pocketed the phone and squeezed Kate's hand. Checking the lay of the building, she moved toward a spot where she could capture the entire run. Harry watched Kate's entourage spread out around the venue, all watching the crowd for any sign of irregularities. He spotted Cathy with Yerik making a slow circuit of the arena. Harry glanced up at the broadcast booth above them on the left and spotted a pair of policemen, one inside and one by the door. Glasmann handed him an earpiece. He inserted it, and it buzzed with a signal check. He acknowledged he could hear them loud and clear. To his right, Maeve and Brownridge talked together and then began to move through the crowd in a slow pattern, separate but nodding to one another and each placing a hand to their earpiece as the checks continued.

At the far end, in the stands above the weave poles, the two policemen conferred. Kate was protected. Now, all she needed was to relax. Harry stepped up to stand behind her, his fingers working slowly over her shoulders to her neck. After a minute, Kate let out a moan. Harry laughed. He leaned in and whispered, "There are other ways I could ease your tension and make you moan."

Kate turned and smiled over her shoulder. "You seem to be a good teacher, kind sir. I'm looking forward to learning them all." The warmth of her smile and the images in his head had his temperature rising.

They silently watched the other runs, the situation too strained to say anything. He wondered why, as she watched each Sam clearing jumps, Kate remained calm. He didn't know how she could stand the waiting since her run would be last. Finally, one of the ring stewards approached and signaled Kate to the ready area. She moved as the pair before her started their run. Harry squeezed her hand and headed toward the wooden barrier. As the pair before them raced across the finish line, Kate stepped up to the start line, preparing to remove Dillon's lead.

Breaking his gaze from Kate, Harry scanned the crowd. Their friends were spread out, checking people from every angle. His focus returned to Kate in time to see her shoulders relax, her head lift, and back straighten. Harry didn't believe in ghosts, but he'd seen this sequence of moves once before. She had told him she'd felt the presence of Tom and John Killoy, her late grandfather and father. They always seemed to be with her in her time of need. Kate had told him, though she couldn't see them, she'd feel their hands on her shoulders as they had done every time she'd gone into the ring as a child. It was recalling the feeling, be it real or imagined, that restored her natural courage. He watched Kate study the pattern of jumps and close her eyes as though speaking to God to get them through this safely. When she turned her gaze on him, she was aglow and smiling. Her spark was back.

Dillon appeared frozen in anticipation. The dog's eyes followed Kate, not distracted by anything around him. She bent to remove Dillon's lead. Then, after telling Dillon to wait, she walked to the start position.

The judge nodded and, with a flick of Kate's finger, a bomb seemed to go off under Dillon, and he flew forward, attacking the course. That was when Harry spotted the man from the elevator standing at ringside off to his right. The guy glanced around and reached into his coat. Harry couldn't see what he was pulling out at first, but when he spotted the snub nose revolver, he didn't wait. Keeping his focus on the man's hand, he ran along the bleachers, dodging spectators. With one final burst of speed, Harry reached the section where the man stood. The man turned toward him, his eyes widened and, pocketing the gun, he quickly disappeared into the crowd, gone without a trace.

# CHAPTER TWENTY-TWO
## *Tuesday, still later in the morning*

"Need eyes on man dressed in charcoal-gray pinstripe suit and blue tie, armed, left side of the building, find and hold," Harry spoke into his mic. He shifted his attention back to Kate then swiveled his head around searching for more danger. Still searching, he reversed direction, weaving back through the crowd, pressing against the boards, yelling. He dodged up a few steps and ran along a clear row of seats then jumped down when he reached an opening in the boards. Without really taking his eyes off Kate, he slammed his hand against his ear.

"What's going on? Anyone spot the gunman? Talk to me."

He heard nothing for a few seconds then someone said, "Over to your left. He's exiting the building."

Harry turned but could see nothing. Without trying to follow, he turned his attention back on Kate and Dillon.

Calling into his mic again, he shouted, "What's happening? Is Kate in danger?"

Kate and Dillon flew around the ring. Everything

inside him yelled, jump, jump faster, don't slow down on the dog walk, you're too exposed, through tunnel, change direction, Dillon faster, jump, long jump, up the seesaw, into the second tunnel. The A-frame, too exposed. Unable to stand it, he started into the ring only to feel hands holding him back.

"Let them finish," a voice spoke in his ear.

"What's happening?" His anguished cry was drowned out as Dillon shot from the tunnel then over one jump, two jumps, onto the pause table where Kate froze, along with Dillon. Then they were again in motion, Dillon flying over two jumps, slamming through the weave poles, as Kate kept pace, followed by two more jumps and the last tunnel. Harry, not daring to tear his eyes from Kate, saw when she spotted the end mark and urged Dillon to soar over the last two jumps and tear toward the finish. As Dillon streaked across the line, Harry wrenched free from whoever was holding him and raced to meet them. Dillon whirled, sprang up for Kate's hug and knocked them both against Harry as static sounded in Harry's ear. The sound was instantly drowned out by the cheers of the crowd. Harry scooped her into his arms and dove behind the ring barrier. He set her feet on the ground but couldn't stop hugging her tight to his chest.

"Harry, what's wrong? You're squeezing the life out of me." Kate tipped her head back to look up at him. He smiled and loosened his grip. "Kate, I…"

"Did you see the run? Dillon was on fire." Dillon jumped up again, his front legs hugging them both.

A voice in Harry's earpiece spoke. "We lost him.

He ran into the crowd of people outside. He never came out. Must have changed his appearance." He drew a slightly shuddering breath, leaned in, and gave Kate a quick kiss. "You were fantastic."

"Let her go, Harry. She needs to go into the ring. They're giving out the scores." He turned and spotted Maeve behind them, pale but determined. Hers had been the voice that had stopped him from running into the ring. He couldn't look at her. She'd kept him from protecting Kate, and he'd need time to forgive her.

Kate kissed him and whispered, "I'll be right back." Moving proudly with Dillon at her side, she headed back into the ring behind the other competitors. The loudspeaker began to announce the scores. They ran the gamut, though most were qualifying. Harry didn't know if their speed had been the luck of the Irish or just the dog's skill, but Dillon had flown through the course in record time with no faults so he ended up the winner. Kate smiled and hugged her dog. She thanked the judge and posed for photos as she accepted the trophy and ribbon.

Their friendly spy master pushed his cart by Harry and whispered, "The NSA, police, and FBI did their job today but this guy is good. He'd probably changed his appearance as soon as he cleared the door. They were waiting for a shooter and ran into the invisible man." He turned toward Kate and said, "She hasn't changed that much since she was a child. You should have seen her with her Sams back then. It was magic." He gave a quick nod and pushed his cart toward the smaller garbage receptacle. Joyce and Cathy joined Maeve as all of them swept into the ring and gave Kate hugs and congratulations. He saw her smile but at the same time, her exhaustion. Lily was telling her she could check out the run on the video she shot and shoved the phone into Kate's pocket. Joyce glanced back at the door but didn't say anything. Instead, she excused herself and headed off in the direction of Captain Glasmann and agent Xiang.

Maeve hugged Kate and said, "You are all done in. It was quite a run. Time to go back to Charlie because your day is not over yet."

Harry scrutinized the area as he tried to shake off the terror and helplessness he'd felt.

His head snapped in her direction when she said, "I can't believe we made it through the morning with no attacks. The police must have put up a huge protective area around the building."

Harry caught her to him, wrapped his arms around her back, and held her tight. "Kate, there was an armed man at ringside." He took her face in his hands. "He got through FBI and police traps but wasn't able to get off his shot."

Kate stared at him in silence for a minute then took a breath, reached up to pull his head down for a quick kiss, and grinned a slightly lopsided half smile. "I think I need to find a place to sit down."

Harry scooped her up and gently carried her to the motor home. Once inside, he sat her on the sofa, pushed her head down between her legs, wet a couple of cloths at the sink, placed one on the back of her neck, and used the other to wipe her face as he rubbed gentle circles on her back.

Maeve, who was standing in the doorway said, “I’m sorry, Kate. I underestimated you. It seems this man you’re marrying knows you pretty well. I’ll leave you to it. I need to talk to Wetherly. Padraig’s here, so we’ll take the major and go back with him.”

After a few minutes, G arrived. He didn’t say anything but helped Harry get the dogs inside and put the pens away. Then he spoke with Harry for a minute, checking to see if he could manage. Like all law enforcement, he had reports to file. He left, telling them he’d see them later.

“Ready to go back to the hotel, or would you rather go somewhere else?” Harry asked, watching her face for shock.

“I’d rather go for a drive and find a quiet, open place where we can talk and nobody can overhear us.”

“It sounds good to me. I’m hungry. Let’s find a place where we can park and have a picnic.” Harry moved to the driver’s seat while Kate checked all the dogs were secure then sat in the passenger seat.

Harry steered Charlie out of the parking lot and turned right. About a hundred yards down the road, he stopped at a light and Kate yelled, “Don’t go yet.” Scrambling into the back, she opened the side door. Harry started to turn his head when someone in a car behind him beeped his horn and Kate called out, “Go.”

She slipped back into her seat, fastened her seat belt then pulled out her new phone and began to search. “There is a city park with a picnic area five miles ahead. Let’s try that.”

"It sounds good to me." A voice from the cabin had Harry's head whipping around.

"Harry, watch the road," Kate yelled.

"Kate, what's going on?"

"Plan B," Kate told him, smiling.

"Are you okay, Kate?" The Coyote knelt between them, looking very much like a drifter thumbing his way across the country and said, "You're Wonder Woman. The shooter never would have stood a chance of hitting you if he tried. You really were faster than a speeding bullet today with Dillon flying around the ring."

"The speeding bullet was Superman not Wonder Woman," Kate told him as she sat back with a smile on her face. The smile became a frown as she asked him, "Why is someone trying to kill me? I don't know anything. I'm a threat to nobody."

"I am finding someone had been monitoring Krystyn's communications for a while," Coyote said.

Harry added, "She must have hinted at something to the major. Some information about Kate they picked up when they tapped his phone." He pulled into the lot at the park and drove until he found an out-of-the-way place for the motor home.

Coyote added, "I'm sure it has something to do with my arrest years ago. Ask your father or grandfather. They might have an idea if it does."

"I'm afraid we can't ask. Gramps lost his life to cancer almost two years ago and, three months after that, Dad died of an aneurysm."

"Oh, I'm so sorry, Kate. I didn't know. They were

both such good men. They loved you and were so proud of all you did."

"I know." Her voice choked, and she blinked away tears. "I miss them all the time. But you still haven't told me if you have any idea what they're searching for. I don't even have an idea what this thing, whatever it is, would look like if I found it."

"The end of my career as a spy came with very little hoopla. I suppose I should tell you the whole story." He helped Kate put the last dog into the pen attached to Charlie, and then Harry stepped out of the motor home with sandwiches, chips, and drinks on a large tray, and they sat at one of the empty picnic tables to eat.

"I had wanted to stop the game for quite a while. Life as a spook is not fun. You live in secrecy, not daring to say a thing even to those you trust most. I knew my handlers were beginning to feel I was expendable. My previous two assignments had been very dangerous, and I'd barely escaped with my life. This one, if anything, was worse.

"It takes a spook to know a spook, and I'd already realized Krystyn recently had been recruited to the hunt for the Coyote. This alone changed the game. The other spy hunters were clueless, but I knew she would figure it out. My goal was to get out without getting killed. The show was a National, though smaller than this one, with fewer activities going on. I was handling a puppy in Sweepstakes, an open dog, an open bitch, and a special. The owner wasn't at the show because it was too far for her to travel. Krystyn was on the committee and chose not to compete even though she could have. We talked, even ate lunch together several times during the week. On Thursday, after the judging, I made my move. The house had just quieted for the evening following the funeral of the owner. People had come and gone during the post-funeral gathering, and I had no trouble blending in and then concealing myself when people left. Once the house was quiet, I emerged from where I'd hidden and went to the library because I'd been told to find a specific book. I found it open on a table by an easy chair. I took it and quickly left. No sooner was I off the property than several police cars arrived, so I must have set off a silent alarm.

"As I did with every score, I hid what I'd taken rather than keeping it on me. On Friday morning, Krystyn came to my grooming area and told me I'd been spotted on camera, leaving the home. I didn't deny I had been there, but pointed out it wasn't a crime. She agreed and we both sat and enjoyed the sunshine. She told me she'd found out the owner of the house had been a high-powered publisher with some rather shady friends. He'd died under suspicious circumstances on the previous Monday, and his death was being investigated. I told Krystyn I was handling dogs on a four-day circuit six states away on Monday. She told me she didn't suspect I'd killed the man, but word was out he had some secret information he was about to publish that could destroy a lot of people's lives and could shake the government at the highest levels. She asked me what I'd done with it because she had no doubt I'd taken the information.

"I had smelled a rat when I was originally given my assignment since the request came from the FSB, the Federal Security Service, rather than my usual handlers. Those people could care less about corporate espionage, which was what I had been doing. I wasn't told what I was taking, but only that it would be in a specific paperback detective story in this house, probably in the man's library. I was given instructions on Friday evening, to bring the book and go with a man who would be waiting for me on the bench for the airport shuttle outside the hotel. They would take care of checking me out of the hotel. I don't know what they planned for the dogs.

"This was a complete change of routine for me so I was pretty sure I would meet with an accident as soon as I handed over the book. With that in mind, before the judging, I drove to a drugstore in a nearby strip mall and picked up a duplicate copy of the paperback novel. Then I made sure it was dog-eared to resemble exactly the original, including the coffee stain on page seventy-eight. I contacted Krystyn and arranged for her to arrest me on Friday evening as I approached the bench. While they were arresting me, I surreptitiously dropped the duplicate book into the bushes behind the bench. I figured it would take time for my handlers to analyze the book and find whatever was supposed to be hidden there wasn't, and to notify the people pulling the strings at FSB.

"I needed a personal favor from Krystyn. I told her I'd give her what she needed for the arrest if she would promise to hide my wife and baby for me and tell nobody, not even me, where they were. She agreed, and I trusted her. So I explained my assignment and what I'd found. I gave her the book I'd taken. I left it up to her to decide what to do with it. When the arrest was made, she was filmed taking me captive. It was the top story on the nightly news cycle. She told me later she'd taken the special I'd been showing into the ring for me. Then she made sure the dogs got safely back to their owner. It was the last contact we had with each other until recently. I was jailed and later returned to Russia. I managed to disappear eventually and after I changed my appearance, work my way back here."

"So you have no clue what was in the book that was so dangerous?" Kate asked.

"No, I saw in the book jumbled words. They didn't make sense. It must have been a code or something worked into the text. No one mentioned a book during my hearing, so I suspected Krystyn had kept it. My Russian handlers thought they had it. I called her to ask about my family before coming here. She said she'd contact them and see if they wanted to meet me. At the same time, I asked if she'd found what was hidden in the book. She said she had decoded it, but it was too dangerous to release. She called it explosive."

# CHAPTER TWENTY-THREE
*Tuesday, noon*

Kate stared at Coyote. "I assume the people who killed Krystyn are trying to find what was in the book to either expose it or hide it. They probably figured out she had it when they listened in on the conversation with you. They knew it still existed and the Russians didn't have it."

"When I contacted Krystyn, I asked her if she had hidden what she promised. She said she had. She also said if anything happened to her, the one with the long golden braid would have the answers. I asked about her dogs. We chatted for a few minutes and then rang off. Two weeks later, I heard she was dead and realized it was probably my fault for calling her."

"She kept the book that got her killed," Harry spoke up. "Neither of you knew her phone was tapped."

"The information was in code."

"Like Maeve, Krystyn loved codes and was good at solving them. Whereas, when I glanced through the story before giving it to her, there were many pages of jumbled words."

"Did she give you a clue where your family is?"

"No, she wanted to check and see if they wanted to meet me. With her death, the connection was lost."

Kate studied his serious, sad expression and asked, "Do you think that was what she was going to tell me?"

"It's not important. What's vital is catching the people who are trying to get the information over your dead body."

His face was a picture of loss, and she knew he'd just lied to her. Finding his family was vital to him. Whatever Krystyn had been going to tell her was vital to him. However, his family's information had nothing to do with the shooters who were after her.

Kate snorted. "Well the rest of show week is going to be fun. I'll go on being Kate Killoy, the clown in this circus, until all the players are caught or I'm dead. And to think I was actually looking forward to attending the National so much after not having gone last year. I suspect I won't remember this week, with fondness—if I survive."

The Coyote turned to Harry. "Having second thoughts about marrying her?"

"Oh, yeah. I think I'm going to have a permanent bruise on my ego from her stating the obvious."

"It's a good thing you love her, man, because she can be scary sometimes."

Harry drove into the motor home area at the show venue and parked Charlie. The three of them had reviewed again what they knew but hadn't come up with any workable plan about what to do next. The Coyote glanced through the windshield and smiled. "Here comes the Irish beauty. I'd better make tracks. We'll talk soon." He patted

Kate on the shoulder then ducked out the door and vanished among the motor homes.

Minutes later, Maeve slipped inside the door and said, "Say hello to him for me when you next talk."

Kate made her face blank. "Hello? To whom?"

Maeve ignored the question. "He always was a handsome devil and worth watching whether moving around the ring on the human end of the lead or just strolling along. There were few of us poor females who could resist taking a peek. I was sure I recognized his hand movement when you were chatting by the exercise pen earlier. Even in disguise, he has style. Luckily, people here don't know the tell he does with his hand."

"Are you going to expose him to Agent Brownridge?"

"Why would I do that? He's not a spy anymore is he? I assume he's helping you try to find Krystyn's killer. They were good friends, and it was hard on her to arrest him, though I think she only did it to save his life. He had a target on his back. Did you know it was Tom who made sure it happened peacefully? Your grandfather would have made a good agent. Believe me, both MI-5 and the CIA tried to recruit him, but he always put family first and said he was happier doing what he did."

"I didn't know they wanted him to be an agent, but I think you're wrong about him being agent material. Gramps was never a company man. He was more interested in justice than getting his man."

"Much as we could have used his talents, you're probably right. He would have driven the powers that be up the wall."

Kate smiled. "You know the world of spies would never have allowed either Dad or Gramps to go around with a Sammy sidekick, and I can't imagine them any other way."

She debated telling Maeve about feeling her father's hand on her shoulder as she headed onto the course. But she didn't want her to think she was cracking under the strain.

Then Maeve leaned in and shocked Kate by saying, "Both Tom and John were with you today. I felt them. They would have been so proud of you and Dillon in the ring. They would also have liked the way you've been handling what's been going on here. You should be aware there's an inner circle of law enforcement and agents working as hard as they can to protect you and capture these people trying to hurt you, be they agents for foreign powers or just evil people."

She wondered how this group of agents would feel knowing part of "her inner circle" was a former master spy.

Kate was startled when Harry spoke up. "Pardon me if I'm not impressed with the 'protecting' element in the game they have laid out. It seems to me they're using her as bait. They knew she'd be exposed in the ring and vulnerable. The powers that be seem to be hoping the shooter would take advantage of the situation. They were having no trouble using Kate as an enticement in the capture attempt."

Maeve stepped down into the parking lot and slammed the door without answering. After they finished putting everything away in Charlie, Kate stepped into the bathroom area and changed into her ring clothes.

"You need any help?" She heard Harry ask.

A few minutes later Kate pulled the curtain aside. "As a matter of fact, I could use some help." She walked forward wearing a sleeveless dress in royal blue with a flip skirt ending a couple of inches above the knee and was carrying a short light-blue jacket with patch pockets. She turned showing the dress zipper was barely started. "I need help with my zipper."

Harry took hold of the zipper bottom with one hand and the slide with the other and slowly pulled it up, stroking the skin of her back as he did. He kissed her neck before giving the zipper a final tug and hooking the tiny hook at the top. They both let out shuddering breaths and then laughed. He held her jacket while she slipped it on. The sterling silver Samoyed pin her grandfather had given her was attached to the jacket. She wore it into the breed ring for luck, and she'd need all the luck she could get.

Kate grabbed the old lab coat she wore to keep her ring clothes nice while she finished grooming before going in the ring, and then they gathered the dogs and headed into the building. G, who was coming out the door, did an about-turn and followed them.

Inside, Maeve had Pavlik up on the table doing his finish grooming. Kate put Dillon, Quinn, and Shelagh in crates then got Liam on the table and began to work. Harry picked up the dryer and, adjusting it to a cooler setting, moved the blowing air to follow her hands as she back-combed Liam's coat, forcing each hair to stand straight out from the dog's body.

With ten minutes to go, Joyce walked up, carrying armbands both for her and the major. Harry lifted Liam from the table and had him shake. Then, nodding to Kate, he took him outside for one last chance to pee. G kept surveying the crowd, but told Kate he'd spotted nothing. Kate packed up her grooming case and, by the time Harry returned, it was time to head to the ring. She looked over at Maeve who only smiled and nodded.

When they got to the ring, Kate spotted Joceline with one of her champions. Consulting the catalog, Kate saw she would be up against some very nice dogs, but Liam was in fantastic shape. So many of the ring moves she'd worked with Dillon had come from working with his father. Liam loved the ring, and she could feel his eagerness coming up the lead. She had the highest armband number of this group, so she'd be the last into the ring, meaning she could use as much room as she needed to show him off without crowding anyone. As the other exhibitors filed past her, she felt a hand on her shoulder and turned to see Harry standing just as her father had, encouraging her. "Do your best and give them a good show," he whispered. Kate straightened her shoulders, smiled, and headed into the ring.

She had never been under this judge before, a Siberian Husky breeder from Washington State who'd been licensed to judge Samoyeds for about six years. Kate had checked her record online and was not disappointed in the dogs she'd put up. Her ring management would require watching. They all circled the ring with their dogs. Kate waited an extra two seconds before starting so Liam could make full use of the room to extend his gait. When they reached the spot where they'd wait to be examined, Liam stacked himself and watched Kate, alert but relaxed. She checked out the first dog in line, Joceline's male. She was setting him up for the judge, moving his feet so he'd be stacked perfectly and jerking his collar, giving him a command to hold.

The judge approached, established a rapport with the dog then had the handler show the bite. She proceeded to examine the dog, her hands mapping his body and recording his assets and faults. The judge next instructed Joceline to move him to the far corner of the ring and back. When Joceline returned from gaiting, she baited the dog, swinging her hand around to keep him alert. The judge then had her move the dog around the ring to the end of the line and turned to the next dog to be judged.

Joceline ran her dog right up to Liam, crowding him. She moved around, baiting her dog and playing with him to the point of bumping into Liam. The old Joceline was trying to shake up and distract her competition. Kate stepped to the side, moving Liam out of line, and placed herself between Liam and Joceline's male, hiding Liam from the judge's view as the woman checked out the line of dogs between examinations. That had been Joceline's aim. Kate stayed calm, smiling at her dog and talking to him quietly. She glanced over at the judge as she finished the fourth dog in the class. The judge raised an eyebrow when she spotted the spacing flaw but didn't do anything. The dog before her stepped into the box to be examined.

Joceline went to move forward, but Kate held up her hand to stop her, looking her in the eye and challenging her to try one of her stunts where the judge could see her. Kate reached down and scratched Liam's ears, relaxed her shoulders, and watched the judge's hands, to see exactly what she was feeling for as they moved through the coat. The dog went up and back, posed and then moved around the ring.

Kate walked Liam into the box, glanced down to be sure he was perfectly stacked and then stepped to the end of her lead so as not to interfere with the judge's view of the dog. The judge stood focusing him and then moved to his other side before returning to approach. Kate stepped in to show the judge his bite then, giving him a scratch under the chin, returned to the end of the lead as the judge's examination continued. Liam was a charmer and gazed at the judge, wagging his tail and arching his neck to show off. Kate was tempted to laugh since Dillon did the same thing when he wanted to charm a judge. The judge stepped back to get a good view of him then asked Kate to move him down and back. She slowly turned in a circle to get Liam in position for the judge to get the best view of his rear gait and, with a tiny flick of the lead, moved out. She could have sat at ringside and watched for all Liam needed her. He knew this game. Taking just the right number of steps, he moved smoothly across the ring, slowing, turning, focusing on the judge, and moving back. When he reached the judge, he slowed and then stopped perfectly four square and held the pose with Kate standing off to the side, giving him the appearance of showing himself. The judge circled him completely and then nodded to Kate.

She moved him around the ring, giving him the full lead to move at his own pace.

The judge then pulled Kate up front, put the third dog in line into second place. Joceline went third, and the fifth dog took fourth place. Kate reached down, hugged Liam, and thanked the judge who said, “He really doesn’t need you in the ring to win, does he?”

Kate laughed and answered, “Not at all,” and headed out of the ring.

## Chapter Twenty-Four
### *Tuesday, early afternoon*

Harry met her, took Liam's lead, and gave her a kiss.

He put Liam in his crate and hitched the ribbon to the outside. Kate would have to go back into the ring to compete for Best Veteran in Sweepstakes but, for the moment, she could relax and watch the other classes. The ten-to under twelve-year-old veteran dog class was just finishing and she saw the major, appearing quite spiffy in his charcoal-gray suit, standing at ringside with Pavlik. The dog's attention was focused completely on the major, and Kate thought they made a striking pair. He had a good chance of winning.

There were four males in the class. The major and Pavlik were third into the ring,, and the dog moved to a perfect stack and held the position, not requiring any adjustment on the major's part. He seemed much younger than his age, the best in the ring, provided he showed for the major. At the judge's signal, the group moved around the ring, and though it didn't seem to impact the dog's gait, the major had a slight limp with his left leg. The judge, with the same efficiency she'd shown in the earlier classes, moved quickly in her examination, only this time she gave a slight hug to each of these old troupers. When their turn came, the major stood back as Kate had, allowing the dog to show himself and then, at the judge's request, moved in to show the bite. As the judge's hands moved over Pavlik's back, the dog turned his head and looked over his shoulder, but other than that, didn't move. She indicated to the major to take him down and back. Pavlik moved on a completely loose lead. When they stopped, the dog was four square gazing at the major. The judge stepped forward and made a sound, but Pavlik barely gave her more than a glance and returned his focus to the major. She had them move around, and Kate could see the major's limp, though it wasn't obvious, was holding the dog back.

The judge completed the judging, putting Pavlik first. The major thanked her and rather than waiting in the ring for the final judging, stepped outside and nodded to Maeve. Kate and Liam were headed back to compete for Best Veteran dog in Sweepstakes when she saw her great-aunt remove the armband from the major's arm and slip it onto her own. She took Pavlik's lead and moved into the ring ahead of the winner of the ten to under twelve class winner and Kate. Kate walked Liam into his stack and then glanced over her shoulder to see her great-aunt silently laying down the challenge. She smiled and nodded. This was going to be tough. The judge checked the armbands, noting the change in handler, and then had them move the dogs around the ring, leaving plenty of room in between. The crowd at ringside stood and cheered. Samoyed owners took great pride in the breed's senior dogs. Kate gave Liam his head and the full length of lead, and he moved with grace and ease around the ring. Maeve did an equally good job with Pavlik.

The pattern for the individual gaiting repeated, and Pavlik was perfect on the up and back, stacking himself for the judge, but as they started to move around the ring, he broke gait when he spotted the major hiding partially behind a pillar. Maeve flicked the lead, and the dog went back to work immediately. The second dog moved, but his quality wasn't up to the other two dogs. Kate stepped in with Liam and watched him pull Dillon's trick of charming the judge. He made it quite clear he was showing just for her, and she should watch. His movement down and back was perfect, and he stacked and smiled at the judge, tail wagging throughout. He moved around the ring, smooth and powerful. The judge then asked them to move their dogs around the ring together. Maeve patted Pavlik's chest to make sure she had his attention and slipped him a treat then nodding to Kate, moved out. Kate gave her several steps and then followed. The crowd at ringside went nuts, cheering. They finished the circuit, and the judge told the other dog to step in behind Kate and for them to circle again as she joined in the applause. Halfway around the ring, she stepped forward and pointed at Pavlik.

Kate gave her aunt a hug, congratulating her, and joining in the applause. After giving Liam a hug and kiss on the nose she put him into his crate giving him a treat. Then she walked over to the major. "Krystyn would have been proud," she told him.

"She would have also said Pavlik had the sentimental edge over Liam," he answered. "The judge knew what happened to Krystyn because Cathy just told me she was a member of the kennel club with them."

"Well, I'd like to thank you for giving me a chance to compete against Maeve. It's something I've never done during all my years in the ring. She's absolutely wonderful." Kate gave him a hug.

The lady in question arrived with Padraig carrying the rosette and handed Pavlik back to the major. "That was fun." She grinned at Kate with a twinkle in her eye. Kate reached over to hug her, and then felt a hand on her shoulder as Harry stepped in.

"Are you done for the day or is there more competition?" he asked.

"Well, it's done for me except for getting the photo. Pavlik has to go back in the ring to compete against the best bitch for Best Veteran Samoyed in Sweepstakes." Kate glanced at the ring and saw the judge had already finished the first class of bitches and was almost done with the second. "It won't be long." She picked up the catalog and checked out the entry. "There are only two in the twelve-and-up class, so we should be ready to head back to the hotel in half an hour."

Deshi Xiang approached with a cardboard container filled with cups and a large bag in the center. "I've brought treats for the people since the dogs have had theirs: hot chocolate and donuts."

Kate reached for a cup as Maeve cleared the top of Pavlik's crate and somehow produced a paper plate to hold the treats.

"Thanks, Agent Xiang," she said.

"Call me Des," he told her.

Kate snatched one of the donuts and leaned against Harry who had Dillon at his side. She suddenly realized she'd been in the ring twice, as well as sitting around at ringside, an easy target, and nobody had tried to kill her. He body tensed but then relaxed as she accepted, at least for the moment, she seemed to be safe.

While waiting, Kate put on her lab coat and let Shelagh out of her crate. She stood her on the grooming table and still keeping an eye on the ring, went to work getting any stray loose hairs out of the bitch's coat so when she bathed her in the morning, she'd dry fast. Shelagh laid her head on Kate's shoulder. Most of Kate's bitches were take-charge bossy types, but Shelagh was more of a snuggly cuddly girl. She had style, but she left it to her mother to whip everyone in shape in the kennel. She was so feminine in both style and actions, people were tempted to think of her as delicate, something Kate knew wasn't true. Shelagh was a strong wheel dog on the sled and could go for hours without showing any fatigue. Kate planted a kiss on her nose and then moved to brush her rear as she watched the older bitches move around the ring. Des stroked Shelagh's ears. He smiled. "This one is a real flirt, Kate."

"Shelagh knows how to turn on the charm, and she knows she's beautiful. She only needs her second major to finish. She's got the points, but not the major. I've been too busy to show her for the last few months. If she takes the points tomorrow, I'm going to need extra hands in the Best of Breed ring because I already have two entered."

Dillon is entered as a special, and if Liam wins the veteran dog class he'll also compete for Best of Breed. At least I don't have a class dog entered. Tomorrow, Shelagh will compete in Obedience and Rally. Then, on Thursday, there will be the dog competition with lots and lots of dogs. Then they'll have the veteran dog competition, working dog competition, and the stud dog competition. The judging will take most of the day. On Friday, Shelagh and I will be in the Bred by Exhibitor Bitch class, which, this being a National, will be a very large class. We'll get our exercise."

G came up with Quinn and put him into his crate. "I think I wore him out. We've been all over this place, checking it out. You told Harry you thought you were being watched yesterday. Well, you were. We all were. Big Brother has eyes everywhere. A friend of mine was assigned to be on one of the shifts in the control room. I checked it out. The place is like the cockpit of a 747. There are screens, dials, sensors, etc., everywhere. They can turn on as many or as few as they need at the time. They can lock and unlock the doors, control the temperature, lights, water, Wi-Fi, ventilation, fire extinguishers, everything. Usually, there's only one man up there, but with the cops running checks, the management decided to add an extra man to give more eyes on what's happening. Harry was squatting next to Dillon, listening to what G said, frowning.

"Harry, what's the matter?"

He shook his head. "Later."

Kate didn't press. Harry had said something about smart buildings when they were traveling to the show, but she couldn't remember what.

The bitch judging was coming to a conclusion with the twelve years and older bitches. Maeve had Pavlik up on the table and was giving him a final brushing. At the sound of the applause indicating the judge had selected a winner, she lifted Pavlik down and got him to shake. Padraig took her lab coat, which had been protecting her show clothes, and checked to be sure she had bait. They all joined in the applause for the one selected Best Veteran bitch. Then Maeve moved to ringside, and the judge called her into the ring.

Pavlik was obviously enjoying himself, now used to having Maeve on the other end of the lead. The judge had them move up and back, side by side, and then had both move around the ring. This time, when she made her noise, Pavlik smiled at her and wagged his tail, which was apparently all it took to make the difference since the bitch never took her eyes off the bait the handler held. She pointed to Pavlik, and Maeve grinned, thanked the judge then after hugging the dog she bent and clapped her hands at him. The clap was something Krystyn had always done with her dogs whenever she'd won. Pavlik began bouncing around like a puppy and barking.

Kate swiped at the tears in her eyes watching Pavlik play. She heard a sniff and turned to see the major wiping his eyes as well. Kate squeezed his arm, and he managed a smile. Harry placed a lead in her hand and she saw Liam. Shelagh was back in her crate, and Des handed her the rosette as they all moved to the area where the judge would do the photos. Maeve insisted the major stand beside her in the photo, and then Kate quickly got Liam's photo done. They finally all headed back to the crates to round up the dogs and return to the hotel. As they walked, Harry, Des, and G were surrounding her, not being obvious but simply there. As she glanced around the quickly emptying building, she was glad for the company.

# Chapter Twenty-Five
*Tuesday, still early afternoon*

When they arrived back at the hotel, Kate was more than ready for a hot shower and rest. They made slow progress through the lobby, constantly stopping to chat with old friends. She waved to Lily and Cathy who were probably heading into a board of directors meeting, seeing the other board members stood nearby. Kate figured they would be trying to figure how to handle the election thanks to the chaos created by the hacked email. She didn't envy them. In spite of the many years as a member, she'd never wanted to run for office. She'd done a lot of hands-on work for the club over the years working on National committees. However, she was perfectly happy to let others sit and argue over all the minutiae running an organization of this size entailed. At the elevator, she yawned.

"What you need, lady, is a nap until it's time to talk to Seamus and Satu. They'll still be in class, so you should get some rest."

"It feels funny to need to sleep in the middle of the day, but I'll admit, I'm exhausted. I keep trying to figure out why Krystyn told people I had all the answers without giving me any. She told the major to come to me for information if she were killed. She was obviously afraid for her life, and she felt I needed to have this information everyone's trying to find, but you'd have thought she might have talked to me about it instead of just telling others. The curious thing is, except for the letter and the card, I hadn't heard from her since my dad's funeral."

"She described you as the girl with the golden braid. You haven't had long hair for a year. Could something she gave you years ago hold the secret?"

She stared at him. Krystyn had always brought them presents, especially when she was returning from abroad. Kate had at least a dozen things from statues, to paintings, to music boxes, and even a tea set. Could any of them have hidden a secret? When she described the pieces to Harry, he thought it might be possible to hide a clue among them, but Kate argued. "These were presents given to an active kid. They got used. The tea set was washed numerous times, so a microdot with information would have gone down the drain long ago. No, this must be recent, or else why would it be happening at this moment?" They entered the elevator, but Kate spotted Des heading their way. What did he want? Harry held the elevator door open, but the agent just entered without speaking. When they reached the room, Kate got the dogs taken care of and Harry asked Agent Xiang what he wanted.

"Please, call me Des. Everybody does." He pulled out the desk chair and sat. Quinn took it as an invitation to play and plopped his favorite toy into the man's lap. Kate was surprised when Des picked up the toy and tossed it for the puppy to chase. Quinn was back in barely a second, delighted with the game. Des reached for the toy, but the puppy tugged it from his hand. Kate watched the man release it, not taking the challenge of tug of war, and let his hand sit palm up in his lap. Quinn placed the toy in his lap, but this time he didn't move but instead waited for Quinn to back up. As soon as he did, he tossed the toy over toward the door, and the puppy jumped and caught it and danced around, swinging his trophy.

"I miss my dog. I grew up with a Lab, but my lifestyle doesn't allow me to have a pet. I always counted on Jep, my Lab, to cheer me up no matter how difficult the day had been. He lived to be fourteen, a lot for the breed, but it was too short for me. I'm here to let you know there is a strategy meeting. Wetherly just called me. I'll pick you up at three thirty. If you think of any questions that might help to get information out of this hacker, let me know." He stood and, with one more toss for Quinn, he left.

Kate reached for her tablet but before she could turn it on, Harry took it. "No. I'll do the research. You get some sleep. You'll be sharper during the questioning if you're not falling asleep standing up. He set the tablet down, eased her back onto the bed, slipped off her shoes, and lifting her feet to follow her body onto the bed, kissed her gently and said, "Dream of me."

"So that's all you know about the arrest from your dad?" Harry's quiet voice brought her awake. "Well, thanks, Tom. If you think of anything else, call me. Yeah, I'll tell her, for all the good it will do. She's Kate, and she'll do whatever she thinks is best." The conversation ended.

Kate rolled over and stared at Harry lounging on the other bed and the dogs sleeping peacefully in their crates by the wall. "What does Tom want you to tell me?"

"He wanted you to be safe, though he didn't quite phrase it that way."

"I can imagine what he said and why you don't want to repeat it." She grinned, climbed out from under the covers, and stretched. "I feel much better."

"Good. I was about to wake you. We need to be down in the lobby to meet Des in ten minutes."

Kate grabbed a blouse from her suitcase and headed for the bathroom. Three minutes later, she was back refreshed and ready to take on the world. She took her royal-blue cardigan off the dresser. It was one with a scene on the back depicting a Sam high on a mountain, standing at the edge of a forest, gazing down at a cabin with smoke coming from its chimney and a sled beside the door. She held up the sweater to show Harry. The design on the sweater was too complex for the commercial line, but she loved it. On the front, there was a puppy peeking out of a pocket. It was warm, but she'd need it if they got back after dark. Grabbing a fistful of biscuits, she handed them out as they headed for the door.

Someone pushed in at the last second as the door closed on the elevator. It was Mr. Sartorial Splendor. He turned to Kate and said, "I need to speak with you. I want you to come with me." Harry reacted by stepping in front of Kate as he recognized the man who'd pulled the gun at the agility competition, and Kate peeked around him.

The man put his hand into his pocket and pulled the same small snub-nose pistol like the one he'd tried to use to kill Kate before. He stepped in close to her side, telling Harry to walk in front of them. The elevator stopped and the door opened. Harry's scowl turned to a grin. "Agent Xiang. I'd like you to meet an acquaintance of ours." Harry swung about, pulling Kate to his side and leaving the man exposed and quickly shoving his hand back into his pocket. "I didn't catch your name, sir…"

"Smith, John Smith," he growled shoving by them and out of the elevator.

"Snappy dresser," Des said staring after the man. "He looks familiar." He continued to watch the man who was met by someone Des knew very well. Then both men rapidly exited the building.

"He wanted to chat with Kate," Harry told him. "Your timing couldn't have been better. I'm sure he's the man with the gun yesterday who got away. I think a police station could be the safest place for us at this minute."

Des grinned. "Brownridge and Glasmann would love to sit down with you and get a better handle on this. So, allow me to escort you to police headquarters, and we'll see if we can get this under control."

When they got to the station, a young red-headed officer escorted them into Glasmann's office. He and the agent were sitting and arguing over who had jurisdiction once the criminals were captured. Kate was reminded of her brothers growing up squabbling over toys.

They had little new information. Harry pointed out he'd spotted the guy from yesterday, but he had taken off quickly, and Harry didn't want a gun battle in the hotel lobby. Des didn't say anything about the encounter but nodded at Brownridge. The men spoke about the plan for guarding Kate, and both requested she not go into the ring. Needless to say, that didn't fly. Kate was tired of men trying to wrap her in cotton wool and put her safely away, while the big strong men floundered around in the dark.

She may have been safe for the last two hours, but her frustration reached new heights. She needed to figure this out and quickly. If she were home, she could go off by herself into the woods and think.

# Chapter Twenty-Six
*Tuesday, mid-afternoon*

As they left the building, Harry stopped. "Des drove us here. How do we get back to the hotel?"

"Not a problem," G said, walking up behind them and pointing toward a sedan parked at the curb. "Agent Xiang arranged for you to be taken safely back to your hotel. There will be a rotation of officers assigned to keep you safe until this person is caught. Louisville doesn't usually treat tourists this badly when they visit. You should come sometime when no one is shooting at you."

Harry coughed to hide his laugh, but Kate still scowled at him. She had taken the back seat and, ignoring the banter in the front, leaned against the seat, stretched her legs to the side to get more room, and closed her eyes, fighting the frustration. The fact Krystyn had told people she had what they wanted was strange. It didn't fit the personality of someone so organized to throw out remarks without dotting every I and crossing every T to make sure Kate really did have what was needed. The logical supposition would be that Krystyn had sent her whatever it was.

So, what had she gotten from Krystyn? She'd gotten a note, a card congratulating her on the coming wedding, and perhaps a wedding present. She should call Gram tonight and ask if the major and Krystyn had sent a gift. Kate was lost in thought, sorting facts like cards in a game of solitaire, as they drew up at the hotel. She reached for the handle, but the door wouldn't open. Shocked, she turned toward Harry.

"It may look like a sedan, but it's still a police car, and if they put a prisoner in the back, they want them to stay there." He and G laughed, and he stepped out to open the door for her, automatically placing a hand on her head to keep it from bumping the doorframe as she exited. His thoughtfulness got him a scowl. Kate charged ahead into the lobby as Harry thanked G and told him he'd see him later. She had reached the elevator and was entering, when Harry caught up with her. "Kate, stop."

"What?"

"You're letting your temper make you behave stupidly. Racing unguarded across the entry and the lobby? People are working hard to keep you safe, and you're making it harder on them."

Harry's words felt like a slap in the face. Kate looked at him to argue but instead gave up and turned away. Without a word, she rode up to their floor. As soon as they got to the room, she slipped into the bathroom and locked the door. Slumping to the floor, she stared at the black-and-white tiles stretching out before her, refusing to let the tears flow. She couldn't let tears get in the way. She had to figure this out even if it meant nobody would understand, even Harry. God, she missed her dad and grandfather so much, she felt sick and scared and lonely.

"Kate?" Harry's voice was calm, in his "always use a calm voice when dealing with the unhinged" sort of way.

She didn't answer.

"Kate, please come out."

Nothing.

"Kate, I've got to use the bathroom."

With a growl, she got to her feet and unlocked the door then walked past him.

He stood there watching her.

"Go ahead. Use the bathroom."

"I lied."

She stared at him. "What are you, two?" She turned away. "The dogs need to go out."

"Stay here and don't open the door," he said, clipping on leads. "I'll take them out. I've got my key to let myself back in."

She turned on her heel, went back into the bathroom, and slammed the door. She stared at herself in the mirror, hating the person gazing back at her, and listened as the hall door shut. She was being a bitch. Frustration was making her strike out, and she hated herself for it. So many questions and no answers.

She walked back into the room, and kicking off her shoes, crawled under the covers and let the tears flow. Ugly sobbing tears boiled up from deep inside soaking the pillow and leaving her with a case of the hiccups, empty and exhausted but unable to sleep.

The door opened, and dogs flowed around the bed.

Dillon leaped up and stuck his head under the covers, licking her face. Kate tried to turn away, but he went after her from the other side. She felt the other dogs jump onto the bed and lie down, heads on her shoulder and back. Quinn had managed to get up there, too, and for once, he didn't bite. He crawled up and wrapped himself around her head. His head rested on the pillow as he stared at her face from two inches away. Another series of sobs escaped her, but then she stopped. The angst that had been fueling her tantrum slowly drained away. The soft, rhythmic breathing from the dogs dragged her under, and Kate finally slept.

The weight of an arm wrapped around her waist brought Kate awake slowly. Turning her head to look out from under the covers, she saw all the dogs on the floor and her husband-to-be lying next to her, on top of the bedspread, holding her in his arms. His beautiful green eyes opened and he kissed her gently. "I want to wake up to your sweet face staring back at mine every day for the rest of my life," he said.

She laid her hand on his cheek. "Do you still love me, in spite of my being a complete bitch and having a meltdown?"

"I still love you, even then." He smiled.

"Harry, this is getting scary, and it's driving me nuts. I just want to be me again, free to move about without having to peek over my shoulder every minute, without having to question everything people say, without being afraid. We've got to find out not only who's behind this but why they want me dead. Maeve's buddies are only going to pat us on the head and tell us to sit quietly at the children's table while the grown-ups fix things."

"Not happening," Harry growled.

"You bet it's not." She glanced at the clock. "How about an early supper, and we'll go over the footage Cathy shot on my phone and knock some ideas around. We could even eat in the hotel restaurant so I can scope out who has arrived. After all these years, I should know most of the exhibitors and almost everyone is suspect. Maybe I'll spot someone who'll give me some ideas. I'm coming up blank, and it just pisses me off." She stood. "I feel grungy. I'm going to grab a quick shower and change." She pulled some clothes from her suitcase and moved into the bathroom.

"Let me know if you need any help in there," Harry shouted, smiling as he heard her laugh, but he stopped smiling when he got a text from Seamus. They'd found something else about the equipment purchased at the tech show. Satu had asked one of the vendors to let her know if any hefty purchases were being made by the guy who hacked the emails. Apparently there were, and they'd be available at eight tonight to fill them in. Harry sent him an okay and then quickly shed his shirt to put on a clean one for dinner. He heard Kate's quick intake of breath behind him as he bent over his suitcase. He turned. She was just standing and watching.

"Like what you see?" he asked, raising an eyebrow.

"Oh, yeah."

Harry laughed, slipping on the shirt.

"Killjoy." Kate straightened his collar and he tugged her in for a quick kiss.

He stared down at her then, glancing at his watch he muttered, "Only nine hundred and twenty-eight hours and twenty-five minutes left until we'll be man and wife."

She looked up at him, suddenly serious. "Worth the wait?"

"Every second."

At a knock, they separated reluctantly, with Harry going to the door and Kate getting biscuits to pass out to the dogs to hold them until their dinners.

A police officer stood in the hall. He glanced first at Harry and then past him at Kate. "Miss Kate Killoy?"

Kate nodded.

"Miss Killoy, I have orders to bring you in to headquarters."

"What is this about, officer?" Harry asked.

"I'm not at liberty to say, sir. My orders are to bring Miss Killoy to headquarters. I'm told it is in reference to an attempted shooting this afternoon. I need you to come with me immediately, miss. I was told not to let you argue."

Kate let out an unladylike snort. She handed the last biscuit to Dillon whose hackles were up and who ignored the treat—staring at the intruder with his tail raised in a challenging position. Kate reached for the crate latch, transferring the biscuit to her other hand as though to hand it to the dog. Instead, she opened the crate letting Dillon fly past her. Before she could turn, he had the cop plastered against the door and reaching for his gun. Harry's arm shot out and captured the man's hand as it pulled the weapon from its holster. He wrenched the gun away.

# NATIONAL SECURITY

Kate moved into position behind Dillon and said, "I wouldn't do that if I were you. He has more police credentials than you do, and he's a lot faster. Harry's just protecting you from getting your throat torn out." Kate pointed to his badge and ID tag. "I've seen a lot of Louisville police today, and it's interesting that the one they sent to bring me to the station, Officer Standish," she said reading his tag, "is one whose ID badge is white with blue lettering instead of blue with white letters. You're also not wearing a summer uniform, even though it's in the high seventies. And you're not wearing regulation shoes. I think Harry should hold your gun until we have a chance to talk to your boss." Kate pulled out her phone, clicking a photo of the man before hitting speed dial for Captain Glasmann.

"Kate?" The cop was suddenly pushed forward as Cathy walked in.

He quickly pulled Cathy in front of him and shoved her at Dillon, knocking Harry aside as he raced from the room. The door shut behind him. Cathy rolled to one side, freeing Dillon, and the dog leaped up to claw door at the to get out. Harry regained his balance and yanked the door open. Dillon shot by him down the hall toward the stairs. Harry tore after him. A second later, the dog threw his body at the stair door trying to force it open. Harry pushed past and grabbed the handle.

Two shots rang out.

# Chapter Twenty-Seven

*Tuesday, late afternoon*

Harry seized Dillon's collar, and braced himself to hold back against the force of the dog's pull. Kate arrived and snapped a lead onto the dog, telling him to wait. Harry slowly pushed the door open, but it stopped after moving only about six inches. Something blocked it. He inched forward, using his knee to keep Dillon back, and eased his head through the gap. He stiffened, backed up, and let it close. Reaching for Kate's arm, he asked, "Did you get through to Glasmann?"

"Yeah, he was down in the lobby and is on his way up." They turned as the elevator bell dinged. The police captain, along with several uniformed officers and Brownridge, exited the elevator and hurried in their direction. Kate stepped back, keeping Dillon in heel position. He glanced their way but then quickly turned back toward the door to the stairs.

"You two want to tell me what's going on?" Glasmann asked. "I got a report of shots from this floor."

Harry signaled him forward and held his hand up, signaling the others to wait. The captain peered inside.

Glasmann stiffened and swore. "A cop!"

Pulling back, he told everyone to wait. With one of the officers accompanying him, he raced back to the elevator.

Brownridge moved forward and, with a nod at Harry, peered around the door and added to the ever-growing collection of expletives from the men waiting. All talking stopped at the sounds of feet coming down the stairs. There were muffled voices from inside the stairwell. Finally, inching the door slightly open, the captain gave his men instructions. "Get a picture of the opening with the body blocking it." They could hear more voices with the occasional click of a camera. Finally, the door opened enough to allow Glasmann to squeeze through.

The captain carefully avoided the pool of blood as he stepped onto the hallway carpet. Posting one of his men as guard, he waved everyone back toward their room with Kate in the lead. She stopped when she realized she'd left her key inside.

"I've got it." Harry stepped forward, used his key, and Kate, Cathy, and the men entered the room. Kate, once everyone was inside, let the other dogs out of their crates. Quinn dashed from one person to another, making sure they all knew he was there then dove for Dillon's crate to consume the biscuit Kate had dropped when Dillon went for the cop. Kate, with a speed gained from years of practice, snatched the treat and using it as bait, shuffled him back into his own crate along with his treat, and latched it, to gain a semblance of order. The other Sams had politely greeted those present and lay quietly watching.

Glasmann collapsed into the desk chair, causing it to grown under his weight, and Agent Brownridge took the overstuffed chair. Kate, Harry, and Cathy sat on the end of the bed. The two officers responded to a knock allowing G and Des inside. The captain glared at Kate, cleared his throat, and began, "The police in New York and Lubbock warned me about the body count with you two around. Tell me what happened here."

Kate quickly relayed what had happened. At this, Glasmann frowned but didn't interrupt. "As I heard him demand to take me to headquarters, I saw Dillon had gone into protection mode, hackles up and focused on the man, ignoring his biscuit. Dillon is a trained police dog, and I pay attention to his instincts. So, while going through the motions of giving Dillon a biscuit, I released the latch on his crate, and Dillon charged forward. He forced the guy up against the wall by the door and then froze, in hold position, ready to do damage if the guy moved."

"You had your dog attack a police officer?" Glasmann shouted, jumping up, pulling out handcuffs, and moving toward her. Kate held out a small leather folder she'd taken from her purse, flipped it open, and handed it to the captain. He scrutinized it, and then Dillon who sat at Kate's side, calmly watching the situation unfold. Kate began speaking again. "As you can see, Dillon's credentials are up-to-date. He followed procedure for a stop and hold. When the man pulled his gun and pointed it toward me, Harry grabbed his arm and the weapon. While this was going on, I saw he wasn't dressed like your officers. He had on a uniform with long sleeves even though it was hot, his badge was very shiny, seemed brand new, but what really caught my eye was his name tag. It was white with blue letters though I had noticed all of your officers' tags are blue with white, and his shoes were older, and scuffed, with a pointed toe. I had out my phone to call you so I snapped a photo of him first. Then, while I called you, Cathy arrived, and since the door was slightly ajar, she walked in, breaking Harry's hold. The man grabbed her, shoving her down onto Dillon and fled. Dillon got out from under Cathy, and he and Harry ran after the guy. I helped Cathy up and followed. Dillon and Harry had almost reached the entrance to the stairs, but before they could enter, there were two shots."

Harry interrupted. "Following the shots, I heard footsteps on the stairs, sounding as though they were going up. After the sound of steps died, I tried to push the door open but found it only opened about six inches and then stopped. I stuck my head into the opening and saw the body. And then you arrived."

Kate reached into her pocket, pulled out her phone, pressed a few keys and Glasmann's phone beeped. He reached for it, glaring at Kate. Opening the message she'd sent, he stared.

"Is he a Louisville cop? Is he one of yours?" she asked.

The captain studied the photo. "No."

Silence filled the room, and Kate felt Harry tense up as he looked from Brownridge to Glasmann.

Harry's anger spilled over in spite of Kate's grip

tightening on his arm. "So, this person, sent to remove Kate from my protection, was able to gain access to her by walking through the hotel and up to our room disguised as a cop. If it hadn't been for Dillon's cop instincts, Kate would probably be dead by now." Silence filled the room. "And, while we're on the subject of her being endangered, who was the genius who decided to use Kate as bait to draw out the shooter today? Were you trying to get her killed? If I hadn't spotted him and forced him to run, he would have had a clear shot. Was it worth it? You didn't catch him. You didn't find out what was going on. You don't know who he's working for. And this guy. Was the shot meant for Kate, or did someone who had planned to shoot her while this pseudo-cop took her down the stairs, instead shoot him because he had failed?" Harry scanned the faces of the men and added, "Three attempts on her life two days? Even for Kate—that's high."

Kate scowled. Even for Kate…? She turned to look at the captain. "I'm sorry if my presence is an inconvenience, but I didn't bring this on myself. My only crime was a longtime friendship with Krystyn. These bastards assume I know her secrets. I don't. She told others I had information, but she never gave it to me. I'm not going out of my way to hurt your capital crime statistics, Captain. But, as of this moment, I want to make it clear, if you, the NSA, the police, and the FBI can't find the person behind this crime spree, Harry and I will. I still have multiple trips into the ring this week where I will be standing still a lot of the time, a perfect target."

Brownridge's face paled.

"I think we should take you into protective custody until this person is found," Glasmann said.

"No," Kate replied.

Des stood and spoke up. "Sorry I was late for this party, but I was updating my superiors. I'm now assigned 24/7 to guarding Kate and trying to undercover who's behind all this. There's been a sudden burst of chatter on the deep web about these attempted hits and the possible danger of failing. Two more agents are on their way to provide backup.

G stood and nodded at Glasmann. "The next room to this has been cleared for us to use as a base. Agent Xiang and I will work from there and be available to shadow Kate until the perp is caught."

"This is NSA business," Brownridge argued.

"Not anymore," Glasmann growled back. "It's attempted murder in Louisville."

They glared at each other in silence.

Kate's stomach suddenly grumbled. "Sorry about this, but Harry and I haven't eaten a meal in a while, so we were going to have an early supper." She stood and signaled the dogs into their crates, took Dillon's ID from Glasmann's hand, and shoved it in the side pocket of her purse then walked to the door and waited for the officer to open it. "Let 'em go," Glasmann muttered. "G, this is on you."

They parted ways in the hall, the others heading for the stairway while Kate and the three men took the elevator.

As they entered the crowded restaurant, she spotted

a group leaving a booth at the far end of the room and G, with a burst of speed, nabbed it telling the busboy clearing it to go ahead and finish, they'd wait for a server. As they sat, Harry's phone buzzed with a text "Be back in a minute."

Kate leaned back and closed her eyes, too tired for small talk. She needed to stop letting what was happening keep her from focusing on the initial question of why Krystyn was killed. Her mind drifted back to the video. What had the shooter thought he'd gotten from the safe before shooting Krystyn? Considering what was happening now, it was clear he didn't get what he was after. The Coyote had called it a book filled with pages of garbled words. Kate suddenly opened her eyes. He'd never said what the book was. She had to ask.

Harry slipped into the booth, stuffing a package under the table. A minute later, the waiter came with menus and asked about drinks. They ordered quickly, and Kate dug in as soon as the food arrived. She had chicken, mashed potatoes, and squash, whereas the guys all selected different cuts of steak. When their waiter returned with the dessert menu, Kate said she needed an idea for a book to read tonight. She asked the guys for suggestions. Harry suggested one of the Kate Flora Joe Burgess Mysteries, which he'd gotten hooked on recently. G mentioned a Stephen King book, but Kate said it would give her nightmares. Des suggested she go for a classic like a John Le Carré. As the waiter took their dessert order, she asked him for a suggestion.

"I've always been partial to Agatha Christie if I

want a good relaxing read before sleep. Perhaps you might try one of the Tommy and Tuppence books like The Secret Adversary. That's the first in the series. It's fun as well as an interesting mystery." He returned with their desserts and brought the check. Kate grabbed it and signed before the guys could say anything. The waiter handed her another slip of paper. "I thought of some more books you might like," he said.

Kate glanced at the paper and shoved it into her pocket. "Thanks."

Back in the room, she quickly fed the dogs and then Harry and G took them out while Des stayed. She cleaned the dog bowls and packed everything away tightly, making sure the room was neat. Des had buried his head in his smart phone, texting as she worked. When she finished, she sat and asked him how long he'd been with the Bureau and why he decided to be an agent.

"I've been in six years, working in different cities. I've even heard about 'Numbers' but never met him."

"Numbers?"

"Foyle. It's what they called him in the DC office. He was famous for solving cases without ever leaving his desk, simply using calculations."

Kate smiled. "Numbers, I'll have to remember that."

"Yeah, I got in because the brother of my best friend was gunned down in the street in the part of Brooklyn where I grew up. The police treated it like just another drive-by shooting, but an agent from the New York office, who spent a month talking to everybody in the neighborhood, found the guys who killed him, and at the same time arrested several triad members who were involved. It turned out Hu's brother was working as an informant for the Bureau, and the agent figured they owed him. I remember watching the agent work his way through our neighborhood. He was as out of place as possible since he was black, about six foot six, and built like a linebacker. But he just calmly asked his questions and apparently managed to find out enough to get arrest warrants. They made the charges stick, and everyone involved is still in prison. That's when I decided to become an agent."

"Good to know. Is the agent still around?"

"Yeah, he's my boss." Des grinned.

Harry came back with G laughing at Quinn getting knock flat by Shelagh, when he decided to jump up and grab her lead, trying to pull her in a game of tug of war. Harry explained, "The bitches are tougher than the males in this breed."

"I believe it, watching her flatten him. She also held him down until he let go of the lead. Harry wouldn't let me interfere, saying Quinn needed to learn and wouldn't be hurt. When my girlfriend and I get married and have kids, I may borrow Shelagh to do some training for me," G said.

"I think your boss might not take kindly to you using a bitch to knock your kids around," Kate told him, laughing.

Kate bumped the package Harry had gotten at suppertime, and it fell to the floor. Kate stooped, picked it up, and asked what it was. Harry looked a little uncomfortable. "It's an early wedding present from Sadie for you."

"It's for me? May I open it?"

Harry nodded, and Kate tore the brown paper wrapping only to find fancy bridal shower paper underneath. She gently removed the pretty paper from a box. Opening it, she pushed back the lavender tissue paper aside to uncover a dark-blue relatively heavy vest when she lifted it out. Both G and Des chuckled, and Harry looked a little sheepish. "She's worried about you. It's a newer, lighter-weight version of the vest Agnes had to wear in New York when they were trying to kill her."

"Well, this means I'm going to have to change my ring wardrobe."

"You'll wear it?" The relief on Harry's face would have been comical if it weren't so endearing.

"Oh yeah. Sadie would kill me if I didn't. She's coming to the wedding to see all the dogs."

She slipped on the bulletproof vest, latched the closures, and then twirled in the middle of the room. "How do I look?"

"Fabulous!" they all said together.

# Chapter Twenty-Eight

*Tuesday, night*

Kate carefully removed her vest and bid her protectors good night as G and Des left. Quinn banged against the door of his crate, unhappy people were leaving. When the hall door closed, she sank to the carpet, flipped the latches on each crate, and was immediately jumped by Quinn, and the white hairy bodies all crowded as close to her as possible.

Kate buried her face in Dillon's ruff, and Shelagh wiggled until her head was tucked under Kate's arm, Liam's head rested on her shoulder as he gently licked her face, and Quinn crawled into her lap. The dogs' snuggling hid her grumbles, but when Harry pulled off her white fluffy covering, she let a stream of nonsense words fill the room. The dogs still cuddled against her legs as Quinn clawed at the bedspread, trying to get up next to her.

"Kate, what are you saying?"

"I'm just blowing off steam. My parents never let me swear, so I used to make up imaginary words sounding like curses to use when I got pissed. Over the years, it's become a long list, and I was just reciting every one. I've had it with being a target and an object of pity. I'm pissed. So, I'm going to find out what this is all about and stop it. It's crapping up my National. I was going to go watch Elements of the Standard tonight, but I don't want to walk into a room filled with my Sam friends who might get shot if the bad guy misses me."

"What's Elements of the Standard?"

"It's fun. They bring a bunch of Sams together with a group of judges and pick the one with each of the elements making up the Samoyed standard. One wins best head, one for best front, best rear, best side gait, etc. The thing is, there is no perfect Samoyed. You breed to have as many of these elements in your line as possible. Of course, judges are people, and some like one type of head and some another, and so the results are by committee. I'll often see a dog win and think to myself, he's a good Sam, but he's not my kind of Sam, so in spite of how much he wins, I wouldn't want him in my kennel."

"Does it happen often?"

"Enough. This is what competition is all about."

"Sounds like fun. Are you sure you don't want to go?"

"I'll stay here."

"Okay, then, to begin with, you can think about what it is they don't want you to find?"

"What do you mean don't want me to find?"

"Well, if they wanted this thing found, they'd keep you alive to make it possible to find it since Krystyn said you had it. If they kill you, it won't be found."

Suddenly Kate heard Seamus and Satu talking, and

Harry turned the laptop so she could see.

"How did Dillon do in agility today, Kate?"

"He blew them away and came in first. I am really proud of him."

"Congratulations. Did you make it through the day without people trying to shoot you?" Seamus asked, laughing.

Kate and Harry both paused before answering, and Satu interrupted, shouting, "Someone shot at you again. Kate, were you hurt?"

"Actually, they didn't get the chance to shoot at me. But one of them is dead."

"Two? Two shooters?"

"Technically there was one shooter I spotted, but the cops lost him before he got off his shot then, later, a fake cop tried to grab Kate. Dillon stopped him. He was shot by someone probably waiting to shoot Kate," Harry explained.

"Sal will go batshit," Seamus yelled.

"You can't tell him, you two," Harry said. "We're working with the NSA, FBI, and the Louisville police. If Sal starts throwing his weight around, he could make things difficult here. We're counting on you to keep this to yourselves. I know you're loyal to Sal. But it is important. The delicate balance of this investigation ongoing here is not be disrupted. There may come a time when we need Sal's help and then we'll ask, but, in the meantime, you've got to stay quiet. I know it's not easy, but it is something you will be asked to do if you want a career in security."

Seamus and Satu whispered to each other for a

minute. Satu turned back to Harry. "Please let us know when we can discuss this with Sal. We'll respect your wishes. We also have more information about the purchases being made using the credit card and Bitcoin account involved previously. They have been purchasing more items, but we have not been able to find out what these items are, only that the purchases were made from sources dealing primarily with hacking, especially of smart phones, smart cars, smart buildings, and similar technology-driven items. We will keep working to get more specific details and get them to you as soon as we can."

Harry stared at Seamus. "I need to hear from you, too, Seamus."

Seamus switched his gaze from Harry to his sister. "Kate. Talk to me, please?"

Kate laid her hand on Harry's arm and moved closer to the laptop. "Seamus, I love you dearly, all of you. I'll be honest. I'm scared. I've been dropped into a situation here not of my making, and much of the time I feel helpless. You know me better than anyone in the family now that Gramps and Dad are gone. You know how much I despise not being able to fight. What Harry is asking you to do is more than keeping a secret from Sal; he's asking you to keep it from the whole family, including your twin. There is a very dangerous situation here. With the attention focused on me, you and the others in the family are safe. If you say anything about knowing of an investigation going on here, the people who murdered Krystyn could decide to find out what the family knows. These people will kill you whether you know anything or not. So, both of you, don't think of what's going on with me but rather of your responsibility to keep silent and save everyone we love. This is scary stuff I'm asking you to do, especially since you're still in high school, but I believe you're ready to take on this responsibility. I love you all so much, and I never want you to forget that, but you're going to have to let this investigation go forward, and remain our backup." Silence followed for several minutes while the four of them just watched each other. Then Harry spoke.

"On the bright side, I showed your report to the head of the NSA investigation team, and he said he'd never gotten such a thoroughly insightful report from any of his agents. He wanted to talk to you, but I told him he couldn't because you were undercover. I think if you ever want to work for him, he'd take you in a flash."

"Undercover? He was convinced we were undercover agents and part of your security team?"

"Yup." The faces on the screen lit up. Kate gave Harry's hand a squeeze.

"Cool," both Seamus and Satu said simultaneously.

"Okay. You two, keep up the good work. I'll make it easier to steer the conversation by sending you the video of Dillon's run today. It was magic, and everyone but Mom will love to see it," Kate said. "We'll keep you posted. I may need you to do some hands-on hacking for me soon as well as some other investigating. In the meantime, take care and send my love to everyone."

"Will do," Seamus responded, and the screen went black.

Harry frowned at Kate. "When did you figure out

your family might be in danger?"

"Just now when I realized if these killers couldn't get whatever this is from me here, they might go hunting for it back home. Remember, Krystyn told the major I had whatever it was when she spoke to him long before we left to come here. Whoever is after this is desperate and a danger to all of us. The focus has to be not just on me trying to stay alive but on finding this 'explosive' information Krystyn supposedly sent me. Oh, and we have one other problem. We've got to keep Sal out of it."

Harry dropped his head into his hands. "You had to remind me about Sal?" Kate kissed his cheek.

When she stood, something fell out of her pocket. The slip of paper the waiter, who Kate knew was the Coyote, had given her at supper. She opened it and then pulled out her phone and called the major, asking if he could join them in their room for a few minutes before the end of the evening. He said he would be right there.

When he arrived after being checked by the men next door, Kate sat at the desk, offering the major the chair. After Harry let the dogs out, he stretched out on the bed.

Kate cleared her throat, wondering how to phrase her question without sounding idiotic. "Major, you said when you spoke with Krystyn she told you, 'Kate will have the answer.' Am I right in the phrasing?"

The major sat and thought for a few seconds then said, "Yes. I can hear her saying, 'Don't worry. All will be good. If anything were to happen to me, Kate Killoy will have the answer."

"Okay." She turned to face him. "What I need to

know is, the answer to what."

The major gaped. "You really don't know? She didn't tell you?"

"No, Major, she didn't."

"Well my original question to her was, 'What are you going to do with the information in the book the Coyote stole?' She told me not to worry about it."

"And, I'm supposed to have this secret information? I was fourteen when all this happened. I knew nothing about it. All I knew was my friend disappeared and my father, Gramps, and Krystyn were all unhappy about it."

The major stared at her. "She really never told you?"

"No."

"Then we have a problem. I don't know what she found out when she decoded the information, but I do know she was very upset by it. I asked her at the time what she'd found and was told I was better off not knowing because the information was extremely dangerous."

"Okay, so I've got to figure out what was in the book. Do you know the title?"

"The Secret Adversary."

"Right, by Agatha Christie." Kate did not reveal she already had the information from the Coyote. "It was the first Tommy and Tuppence book."

"Krystyn read all of Agatha Christie. She had several shelves of them in the den. She thought she was an exceptional writer. I'm afraid I haven't read them. Perhaps I should."

"You would probably enjoy Hercule Poirot stories. He's a Belgian detective in England and very methodical in his approach to solving crime."

"You understand me very well," the major laughed.

"Was the book hardbound or paperback?"

"Paperback."

"Can you give me an idea of what the cover looked like?"

"The cover? Why? What does the cover have to do with it?"

"If you talk to my cousin who's studied books all his life and works at the Beinecke Rare Book Library at Yale, you would be told the cover is one of the best ways to tell the edition of the book, what changes have been made to the front and back matter, paging, and for those researching older books, how valuable the book is."

"And this is important, why?" Harry asked.

"Important because if it is where a code is hidden, being able to compare the original to a copy of the same edition might make it easier to spot."

The major stared at Kate for a minute and finally said, "That is why my wife was so devoted to your fiancée, Harry. The book showed an ocean liner sinking and a lifeboat full of people moving away."

"Do you think the book is still on the shelf with all the others at your home?"

The major pulled out his phone, dialed, and spoke quickly. "Thomas. Go into my wife's den and check in the bookcase on your left, beginning with the second shelf, for books by Agatha Christie. I'll wait." He began to pace, and Quinn followed along by his side, happy people were moving instead of just sitting around. "You found them.

See if one is The Secret Adversary. It's got a sinking ship and lifeboat on the cover." He paused to listen, and Quinn sat waiting until the walking began again. "Not there? Oh, good thinking. Right, tomorrow morning. You dismantled all the cameras and your phone is now clean? Good. I'll be in touch." He moved to the chair and sat again.

"Was the book there?" Harry asked.

"No and yes. Thomas, my aide, did not spot the book when he looked at the covers. However, he worked for Krystyn before he came to work with me. She must have trained him well because he opened each book and checked to make sure the inside matched the cover. He found the book inside a cover for a book entitled The Body in the Library. He's sending it by courier, and we'll have it by morning."

Kate reached for her phone and dialed. "Rory. It's Kate. Yes, I'm at the National in Louisville. Four, but only showing three. Quinn's along for the ride. I've got a favor to ask. I know Sharon collects Agatha Christie in various editions. Harry and I are working on a problem requiring a certain edition. Okay, I'll wait." She stood and began pacing. Quinn jumped up and began moving at her side, enjoying this game. They'd made it to the door and back, when Kate stopped and Quinn sat. "Sharon, yes, I need the paperback edition of The Secret Adversary with a ship sinking and a lifeboat full of people in the foreground. Oh, you're putting them on display. If I send Seamus over tonight with a hand scanner, could you let him copy the contents before you box it? You're a saint. Back pains? How many weeks? Well, you'd better not deliver in the middle of my wedding. Take care. See you soon."

Kate turned to them. "Shannon has a copy, but she's sending her collection to be part of a display in the Hartford Public Library tomorrow. Harry, text Seamus he's got to go over to Rory's and copy the book pages. Tell him Tom has a hand scanner. I'm sure he'll loan it to him."
"I'm already on it," he said, his thumbs moving fast.

The major stood. "Kate, where will you be at ten thirty tomorrow morning?"

"Showing in either Obedience or Rally with Shelagh."

"I'll see you there." He stood and started for the door then, turning back, he gave Kate a quick hug and left.

# Chapter Twenty-Nine
*Wednesday, early morning*

G called about six o'clock to check when he should be at their door. Kate was in the shower, so Harry told him to be there in ten minutes. Kate's speed in getting herself ready for anything, be it taking dogs out to poop or going to a dinner dance, was one of the things endearing her to him. Four minutes later, Kate emerged dressed except for her shoes. She'd just managed to get her shoes tied, when G arrived. People and dogs headed for the elevator. G had Quinn on lead, which pleased the puppy. The distraction of being with the new person made taking him down in the elevator easy. They were very careful crossing the driveway with Harry and G bracketing Kate as they walked. Once they reached the exercise area, the dogs got down to business and the humans talked.

Kate's mind drifted to the book hopefully holding the answer she needed. Shelagh's snuggling against her knee brought her out of her reverie. She cleaned up after the bitch, after Liam and noticed Harry and Dillon were finished and approaching. A man in coveralls, pulling a wheeled garbage can approached carrying an oversized pooper scooper.

Kate picked up her poop bags and walked over to deposit them in his garbage can as he cleaned up after someone's dog. "So they've got you being the poop fairy this morning."

"Years of practice have made me an expert, Kate."

"I'm with you there." She lowered her voice, still smiling. "Need to talk to you later about the man from whom you took the book. We'll call for tea about four."

Harry tossed his bag as did G, and nodded as the man left to do another area.

"Friend of yours, Kate?" G asked.

"Yes, as a matter of fact. I had the job with the show committee for several years. It's a good way to get to know who is conscientious and who's not when it comes to their dogs. Harvey's a good sort who doesn't mind doing it." As they headed for the parking lot, Kate peeked over her shoulder and received a nod before the man went back to cleaning up the area.

They headed for Charlie to get the dogs relaxed in their crates. As they rounded the end of the building to the motor home area, they spotted the major dressed in jeans, a sweatshirt, and running shoes, carrying a tote, with Pavlik walking quietly at his side. Kate greeted him and offered him a ride to the show venue. As he climbed into Charlie, he said, "I've brought extra towels. Cathy thought you might need them. I know you have both Shelagh and Dillon to wash."

"Great." She reached for the tote bag. It was heavier than it would be with just towels. Looking inside, she noticed a leather pouch with a chain and handcuff attached to one corner. Lifting the bag onto the counter next to the stove, she boosted Quinn into his crate and then stepped back as the other dogs jumped into their own crates. Using her body to block the action, she slid the pouch into a hidden compartment behind the counter. Her father had installed it when he was carrying his gun but doing undercover work for a client. He needed a hiding place so the motor home could be searched and the weapon wouldn't be found. The catch was also hidden. As the men entered, she checked in the overhead compartment for the number of towels stored there and then smiled at the major telling him they now had plenty. She moved forward to her seat, handing him the much lighter bag as she passed.

"Shelagh and Dillon should be washed first," she said as she buckled her seat belt. "Did you double-check to see if Pavlik was entered both in Veteran and in Best of Breed, Major?"

"He's only in Best of Breed. I find it hard to believe he is a veteran. It seems like yesterday he was a puppy. I use to take him into the ring when he was young."

Harry took Kate's hand. "After we're married, will you expect me to learn to handle the dogs?"

She looked at him seriously. "Would you like to?"

"You know, I think I would."

"Great, you and Quinn can train together. By the time he's ready to go into the ring, you'll be ready to take him."

Harry let go and reached back over his head to tap the crate on the platform above him. "Hey, Quinn. The boss says we get to work together. No slacking off. You've got a tough act to follow with my man Dillon."

G leaned over the back of the seat and added, "You get to work with a super puppy. This guy is smart."

"Don't I know it. He's already saved lives." Harry went on to fill G in on what happened in Texas and when they returned to Connecticut from the trip last month.

"He'd make a good police dog," G added.

"Oh, don't worry. It will be part of his training. Dillon has more credentials than most cops. He helps with the police dog training classes."

Harry smiled at Kate with pride and then glanced at G. "You should see the police dog training class Kate runs with her kennel manager, Sal Modigliani. Sal was former chief of police in Western Massachusetts."

"Is he the same guy who use to be head of the chief's association?" G asked.

"One and the same," Harry said. "We haven't told him about what's been happening here because he'd go ballistic and have the police, the NSA, and FBI all walking on eggshells. He's very protective of his boss."

"Turn left at the second light to get into the Coliseum," G said when he saw Harry was in the right lane.

"We're taking a slight detour to the golden arches for some breakfast first. Kate and I haven't eaten, and I imagine everyone could use a fast food fix to start the day."

Five minutes later, they pulled into a parking space sized for motor homes behind the massive building. They finished their food, and Kate noticed people moving in and out of a small door next to the loading entrance.

Harry asked, "Kate, Major, could you please wait here? G and I need to check out the building and make sure the security is in place. Major, are you armed?"

"Yes, I am armed, though the thought of needing a gun at a dog show still boggles my mind. Don't worry. We'll be fine."

"Lock the door when we leave. Don't let anyone in."

Harry and G entered the building. There hadn't been any attack in the building yesterday, so maybe the security the National Committee bragged about would save them. The building had a new smell about it, with fresh paint on the walls and floors. Yesterday had been chaotic with the dog baths, rushing to the second agility trial then, after lunch, back to show in veteran Sweepstakes. It had put a lot of stress on them, and Harry hadn't really checked out the facility.

Oversized television screens were hung overhead in the center of the room, and a staircase on the far side going up to a glass-enclosed viewing box. G reminded him it was filled with enough high-tech gear to fly a 747. The left side was taken up with two rings—each seeming about the size of a football field. The rest was empty, but a sign on a nearby pillar displayed an outline of the building showing where the restrooms, meeting rooms, and food vendors were located. He and G trotted up the stairs to get to see the equipment, but the place was locked and appeared to be unoccupied. He assumed it wouldn't be manned until the show began for the day.

Back in the motor home, Quinn fussed since he couldn't get out, but, eventually as Kate and the major sat, he, along with the other dogs, went back to sleep.

The major sighed. "Kate, I can't tell you how sorry—"

She held up her hand to stop him. "No apologies. What happened isn't your fault."

They sat, each lost in his own thoughts, when a knock sounded at the door, and suddenly Pavlik went ballistic. Kate and the major slipped to the floor, curling out of the view of any windows. All the dogs barked in danger mode. Kate watched a shadow move from the side window in the door to the large front windshield with a view of the interior. She squeezed herself as far as she could into the space under the banquette table and glanced at the major who was half sitting behind the driver's seat. Pavlik had jumped onto the passenger seat and was clawing at the side window and the windshield. Kate had just shouted to the major to call Pavlik when the windshield exploded with a huge bang, and a bullet lodged in the banquette table above her head. Both Kate and the major screamed as the dog jumped onto the dashboard.

"Pavlik!"

The joint screams filled the motor home. The old dog paused only a second before he dove back through the seats to the major. He whined, licked his face then reversed, turning back toward the front of the motor home. The major threw his arms around the dog. Kate crawled on her belly across the floor and threw herself on the dog, using her body and hands to calm him, stopping him from crawling forward as the sound of more bullets hitting the windshield filled the motor home.

His pull toward the shooter was the dog's total focus. He dragged both the major and Kate forward. She heard Harry call her name and the sound of a key in the lock. He threw open the door and was next to her in two steps.

"Kate," he yelled.

"We're fine. Grab Pavlik's lead off the counter." Harry added his hand to those holding the dog's collar and quickly snapped the lead on the old dog as Kate rolled off the pile. The dog was totally focused on the front of the motor home until the major, using a soft voice, told him to heel and moved to the banquette seat. The dog responded instantly and sat obedient, though still tense, at the man's side. Harry pulled Kate to her feet and wrapped his arms around her, just holding her close.

Kate didn't want to move. Her head burrowed into Harry's chest as she tightened her arms around him. Then the door swung open and G pushed in. "I got a look at their car and the plate, so I called it in. It's been spotted heading west, and we should hear something soon. How is everyone here?"

The major turned to him and said, "We are fine."

Kate raised her head and faced them. "One of them was the man who shot Krystyn. I've seen Yerik identify him before, and this time was the same. If they can catch them, we can get an ID."

"What do you want me to tell the people gathering

outside?"

"Tell them to be careful." The major's calm voice gave the instructions. "Some teenagers with a rifle tried to shoot at one of the dogs and broke the window. Tell them the dog is unhurt." He turned. "Harry, you're going to need a new windshield. I'd suggest bulletproof if possible." He took hold of Kate's arm as she stepped back. Picking up leads, he asked, "Are you ready to go wash dogs, my dear?"

Kate looked at him. "Of course, Major, we've got work to do." Harry had his phone out and was talking to his assistant, Sadie. She could do anything. Probably by the time the dogs were washed, and Shelagh had finished obedience and rally, there would be no sign of what happened this morning. She pulled out her phone and checked the time—six forty-five. It seemed as though hours had passed. While Harry took care of getting Charlie repaired, she, G, and the major headed into the building, stopping along the way for the dogs to relieve themselves. They all scanned the area, watching for more trouble. Once the dogs were again relaxed in crates, Kate left the major to watch them. Then, taking Shelagh and her supplies, she and G headed for the bathing area. People were filtering into the building, probably with dog bathing in mind, so she moved across the area.

# Chapter Thirty

*Wednesday, morning*

Kate quickly got the bath ready. Shelagh was a little more clingy than normal. It was probably the stress of the attack on the motor home and Pavlik's reaction to having Krystyn's killer so close. She suspected it would throw the dogs off their normal behavior for a while, but having Shelagh upset was not the best lead up to an obedience competition.

Kate got her wet and began soaping her coat. One of the heavy loading doors off to the right shut, and the bitch jumped and spun around. Kate was glad she hadn't hitched her to the wall ring. She would have hurt herself. She felt a tiny vibration under her hands and knew she had her work cut out for her. If she was this jumpy, it would definitely throw off her work in the ring and might keep her from qualifying.

She had been planning on bathing Dillon today but changed her mind. Shelagh needed her. She needed to be worked, retrained to resist startling noises and other distractions, plus she needed to be spoiled. G handed her the vinegar rinse and asked, "Is there a problem with Shelagh?

She seems tense."

"Yes. She was thrown for a loop by the shooting this morning. Of all my Sams, she is the most dependent. She's tough with Quinn, but she'd never tell off Dillon the way her mother would. She's very much the sweet little lady, a great wheel dog on a sled, but not one I could use as lead dog. She goes along without pushing herself forward as do most of my other dogs. So I've got to get her dry and then squeeze a month-long training program into a twenty-minute retrain. I've got to desensitize her to loud startling noises and get her focus back on me."

Kate quickly toweled the bitch off, thanking Kelly for giving her daughter such a crisp stand-off coat that, since it hadn't come all the way back in after her August shedding, would dry fast. She lifted her out of the tub then stepped back and let her shake. She told G to help her gather the towels and supplies. "I'll do Dillon's bath tomorrow. All three Sams will be in Stud Dog competition following the dog classes since Liam is the sire of both of them. Shelagh should be feeling better by then if nothing else happens, and it will get her into the breed ring before she has to compete in open bitch on Friday." They headed to the crate and the grooming table to finish the drying process.

Maeve was sitting, talking to the major when they got there. Kate lifted the bitch onto the table, threw a large beach towel over her, covering the Sam from nose to tail, and then wrapped her arms around her and rested her head on the back of the bitch's neck. Maeve moved to the bitch's front, and after offering a hand to sniff, began working her thumbs from the base of her ears to their tips, over and over again. Kate finally felt a sigh go through Shelagh and stepped back, removing the towel and starting the blow dryer. A brush appeared in her hand, and she saw Harry smiling at her.

"How's she doing?" He reached out to scratch the bitch's back.

"Shaken and stirred, I'm afraid. She was thrown off by being in the crate and unable to react when the shooting came. I've got to get her head screwed back on before she goes into the ring. Did you get somebody to replace Charlie's window?"

"They're doing it now. It will be back about one o'clock."

"They couldn't do it here?"

"No. I'm using a shop Sadie recommended and they specialize in this kind of repair."

"Good thing I don't have to dress up for obedience competition. All my show clothes are in Charlie. Oh, wretch, so are all the dogs' toys. I don't have anything with me I can use to reward her," Kate grumbled as she finished drying and back-combing the bitch's right side and back and moved to the other side.

"Not a problem," Harry said, disappearing across the room,

By the time Kate had finished blowing her back, sides, chest, feet, and tail then combing out her ears and face, Harry was back. Shelagh had eyes only for her new best friend who walked up carrying a pink elephant and a canister of tennis balls.

"You've got thirty minutes, Kate. There are some rooms off the hall. See if one is empty. I'll text you when it's time." Maeve accepted a cup of tea from Padraig who'd arrived with goodies and sat.

Harry and G flanked Kate and Shelagh as they crossed the room and moved into the hall, and into the second meeting room. Shelagh had been carrying the elephant proudly, and Harry couldn't resist taking a photo of her sitting in perfect heel position with the elephant stuffed in her mouth.

Harry's phone buzzed. It was Sadie, so he stepped outside the room to answer. When he finished the call, he reached for the knob but it didn't turn. He knocked, and G came over to open it, but it wouldn't open. The vents at the side of the room opened and started pouring a white cloud into the room, and he saw Kate start coughing.

Harry turned and ran. Des was just coming in, and Harry shouted for him. They ran up the stairs and along the catwalk. He reached the control room only to find it still empty and locked. He and Des both kicked the door together and it opened. The only monitor on showed the room with Kate and G covering their faces and Kate holding Shelagh's head under her T- shirt. As he scanned the controls, he saw the dial move upward. Outside the booth's window, he saw the man from the elevator with his cell phone pointed in their direction.

Harry pointed to the man, and Des ran out, heading for the stairs, gun drawn. Harry tried moving the dial but couldn't. He reached for the bottom of the control box, followed the cord to the power source, and yanked. He glanced back through the glass and spotted Kate and G running from the room with Shelagh.

Harry raced down only to see Kate opening another door, only this time, blocking it with a garbage can. She took the lid off the can and went inside. Harry checked his watch and was shocked to see less than five minutes had passed. He asked if they were okay, and she told him she didn't have time not to be okay. She could be not okay later.

He quickly filled them in on what had happened as Kate set up her training area. "So now we know why they needed the fancy remote control," Harry grumbled.

She held out her hand for the elephant and took it from Shelagh who was reluctant to give up. Then moving to the side wall, she heeled her bitch. They'd just made the first left turn when the metal lid from a garbage can hit the floor behind them, and at the same time, Kate said, "Heel." Shelagh had started but recovered quickly and was back moving easily at her side. Kate continued through the routine and as they passed Harry there was a high-pitched screech from his phone. This time Shelagh looked over but didn't move her body out of position. Kate moved her into the "stand for examination" position and told her to hold. Harry stepped forward, holding the elephant behind his back, and ran a hand from her head to her rump. Kate returned and told her to heel. Then she hugged her and praised her until Shelagh was bouncing up and down. Kate led the still-happy bitch back to the spot by the wall, took off the lead, and placed it behind her. Then she repeated the heeling routine. This time, the lid clattered behind them after the about-turn. Shelagh gave a glance but continued without breaking stride. The final test came with the recall. Kate had her sit, told her to wait, and then walked to the other side of the ring. Harry tossed a tennis ball to G on the opposite side of the room and though Shelagh watched, she didn't move. G returned the ball by rolling it across in front of her. Harry then sent it back bouncing it once in front of her. G caught it and put it behind his back. Kate called Shelagh whose attention was totally focused on G. She refocused instantly and came straight in with a perfect sit. Kate told her to heel and saw her leap into the air, spin around, and land in place. They were done, and Kate fussed over her, and then G bounced the ball and Shelagh leaped and caught it midair. She dropped the ball when Harry tossed the elephant up into the air. She flew up and snatched it by the trunk, shook it back and forth while dancing in backward swirls. Kate snapped on Shelagh's lead, and they all returned to the main room.

Maeve had Kate's armband waiting. She slipped it on as Maeve removed the toy and ran a quick brush over the bitch. Then they all headed toward the ring.

Kate spotted Joceline Levasseur standing at ringside, holding several shopping bags. She was both surprised and suspicious to see her in the building when there were no breed judging classes today. Performance classes were definitely not Joceline's thing. Deciding silence was golden, Kate stood quietly between the two men. Maeve and Padraig had brought their folding chairs and found a good spot to watch.

Joceline approached and, with a supercilious smile

on her face, eyeing both Harry and G asked, “Collecting men, Kate, to make up for your dateless youth?”

“What can I say, Joceline? When you’ve got it, flaunt it,” Kate answered, smiling and slipping her arms though those of Harry and G. Maeve, laughed, and Joceline turned on her heel and moved away.

“I get the feeling she’s not in your fan club, Kate,” G told her.

“I’m surprised Lady Levasseur deigns to speak to a mere peasant these days since her family will soon be joining Washington’s aristocracy.”

Harry frowned at her but didn’t say anything. Then her number was called.

# CHAPTER THIRTY-ONE
*Wednesday, mid-morning*

Kate smiled at Shelagh and stepped into the ring. They worked together smoothly with Shelagh showing none of her earlier unease. During the heel free, Kate noticed Joceline move close to the edge of the ring near the oversized garbage can but didn't figure out what she was up to until someone called out, "Watch out," and the room filled with the sound of a trash can lid hitting the floor. Shelagh barely spared it a blink and continued the exercise.

When they finished the recall, Kate swept Shelagh up in her arms, giving her a hug and kiss. Harry arrived carrying the elephant, which he presented to the happy bitch. Five minutes later, they went back in the ring for the long sit and long down exercises, and Shelagh was rock solid. In the end, they came in second with a score of one-ninety-six and a half. Kate skipped the photo and checked with the ring steward, asking how much time there would be before rally began. They had half an hour, so they went to sit and relax. Shelagh curled up in her crate and fell asleep with her head resting on the elephant.

Kate sat and snagged one of the jelly donuts from

the box Padraig had just put on the grooming table. She looked down at Shelagh and saw Quinn in the next crate, staring at the elephant, his paw trying to pull it into his crate. She finished the donut and then reached down and undid the latch on Quinn's crate, he came out and she pulled him up into her lap, clipping on a lead and picking up one of the tennis balls they'd used. Since there weren't too many people around, she stepped away from the chairs and bounced the ball. Quinn first ran and picked it up, brought it back and, after a minute, gave it up to be tossed again. This time, he jumped up after it bounced and caught it in the air. Kate fussed over him, telling him what a smart puppy he was. He gave the ball back, and they did it again.

Seeing Maeve standing, she let him keep the ball and quickly put him back into his crate, got Shelagh, and went to the rally ring. Shelagh liked rally. Kate thought it was the constant variation of things to do that attracted her. Kate had G hold the bitch's lead while she walked the ring, reading the signs so she'd be prepared. She was the seventh competitor to do the course, and they made it through with good time, even though there were several commands on the cards she'd never done with Shelagh. The stop-and-go exercises usually threw eager dogs in the classes she taught. Shelagh's head followed her on the last exercise where Kate had to walk around her, but she kept her butt on the floor and didn't move. The judge praised Shelagh, telling her what a good girl she was, and the little princess ate it up as though it was her due. Kate picked up her score and headed back toward the crates with G at her side.

Harry was approaching from the outer door, smiling. Kate told him Shelagh had been her lovely self and added both an obedience title and rally title today, getting her third leg in each.

"Congratulations. My girls did a good job today." Harry said Charlie was back, good as new. So they all packed up and headed out. It was almost lunchtime. Maeve, Padraig, and the major were heading out to eat with old friends. Kate said she just wanted a nap. They parted ways at the parking lot as G's phone rang. He stepped to the side to answer as Harry helped her load the dogs into Charlie. When the dogs were settled, Kate dropped into the passenger seat and Harry slid into the driver's seat. Kate was about to comment on the fact the windows were tinted a deeper blue which should cut down glare when G stepped in.

"They got them. They chased them onto back roads due to the amount of traffic on the highway, and their car hit a Jersey barrier. One man is in the hospital, but the other guy's injuries weren't as bad and he's being held downtown. Glasmann wants you to bring Pavlik to the station this afternoon to let him have a sniff at the one in custody. If the murderer is the one in the hospital, the ID will have to wait.

They took care of the dogs, and Harry walked Kate to the back to lie on the bed. He kissed her, had her sit, took off her shoes, and encouraged her to lie down. Then he picked up his tablet and went to sit in the driver's seat.

"Harry, you shouldn't sit there. If they send another shooter, you'd be a perfect target."

"Don't worry. I took the major's suggestion. It's

bulletproof glass."

"Wow, that must have cost a penny or two. Are they going to bill me?"

"No, it's all taken care of. It's not a problem."

"But, Harry…"

"Sleep."

Harry's glare made her give up, for the time being. He said his business was doing well, but he shouldn't have to fork out huge amounts of money on this trip. She had no idea how much his company made, but though her design business and the kennel were well into the black, she didn't have big bucks to throw around. They were getting married and, eventually, the money conversation would have to come up. Kate sighed. Maybe not just this minute. She closed her eyes, and her mind drifted back to the feeling of being trapped, the horrible gas choking them. She'd have to talk to Harry and find out what exactly happened. She should get up and check whether the pouch with the book was still safely hidden, but she'd do it in a minute, after she rested her eyes.

Harry peered over the back of the seat and noticed Kate had finally fallen asleep. She seemed so sweet and vulnerable. He wanted to start the engine and get them as far away from this madness as possible. But he and Kate both knew it wouldn't do any good because the nightmare would follow them wherever they went.

He stretched, staring out the windshield at the huge coliseum before him. The view took on more of a bluish tint because of the new windows. Sadie said the tires and gas tank were also protected as well as the engine. They'd added extra power to handle the additional weight, but it was worth it. It hadn't been cheap. Harry knew Kate was concerned about what it cost, but he could afford it.

He hoped he could put off the money conversation until after the wedding. Knowing the way Kate thought, he was sure it would be difficult to get her to accept the fact they didn't need to worry about money. His father had worried about money every day. Cops made enough to get by but not enough for many extras. When his teacher had approached his parents when he was entering fourth grade and told them he should go into the program across the country at Caltech, his father said no. When he was informed all expenses would be covered, including living expenses through college, he said yes. It had taken Harry a while to understand how his father could send him away. He knew he made him uncomfortable with his math ability, but for many years, he'd taken it as a rejection of his love. Eventually he'd come to understand the fact that only having to pay to raise only one child instead of two meant there would be safety money to cover emergencies. His father couldn't afford to give Harry the education he'd need since he was so smart. Harry finally came to understand the offer made that day must have seemed like manna from heaven to his parents.

He had discovered something else during those early years, isolated from his family. He had a talent with money. He discovered the stock market in one of his early classes. They were instructed to make "paper" investments for the class. Harry instead took money he'd gotten from his dad for Christmas and made real investments. At the end of the semester, his teacher congratulated him for his outstanding understanding of the market and joked it would have been wonderful if he had invested real money. Harry took his A and never mentioned he was several million dollars richer. He continued investing, but only Sadie knew about his wealth.

When his father was shot and killed on duty, Harry stepped in. He convinced his mother his dad had taken out a separate insurance policy. Without his mother or sister knowing, he paid off the mortgage on his mother's house and arranged for her to get an annuity. He also covered his sister's college education. Neither of them questioned the farsightedness of his dad to take out such a policy but just accepted their good fortune.

Kate knew some of this, but had no idea his little habit of making good investments continued. He hoped the money he'd spent today wouldn't create an uncomfortable conversation. He watched Kate. It was ten thirty, and they were due to be downtown right after the major returned from lunch.

A tap came on his window, and he glanced out to see G standing there. He signaled for him to come around to the passenger seat and let him in. Harry signaled him to keep his voice down.

Harry checked his watch again and headed into the back of the motor home. He squatted beside the bed and placed a hand on Kate's shoulder. Instantly, she was awake.

“Uh, I must have closed my eyes for a minute,” she said, rubbing her eyes and sitting up.

“More like forty minutes,” he told her. But who’s counting? It’s time to get up and eat something before we’re needed downtown.”

# Chapter Thirty-Two
*Wednesday, early afternoon*

Kate spotted G. "Have you told Wetherly Brownridge the men have been caught?"

"No, since he wasn't involved this morning."

"He'll want to know because one of those men is Krystyn's killer. I guarantee it."

"Who's Krystyn?"

"I forgot you've come late to this dance. Krystyn was a former NSA agent who showed Samoyeds and was the major's wife. She was murdered last week by the same people who are after me. I've got to clean up. You'd better go tell Brownridge so he can meet us at the station. We'll need the major and Pavlik as well. If we don't get the confirmation at the station, we can check the guy at the hospital to verify if he's the shooter. We can ask Pavlik."

G glanced at Harry who nodded. So he got out and headed back into the building while Kate grabbed Harry's arm to position him between her and the window, and checked her hiding place. The pouch was still there. Kate pulled it out and found the book. She shoved it back and closed the cover, making it disappear into the woodwork. She sighed and Harry said, “Why don’t I make us some tea?”

“I’d love some. Harry, about the money…”

“Kate, where are we building our house?”

“We agreed it would be attached to the one I have now.”

“And who owns the land?”

“I do.”

“So, you are going into this marriage, supplying the land for our home, land worth…?”

“Okay, you don’t need to drop a brick on my head. I’ll stop. But we’ll have to talk about it sometime.”

“How about on the day after the honeymoon, I’ll sit down with you and Sadie and go over our finances. I’ll even take you for a drive in the 1966 Corvette Stingray I restored while I was working on my PhD and needed relief from the tons of work on Algorithms at MIT. It kept me from going nuts that year.”

“What color?”

“Racing red, of course.”

“My brothers will freak.” Kate grinned.

Harry drew a quiet breath of relief.

They pulled into the police station parking lot, since finding a spot on the street for Charlie would be impossible. The major stepped out of his car and let Pavlik out of his crate. Kate approached and spoke quietly to the major. He handed her the lead, and they all followed G inside. Glasmann was waiting and asked how they wanted to do this.

The major cleared his throat. "Kate pointed out my emotional involvement might distract Pavlik, so I shall wait here."

"If you let me walk down the hall by the room, we'll know. Kate nodded to the others to wait and told Pavlik to heel. Moving swiftly down the hall, they passed the interview rooms then reversed their route. "He's not your man."

Glasmann frowned. "They're not going to let you into intensive care with a dog."

"We may not have to go into the room if we can get a piece of clothing from the other man," Kate suggested.

Glasmann nodded and, after a ten-minute wait, an officer approached the group, carrying a paper bag. Pavlik lunged, a heart-wrenching howl filling the room. Kate held him back from the terrified officer. The captain waved his hand to the man who disappeared down the hall, and Pavlik fought to follow, but, eventually, with the major and Kate wrapping their arms around him, he calmed.

A man approached holding a video camera. "I got it, sir," he said. Glasmann nodded as Des and Brownridge arrived.

We have a positive ID on the murderer of Former Agent Machnicki," he told the men. "It's the guy in the hospital. They say he's just out of surgery, but Kate got the dog to do an identification and there was no mistake. He's your guy. We've got it on video, which I'll get to you."

Agent Brownridge placed his hand on the major's shoulder. "I don't know what to say, Major. Of course, this is only the start. We still need the power behind the man."

"I'd like you to sit in as we question his partner." Glasmann included both men in his nod. "Now, we—"

Harry interrupted. "If you're done with us, Captain, we'd like to get back to the hotel."

The men shook hands, agreeing. The major took Pavlik and left. Once G had checked his assignment with his boss, he spoke with Des and joined them. Kate was quiet as they got Charlie turned around so they could exit the lot. Soon they were back on the road and heading for the hotel. The man she'd seen kill Krystyn was caught, but for some reason she didn't feel relieved or glad. She understood Pavlik's frustration and fought her own scream. It was like striking out and only hitting air. Finding this man didn't give her the answers she needed.

As they were leaving Charlie, Kate slipped the strap of her heavy tote filled with the leftover towels over her head. She pasted on a smile and waved to friends as they approached the lobby, Harry and G scanning the area. Suddenly, Harry grabbed her shoulder. "Isn't that the man from the elevator?"

Kate watched a small group of men and a woman move out of sight around the corner of the building. She stared after them, shocked to see who the woman was. What in the world was Joceline doing with a man who pulled a gun on them? A glance at the clock by the elevator reminded her they had a meeting with the Coyote in half an hour.

Harry stopped at the desk and entered the elevator, carrying two packages. Kate, Harry, and G got the dogs relaxed in the room then G told them if they didn't need him for a while, he had things to do and he'd see them at dinner and left.

Harry set his packages on the bed as Kate pulled the pouch out of her bag. He opened the first box and took out a small printer a lot more high tech than the one Kate kept on the desk in her office at home. From the other box came a hand scanner. She had watched Tom use his so she knew its purpose.

"What's the plan?" she asked.

"You're going to order in tea and some food. I'm going to copy the book and print out the relevant pages. Next we're going to go through and compare the pages to those in the duplicate book. After supper, we'll begin, hopefully, to decode the information.

"Okay. I'm going to use the bathroom and get cleaned up first," Kate said.

Harry nodded. "I'm going to turn on the TV and check the news. I can't believe I haven't watched it in days."

"Hopefully, none of our adventures have made it into the news cycle."

Kate called room service while Harry set up the equipment. He turned off the sound but let the news continue with the crawl along the bottom of the screen, giving them the highlights of what was happening in the world away from dog shows. Then they both got to work scanning. The scanner was fast, especially with Kate turning and holding the pages. By the time there was a knock announcing room service, Harry had the first half of the book done. He quickly marked the page, placed both copies of the book into a plastic bag, and shoved them into a large bag of dog food. Kate threw the towels from her tote over the printer and scanner and dumped some brushes and combs on top of them, along with a show lead and collar.

Harry pulled his gun out of its holster and, holding it at his side, opened the door. The room service cart was wheeled in, and Kate reached for the bill and signed it. As he shifted the food and tea, water, and cups to the desk, she asked, "Before you took the book from the publisher's home, you said there was a funeral. Did you recognize anyone there?"

"No. These weren't my class of people. They were the rich, with fancy cars, though I did see a man I thought I knew from something to do with dogs. Maybe someone I'd seen at the National. I don't know. I recognized him because he was with someone I remembered from my last trip to Russia. However, my focus was on getting out with the objective and not getting caught."

"I have some good news. They've caught the shooter who killed Krystyn. Pavlik identified him today. He's in the hospital in intensive care."

"Pavlik did that?"

"No, though he might have wanted to. When he escaped after shooting up my motor home, he crashed his car."

"Good. I hope he suffers. Krystyn was a good person. I hope he is in much pain."

"Unfortunately, he is just one of the thugs carrying out orders. We need to find the person pulling the strings behind him."

She watched the Coyote turn to leave but stopped, staring at the TV screen. A flood of Russian words filled the room and, looking at his expression, Kate assumed he was swearing.

"What? What do you see?" she asked.

"It was he, the man."

"What man?"

"The one I was just telling you about, the man who was at the funeral. He was there on the television."

Harry turned on the sound, but the show had already gone to commercial. He flipped the channels until he found a station reviewing highlights from today's news. They stood in silence watching reports from the Middle East, of an earthquake in Chile, and the breakup of a Hollywood marriage before the news anchor turned to the latest news from Washington about the nomination of a new Secretary of State.

"That's he. It's the man. He was at the funeral, and he spoke to the widow, asking if her husband had any copies of the new blockbuster book he had told him about. The widow said she knew nothing about a new blockbuster. As far as she knew, her husband didn't have anything special scheduled for release. I suspected he was searching for the same book I was after."

"Harry, he's here. He's at the show."

"Who's at the show?"

"Him. It's Joceline Levasseur's father who's been nominated to be the next Secretary of State. He's here at the show to see her compete."

Harry pulled out his phone, but Kate grabbed his

hand. She told her friend to go but stay in touch. If he found out anything else, be sure to let them know and to be careful. When he had gone, Harry said, "We've got to tell Des and Brownridge."

"Agreed, however, we're not calling them immediately after room service delivered food to our room. These men are smart, and I don't want the Coyote to suffer. Also, what are we going to tell them? A former spy says a nominee for Secretary of State was at the funeral where the spy stole something so dangerous Krystyn was killed to hide it? That and a dollar still won't buy a cup of tea these days. So, we should finish doing what we're doing and then get to work decoding. Plus, I'll work better once I have some food and a cup of hot tea."

"You're probably right about the proof, but I'm going to talk to them later. However, we'd better work fast considering the number of people coming in and out of this room. We don't have much private time."

It took them only fifteen minutes to finish scanning the book and print out the file. Harry packed the original book back into the courier bag and hid it deep in the forty-pound bag of dog food resting on the crates. Then, dividing the pages, they got to work comparing the two versions and marking the discrepancies.

Twenty minutes later, Kate growled, "I don't know about your pages but mine are sheer nonsense. Are you finding any classic coding patterns?"

"Nope. I'm afraid we're going to need the Killoy magic to figure the answer to this one. At least we can get the message written down even if it is garbage."

"It's explosive garbage, according to Krystyn. You know what really bugs me is she told so many people I had the answer. If she expected me to break this code, she definitely chose the wrong Killoy."

"Did she know codes weren't your thing?"

"Oh, yes. Both Maeve and Agnes use to tease me about it in front of her. Gramps and Dad always said I had other talents."

Kate thought about what she'd just said. It was teasing in the back of her mind. Something she said was important, but what?

She stretched after another hour. "Okay, I'm done. I'm sure this is a best seller in whatever country speaks gobbledygook as their first language. It should sell a million copies."

Harry reached over to rub her neck and shoulders.

"Ahhh, don't stop, that feels so good."

"Exactly what I'll hear from you on our wedding night." Harry chuckled as Kate's face heated.

She poured some more hot water from the carafe into her teacup, muttering, "Promises, promises."

A knock came at the door. Kate quickly gathered the papers and shoved them into her tote while Harry moved the printer and scanner into a suitcase he had left open on his bed. Then he pulled his gun and went to check the door. It was G.

"Des called. He and Brownridge want to meet us for supper. They've got some questions for you," G told them.

Kate gave each dog a treat and told them they'd be

back. Then, slipping into the bathroom to put on the vest under her sweatshirt, she grabbed her tote and joined Harry and G waiting at the door.

Harry attached the Do Not Disturb sign to the door as well as his invisible entry detector. Considering what they would be discussing when they got back, he didn't want anyone listening in. He'd brought his backup tool bag from Charlie. If the person behind this had any idea Kate had the book, and they could be decoding it, her life would be worth nothing, and neither would his. What they needed was to find the key to the gobbledygook, as Kate called it. He watched Kate and wondered if that was what Krystyn was talking about when she said Kate had the answer. She hadn't said she would have the answer. No, she said Kate already had it. The answer was just out of reach in the back of his mind. It would come to him. None of them said anything as they took the elevator to the lobby. It didn't feel like a time to chat.

They reached the meeting room and saw Des and Brownridge had been joined by Glasmann, Maeve, and Padraig, none of them smiling. Kate moved to a seat with Harry beside her. The NSA agent shut the door and then turned to stand across the table from them, glowering.

"When were you two going to tell me you've been working with a Russian spy?"

# Chapter Thirty-Three
*Wednesday, early evening*

"I am not working with anyone spying for Russia," Kate said, staring the man in the eye, knowing she must make sure her words were well chosen. "Are you, Harry?"

"Nope."

Maeve interrupted. "Wetherly…" He held up his hand to stop her.

Leaning closer to Kate, he said, "You're lying and you are not going to walk out on me this time, missy. You're going to answer every question I ask, and you're not leaving until you do."

Kate leaned forward, her breathing getting louder, until her face was barely an inch from his. "I did."

"You're not telling me all you know."

"It would take years to tell you all I know. I'm a very intelligent person." Kate heard a snort behind her, but she didn't blink in her stare down with the agent. There was no way she was going to be bullied. Having four brothers had taught her the first to blink loses, big time.

"Maeve, do something with her," he yelled.

"My great-niece doesn't lie. If she says she's not

working with someone spying for Russia, she's not. End of discussion. However, if you ask her if she has any information which could help in your investigation, and you are polite rather than acting like a wounded bull, you might get more cooperation." Maeve drew the agent's glare and was as unmoved as Kate. Des put a hand on the older man's shoulder, urging him back into his chair.

"Kate," Des said, a smile on his face.

"Yes, Des?" she said, smiling back and sitting in her chair, her hands folded in her lap, "what can I do for you?"

"What do you know about Mr. Smith?"

"Oh, you mean the man who pulled a gun on me in the elevator? Absolutely nothing."

Brownridge and Maeve both shouted, "Gun…" Des stopped them with a raised hand and continued.

"Had you ever seen him before?" he asked, his sideways glance telling the others not to interfere.

"Yes, he followed us onto the elevator the other day, but since there were a bunch of us with dogs, he didn't say anything. He was wearing a dark suit so he stood out. The man was a walking dog-hair magnet. Also, we spotted him on the video of my first agility run." Kate pulled out her phone and with a couple of clicks sent him a photo. Des's phone buzzed.

He handed his phone to Wetherly, saying, "He's the person of interest who seems to be a known associate of actor number one."

Harry spoke up, "Don't forget, Kate, he was with a group of men accompanying your best bud, Joceline."

Best bud indeed. But she turned back to Des, saying the last time they'd seen the man, he was with a group of men in suits, accompanying Joceline Levasseur. She assumed they had something to do with her father. "He's been nominated for Secretary of State, so they may work for him. Joceline was enjoying all the adulation."

G spoke up. "What a piece of work that b…uhm, lady is. She tried to ruin your score with Shelagh, and it wasn't any accident."

"Her father is supposedly here this week to watch her compete. The occurrence in itself is strange since I don't remember him coming to her shows." All except one. She decided to share. "It's curious he's here though, since I have it on good authority the last time he attended a National was ten years ago when Krystyn arrested the Coyote."

Both Brownridge and Des stared at her. "You knew all this and didn't tell us?" the older agent yelled. Kate could see his blood pressure rising.

She sighed. "Tell you what? A man has shown up in various places where I've been at the National. It's hardly unusual except for his black suit collecting the hair from over six hundred shedding white dogs. Until he pulled a gun on me, which, considering how my days have been going is becoming less and less unusual, I had no proof he was dangerous. Luckily, Des came along. I thank you, Des, very much for your timely save. The whole thing became a farce as he ran off.

Des turned to Brownridge and said, "The subject approached actor one, and they spoke." He turned back to Kate. "Do you know anything else helpful about this man?"

"About him? No. About Mr. Levasseur, maybe. I have it on good authority from a source who shall remain nameless as they say that Levasseur was trying to get a hold of the same information as the Coyote was when he was arrested."

"Who told you?"

"I'm not going to reveal my source. However, as I learn other information, I will share what I get with you. Believe me, I am the person most interested in having this finished, with me still alive." She kept her eyes on him not glancing at her tote holding the information Krystyn had called explosive. If she gave the still-coded document to Wetherly, it would disappear into the cyber security department of either the NSA or FBI, where it would be studied patiently by good decoders who would work on it, but every moment's delay left her out there with a target on her back.

Brownridge glared around the table, his frustration visible but then he sighed. "You'll call me the minute you have anything else?" he asked, reaching out to grab her hand. Kate nodded, as did Harry and Maeve. "And I want it understood—what we've discussed stays among us. You can't share it with anyone."

"Understood. If nobody minds, I'd like to get my supper and get back to my room."

Des and G accompanied Kate and Harry into the restaurant. Kate was startled so much time had gone by. It was after seven, so it wasn't surprising she was hungry. Kate decided on the baked stuffed sole with sweet-potato fries and zucchini, and the men all had some variation on steak and baked potato. When their food arrived. Kate thanked the waiter. "I appreciated the book suggestion the other evening. I'm reading The Secret Adversary and enjoying it."

The waiter smiled back. "I'm glad you like it. I've found you can't go wrong with Agatha Christie."

Harry watched the interplay between Kate and the man she called the Coyote. She trusted him even though he had confessed to having been a spy ten years ago. His training had taught him to be suspicious of everyone. Kate, on the other hand, seemed to have the ability to tell those who were basically good from those with ulterior motives. Maybe, since she'd grown up surrounded by dogs, she'd picked up some of their instincts. It had been a painful lesson for him in both New York and Texas to learn questioning her instincts had ended up getting him shot and endangering her. The faith she had in some people rattled him. He loved her more than life itself, but there were times when he didn't understand her. The way she took chances when she felt it was the right thing to do and necessary, terrified him. Maybe he should talk to Padraig. Of course, Maeve was a pro. He didn't know which way to hop. He couldn't lose Kate.

"Earth to Harry." Kate leaned into him.

"Excuse me?"

"You disappeared there for a while."

"Oh, just thinking. Are you ready to go?" Harry signaled the waiter to bring the bill.

Kate gathered her things, said goodnight to her

friend when she signed the bill, and headed back up to the room. The dogs needed to be fed and they needed to figure out the key to the code they'd pulled from the book. Her mind kept going back to the fact Krystyn had told the major she had the answer. Could it mean she had the key? It could be anything Krystyn had given her in the last ten years. However, those things were mostly toys or souvenirs.

They reached the room and Des stayed with her while Harry and G took the dogs out. Kate made the food and put the appropriate bowl on top of each crate. As she worked, Des asked her where she'd gotten the information about Joceline's father's involvement ten years ago. She didn't bother to answer. Then she asked what Krystyn was going to share with them when they met her at the show. Des told her he couldn't say. Their silence was broken with the return of the dogs, who hit the crates, stomping their feet in anticipation of their dinners. Kate fed them, and Harry saw Des and G out then sat quietly, trying one decoding pattern after another without success.

"Harry, I've been thinking." She sat on the bed across from him. "When Krystyn told the major I had the answer, she might have meant I had the key to this code. Since she didn't feel threatened until recently, something must have set off her fear. We know, according to the major, she was preparing the documents and thumb drives found in the safe before he left. When the murderer broke in, he thought he was stealing the information the Coyote had taken years ago. This means her death is connected to this code."

"Well, we pretty much thought that from the start."

"But the question is, why now? What things are happening bringing all this together?"

"Well, the National, our wedding, and whatever investigation Des and Wetherly are working on." Harry frowned since there weren't many items on his list. "The National allowed her to meet in a public setting with the agents to pass on information they needed."

"The National and the handoff takes care of two of the three and leaves our wedding. How would the wedding work into this?" Kate reached into her bag and pulled out the note and card she had gotten from Krystyn about her wedding and put them on the bed between them. She picked up the card and read it aloud.

*Dear Kate,*

*I wanted to send this even though I will see you next Monday to let you know how happy I am about your engagement and upcoming wedding. I'll give you and your Harry a hug at the National, and the major and I will be flying out for the wedding. I'm looking forward to chatting with you. I have some information I want to share with you, but I have to check with a third person. I'll see you on Monday.*

*Love,*

*Krystyn*

"Unfortunately, it doesn't give us any help with the code," Harry grumbled. He picked up the card and flipped it open and closed over and over as he thought. Kate watched his hands move, almost mesmerized by the back and forth movement, of the design on the front of the card. Then she saw it. She stared at Harry.

"What?" he asked.

"You're holding the key," she answered.

"How? I don't get it."

Kate reached for the card and placed it between them on the bed. "What do you notice about the wedding cake on this card?"

"It is all swirly and avant-garde."

Kate reached for some of the pages of the code and used them to block out most of the design, leaving only the black-and-white marks in the center of the cake. "What do you see now?"

Harry stared at it and then at her. "It's a QR code. The kind you can scan with your phone, and it takes you to a coupon or information. Wait, let me download a code-reading app to my phone from a safe source." Once it loaded, he pointed the phone's camera at the square filled with black-and-white squiggles on the bed. The phone went ding and, immediately, a block of text with instructions appeared.

Harry clicked a few buttons and sent it to the printer, printing two copies. They divided the stack of coded pages in two, and Kate moved to the desk. Without a word, they got to work. It was ten thirty when they finished. Neither spoke but only stared at each other.

Kate opened her mouth to say something only to have Harry hold up his hand. He picked up his phone. "Des, I need to take the dogs out. Could you and G come by? Thanks." He leaned in and whispered in her ear. "Don't move or say anything."

Harry rolled off the bed and grabbed a black suitcase. He reached into his pocket and unlocked one lock and then opened it to get access to a second lock. He opened the second layer and took out a black box, clicked it on, and checked a reading. He sighed and then said, "G and I will take the dogs outside. You must tell Des what we've discovered. We have no option."

"Harry, this is frightening." She reached for him, shaking as he wrapped his arms around her. Being shot at didn't scare her like this. She just wanted to be at home with her dogs, hiding in her kennel. A knock sounded at the door.

"Don't say anything to G," Harry whispered as he gently kissed her, put everything out of sight, and then moved to the door.

"Thanks, guys. G. you want to take Quinn and Liam and I'll take Dillon and Shelagh."

"Sure. Hi, Kate. After this, I may just have to get a Sammy puppy from you. I'm falling in love with Quinn."

Kate took a quick breath and smiled. "They do tend to grab your heart and not let go." With a flurry of activity and excited yips from Quinn, the dogs left. Harry gave her a nod as he closed the door.

Kate turned toward the agent who had just sat in the overstuffed chair and put his feet up. "Des, I'm terrified. We need about a hundred FBI agents. This is bad, so bad."

"What is it? Harry didn't say anything."

"He said I must tell you." She took a deep breath. "When you came here, it was to see Krystyn. What did you expect to get from her?"

"I can't tell you. It's classified. Sorry."

"Des, I've got what she was going to give you. Harry and I figured it out. It was in code, and Krystyn had sent me the key, but I didn't know it and so I thought everyone was wrong, but they were right, and it is so horrible…"

"Kate, stop. Breathe." He jumped up and grabbed her arms. "What did you find?"

"I found the information Krystyn had. The reason she was killed. The reason they've been trying to kill me—will keep trying to kill me. There's just you and Agent Brownridge. You will both be targets, as well as Harry. This man, these people, need us dead." She handed him the decoded notes they'd written out. He stood and read the first three papers then pulled out his phone and hit a single key. "I need the director, now. No, I don't care if he can't be disturbed. This is vital. Just say Coyote. I'll wait."

# CHAPTER THIRTY-FOUR

## *Wednesday, late night to Thursday, early morning*

"Kate, give me your phone." She took it from her pocket, and Des grabbed it, hitting the keys with his thumb then slapped it to his ear so the pair of phones resembled earmuffs. Kate could hear a ring and then a click. "Brownridge. Kate's room. Alone. Do it. Don't talk to anyone." He turned her phone off while still waiting on his own. Finally, someone must have picked up because Kate heard a click, and the vague sound of talking. "Director, we have an emergency situation here. Wetherly Brownridge of NSA and I are on-site. We've gotten the information we sought. It's explosive. I am not a high enough level to deal with this. So far, only two civilians and I know the contents, and one of the civilians is former FBI, Harry Foyle. Yeah, Numbers." This is the problem you spoke of in May as something we should possibly fear. It became a reality ten minutes ago. Yes, sir. I'll await your call." He disconnected and stared at the phone.

"Des, isn't there an FBI office in Louisville? Can't you contact them?"

"No. I can't tell them what's in the report unless I

have a death wish. I couldn't even tell the director because the call could be intercepted and listened to with today's technology. You and I shouldn't even be talking about this in case someone is listening."

Kate pointed to the black box Harry had set going. "If they try, they won't succeed." Kate picked up a pad and wrote quickly then handed it to Des. "This is where I will be expected to be for the next three days. If I'm not there, people will ask questions. As for the rest of the time, we're flexible if you need to meet with us away from here. We could create an old friend of Harry's we'll be spending time with since we're in the area."

The sounds of dogs arriving and men talking filled the room. Kate picked up a towel and dropped it over the black box. By the time the door opened, Kate was sitting in the chair from the desk next to Des, and they were both staring at what resembled a puzzle on her tablet. "See? Getting it into the final box is the object of the game. If you move these pieces first, then you've got almost a 70 percent chance of winning. Hi, guys. Yes, Quinn, you're back, and I still love you. I love you all," Kate said as the four dogs crowded around her. She hugged them, scratching their backs then she asked, "Who wants a bickie?" They raced to their crates and whirled around in each, smiling and waiting for the promised dog biscuit. She passed out the treats, latching the crate doors as she did. Her timing was perfect. No sooner had the last biscuit been taken than the knock on the door announced Brownridge's arrival.

Agent Brownridge pushed through the door and spotted G standing next to Harry. "You, G, or whatever your name is. I've got to question these two about things above your security level. I need you to watch the hall from your room and make sure we're not interrupted." G glanced at Harry then nodded and left. As the door closed, Kate pulled the towel off the black box, and the NSA agent relaxed slightly. "Okay, what is so important and secret?"

Des nodded at Kate, and she repeated what she'd told him. The agent's expression turned from impatient, to concerned, to horrified as he quickly read the papers Kate handed him. Des' phone buzzed with a text. Des read it, and Kate saw some of the tension leave his shoulders. "Help will be here in two hours."

Kate walked over to where Harry was leaning against the door and straight into his arms. He held her, resting his chin on her head, without either of them saying a word. Then they both slid onto the empty bed and sat up, leaning against the headboard. Harry wrapped his arms around her again and let her head rest on his shoulder.

"How did you discover the QR code?" Wetherly asked.

Harry nodded at Kate who spoke. "Maybe it's because I'm a designer. I tend to see things differently. I knew Albrecht Durer had not done a cake drawing like this, though it was definitely worked in his style. Harry had been waving the card back and forth while he thought. The surrounding lines seemed to blur as I watched him move it, leaving the central square standing out. I had seen the codes used in magazine ads, online, at conferences to gather information, and other places. They are always related to either giving or getting information. Harry downloaded a

QR reader into his phone and, once I'd blocked off most of the irrelevant lines, we were able to scan just the square with the code. It took us to a site, probably housed in the dark web, with the key or, more specifically, the instructions on how to break the code."

Time passed slowly as they waited, the restless man from the NSA again examining the card. "Amazing. I'm astounded Krystyn knew you'd be able to figure this out and not just put the card with all the rest of your wedding stuff. She must have known you well."

"She'd known me since I was seven years old. She was one of my best friends. We would often talk for hours about everything and nothing, and I always felt at home talking to her. My dad and grandfather liked her, too." Brownridge smiled to himself as though he, too, was remembering time spent with Krystyn. The silence descended once more then finally Des' phone buzzed.

"Yes. Got it. Twenty minutes or less. Room two thirty-four." He ended the call and told them, "They've landed at the airport and will be here soon." He stood and gathered up the papers, arranging them in order. The card rested on top, appearing somewhat out of place in such a businesslike environment.

Des called G to let him know more agents would be arriving. Then he moved to the door to watch for them. Kate and Harry sat on the edge of the bed and put on their shoes. Harry stood and reached into a box for dog cookies, handed them to Kate then took out a lead to put on Quinn. The others would be polite during the meet and greet, but Quinn hadn't learned to curb his instinct to greet everyone by jumping on them and trying to attract all their attention. It usually worked because he was so cute, but he wouldn't stay small and cuddly forever. When he got as big as Dillon or Liam, jumping would not be welcome.

The door opened quietly, and four men came into the room, mentally shrinking its size considerably. Des had barely closed the door when Quinn jumped on his crate door, banging with his paws to get out. Kate took the lead from Harry as he released the others. Quinn was a puppy on a mission as soon as he heard the latch release, but Kate had a lifetime of practice at stopping dogs determined to escape. Before he knew what happened, the puppy found himself being made to sit quietly in a row with the others, receiving pats from the men. Then, just as quickly, being returned to his crate along with a long rawhide chew to keep him occupied.

The man in charge was even taller than Harry's six foot four. With his shaved head, mocha coloring, dark eyes, and linebacker physique, he should have been scary, however, the Harry Potter glasses slipping down his nose, the charcoal suit, crisp white shirt, and blue-striped tie, gave him the perfect executive style to soften the thuggishness nature provided. He nodded at Brownridge who introduced him to Kate as the Assistant AIC for the DC office of the FBI, Malcolm Bullock. As he reached out to shake Kate's hand, she glanced at Des for a second and then smiled at this imposing figure. "You're the man who inspired Des to join the Bureau. It's a pleasure to meet you. Des is a great agent."

"Telling tales out of school, Xiang?" He frowned

for a second and then laughed. "You're an insightful young lady. Killoy? Any relation to Tom Killoy, the forensic number cruncher?"

"He's one of my brothers."

"How many brothers do you have?"

"Four, and they all love math."

"Is that how you met Numbers here?"

"No, I'm a knitting designer who shows dogs, as you can see."

Harry walked over from where he had been chatting with the other new arrivals and shook Bullock's hand. "Good to see you again, sir. What you should know is Kate and Agent Machnicki had been friends since Kate was a young child. She sent her a clue to breaking the code located in a book the Coyote stole. It seems he wanted out of the spy business because it was getting too dangerous for him, so she arranged for his arrest. He, in turn, passed her the information he'd stolen. Krystyn apparently thought it too explosive to reveal at the time, so she hid it. She realized the Coyote was not the only one searching for it. For a long time, she was able to keep the knowledge she had it from others. However, someone must have made the connection through the arrest. They had begun tapping her phone, so she set out to hide the information, sent Kate the clue to break the code, and then told people in her life Kate had the answers. Unfortunately, she was killed before she could tell Kate what was going on."

Bullock scanned the room, raising a brow when he spotted the black box resting on the edge of the bed and taking in the stacks of papers topped by the card arranged on the desk. He seated himself into the desk chair, adjusted the lamp for better lighting, and reached for the card. He opened it and read what Krystyn had written. "I see congratulations are in order, Foyle."

"Thank you, sir."

"When's the wedding?"

"Five weeks," he said, reaching for Kate's hand. "If we can get these sons of bitches—sorry, pups—to stop trying to kill her."

"Well, we'll just have to make sure the wedding happens. Xiang, tell me what I'm reading." He picked up a stack of papers.

Des took a moment, seeming to get his thoughts in order, and began. The next two hours were spent with all the men in the room talking. Kate curled up on the bed, her fear growing as she learned more and more about this evil plan. So many people would suffer because of greed. They needed to stop these people. But the book hadn't had the names of those behind the plan. It had all the details and the projected results. It even had the division of profit. It had everything but the names of those behind the operation and, without those, stopping the plan would be next to impossible. Krystyn must have had the names of the people at one time, but the page with that information was missing. Kate could see why she didn't want all her eggs in one basket, but without the names… Her mind went back over the week, took out every piece of information they'd learned, shook it out, and examined it. She was sure, dangerous as this plan was and as devastating its possible results, it couldn't be halted without the names.

The drone of voices became like elevator music, present in the background but unnoticed. Kate reached for her tablet and pulled up the video of Krystyn's murder. There was something the major had said. Kate scrolled through the list of recordings. She fast-forwarded through at high speed until she got to a shot of her desk then stopped. She repeated this, going back one day at a time. Then, she found it. It was a day when the laptop was on the desk and next to it, sat a copy of the book with the code. Krystyn was at the desk typing and double-checking by consulting the book. She finished, closed the laptop, and then ripped a page from the book, crumpled it up, placed it in a saucer on her desk, and burnt it. She stood, returned the book to its spot on the shelf, and pulled a flat square package of wrapping paper from a shopping bag, a bow, and a mailer.

Kate must have made a sound because Harry quickly moved to her side. She reached for his worried face and kissed him. "I know where the names are." She had everyone's attention. She glanced at the clock. It was three thirty in the morning. Yikes, she had dogs to show today and one to bathe, and she'd had no sleep. Well, she'd pulled all-nighters before. She'd just push.

"Kate. Wake up," Harry said, shaking her.

"I'm not asleep, just trying to figure how to bathe a dog and show a bunch of them today." She pulled out her phone and called her brother. "Tom, I need you to do something. I didn't call Gram because she might still be sleeping, but I knew you'd be up. I need you to go into the room where the wedding presents are stored and see if there is a brown mailer with a red stripe across the bottom left corner. I'll wait." Kate gazed around the room, but her audience hadn't moved. "Found it. Good. Open it. If I'm right, it's a laptop computer. Is it password protected? Damn. No, wait. Try Darragh38. You're in, great. Find a file labeled Pavlik and open it. Four names? Read them to me." Kate scribbled them on the pad Harry had just shoved in front of her. "Thanks. One more thing. Lock the laptop in your secure safe and don't mention it to anyone. If Gram notices the package is not there, tell her it's something I had sent I knew would arrive when I was away and didn't want anyone to see. Tell her it's for the honeymoon. Yes, and get your mind out of the gutter, big brother. Thanks. I'll talk to you soon. Love ya." Kate ended the call. Everyone was standing and leaving. Harry showed them out and set the lock on the door, walked to the bed, and handed Kate her pj's.

"Go get changed. You need sleep. I'll wake you in time."

Kate quickly changed and brushed her teeth. She crawled into bed as Harry cleared the equipment off his bed and headed for the bathroom. She waited to say something when he came out, but the next thing she knew she was being shaken, and the sun was streaming in the window. Harry was dressed and the dogs all were chewing on biscuits.

"Relax," Harry told her. "The dogs have already been out. G and I walked them while Des watched over Sleeping Beauty. But if you're going to eat breakfast, get

Dillon bathed, and everyone groomed for the stud dog class, you need to get up now."

Kate raced for the bathroom, grabbing her clothes on the way. As she stood under the shower, she remembered the number Tom had said was at the bottom of the page of names. It had the names Jane and Sacha next to it. She had to make a phone call.

# CHAPTER THIRTY-FIVE
## *Thursday, morning*

G and Des met them in the hall as they headed for the motor home. G was carrying two large bags of breakfast takeout, and Kate's stomach rumbled in response, plus all the dogs were working on becoming G's best friend. Maeve and Padraig met them when they pulled into their parking slot at the show site. Maeve took Dillon's lead and told Kate to relax and eat. She'd see to his bath and meet her inside. She found herself being pushed gently into the banquette with food placed before her. She smiled, thanked G, and dug in. G and Des had already eaten, so they took the remaining dogs to walk, telling Kate they would put them in their crates inside. Harry slid in across from her, placing a mug of tea in her hand and setting down one for himself. They ate silently for a few minutes, and then Harry cleared his throat.

"I need to apologize to you, and it's not easy. I've finally figured out something. You asked me to think about our relationship. I realized I'd been thinking of us as two people in love but separate people. Last night, or maybe it was this morning, it occurred to me since I met you, we haven't been truly separate. Even when we weren't physically together, we were together. I know I'm not making sense, but we may not be married yet, but we've been partners in life from the minute I ran into you, literally if I remember correctly, and as far as I'm concerned that will never end. I'm sorry I got all macho, and feel free to deck me if I do it again. I love you, Kate."

"I love you, Harry, and I'm looking forward to being your wife and your partner in our life together." Harry was kissing her when a knock came at the door.

"Kate, it's Cathy." Harry opened the door, and Cathy came in, followed by Rufus and Jordy.

"Hi, Kate, Harry. Have you seen all the Sammies? There must be a gazillion of them. We came through the building, and this guy was putting dogs in crates, and suddenly a puppy started barking and trying to get to me, and it was Quinn. He remembered me. He's gotten bigger. He'd never fit under an airplane seat now. I told him we'd be back and I'd play with him later because Cathy had to come talk with you." He finally ran out of breath.

"Hi, Jordy," Kate said. "Cathy, I know I asked you a month ago to help with the showing today, but with all this going on, if you'd rather not, I'll understand."

Cathy smiled. "That's why I'm here. I'm going to be with you in the ring. I assume I'll have Shelagh. I will want to work with her for a few minutes before we go in, but with what I've seen, we'll do great together."

"Thanks. I just have to make a call then we'll be right behind you. Maeve is bathing Dillon for me so I am living in the lap of luxury this morning." They left, and

Kate pulled out her phone. She dialed the number from the laptop and didn't have to wait long for a woman to answer.

"Jane, my name is Kate Killoy, and I'm a friend of Krystyn Machnicki. You know who I am? The long braid, right. Well, I don't know if Krystyn has contacted you recently but—oh, she did? You were waiting to hear back. Well, I have to tell you Krystyn was killed last week. Yes, I know, we all miss her. However, she asked me to follow up with you and check to see if you would like to get back together with your husband again. Wonderful. She never told me where you live. Got it. Actually, he's in Louisville now, only an hour away from you. I know he wants to see you. He misses you and his daughter. Tonight? Fine. We'll either be at the Grand Hotel or across the way at the dog show. I'm looking forward to meeting you, too. You're welcome."

Harry reached out and snagged her wrist as she ended the call, pulling her to him, and kissed her. "I'm guessing from your side of the conversation we're going to have a very happy spy, pardon me, ex-spy, on our team." Kate grinned and ducked into the bedroom area to slip into her ring clothes.

As they left Charlie, they were immediately met by two of the agents who had been with Malcolm Bullock last night. Harry introduced them as Karl and Ike. They started teasing Numbers about having gotten such a stunner to fall for him. Ike added, "She's brilliant, too."

Kate laughed and suggested they introduce the guys to her cousin.

"No, not Agnes." Harry cringed.

"Agnes who?" Karl asked.

"Agnes Forester," Harry growled.

"You're kidding, the model?" Ike asked. "Can I get introduced?"

"Sorry, guys, she's engaged." Kate laughed. They had arrived at her crates as Maeve brought Dillon from the grooming area. Kate reached into her tote and pulled on her lab coat to keep her outfit free from massive amounts of white hair. She grabbed a towel and rubbed Dillon all over as he tried to kiss her face. She laughed, pulled up the dryer, and got it started. Brushing and blowing his coat, she and Maeve had him ready to go in about twenty minutes. As Harry lifted Dillon off the table, Cathy and Rufus came up with her two bitches along with Jordy handling Quinn.

"Watch me, Kate. Quinn and I are learning to show." The boy gated the puppy in a circle and brought him to a nice square stop, as Kate, Maeve, and Harry applauded. Kate stepped forward, took Quinn's lead, and put him into his crate, giving him a treat. Then she squatted down in front of Jordy and asked if she could talk to him. He nodded.

"Remember when I was visiting and I got shot at and Harry got wounded?" she asked.

"Of course. But she's in jail now."

"Well, she wasn't the only bad person out there. We've been having a problem here. There are some bad people who want me dead. They have tried twice and failed. However, I don't want anyone else to get hurt if they miss me. So I need you to do something for me. If any of us"—she scanned the group—"including these old friends of Harry's, tells you to do something, I don't care what they tell you, you do it. Will you promise me that?"

"Kate, I don't want you hurt."

"Do you promise me?"

"Yes, I promise. Kate, be careful."

"I promise I'll be careful."

Jordy reached out and hugged her hard as Kate hugged him back.

"Thanks for playing with Quinn. We've been a little busy around here, and it will help for you to play with him."

"I'll help. I like playing with Quinn, and he likes me."

Kate wiped her eyes and stood, nodding at Rufus and Cathy.

She went to Shelagh's crate, took her out, and handed her lead to Cathy who moved off to work with her before the stud dog class. Maeve told her, "They are just finishing up with the open dog class."

Kate looked at the ring. She'd forgotten about Yerik. The open dog class was in. She scanned the line and spotted Krystyn's young dog with Lisa. The major was watching from the side. Kate paused and saw the judge pull out six dogs from which he would make his pick. Yerik was in second place, and that's how he placed them.

"Yerik went second." Kate caught Lisa's eye as she exited the ring, giving her a thumbs-up.

"They've got Winner's Dog judging next then you'll go in for Veteran Dog. Then they'll have Working Dog and, finally, you, I, and Cathy will go in for Stud Dog judging," Maeve said.

"Okay, Liam, my boy. Up you go on the table for a quick brush." Kate opened his crate and patted the grooming table. Liam placed his front feet up and Harry boosted him the rest of the way. Then he grabbed a brush and began brushing his legs and belly while Kate did his back and chest. In less than a minute, they were done, Harry whipped him off the table then he and Liam dashed outside so the dog could relieve himself. Kate took off her lab coat and made sure there was bait in her pocket. Padraig slid on her armband, handed her a bottle of water, and she drank. Harry returned with Liam, placed the lead in her hand, gave Kate a kiss, and stepped back as the steward said, "Veteran Dogs eight to ten years of age into the ring, please." Kate straightened her shoulders, said a small prayer and, when her number was called, walked into the ring.

The team surrounding her grooming area spread out around the ring, looking not at Kate but at everyone watching the competition. G headed up to the control room overlooking the judging. He would remain there until both Veteran and Stud Dog judging was over. G would be able to study the monitors displaying not only the show ring but the hall outside the main room, the food vendors, and the meeting rooms.

Liam was the fourth dog into the ring, two behind Joceline's male with two more behind her. Kate was relieved she wouldn't have to deal with the girl's tricks on top of everything else. She watched the judge and, at his signal, the group began to trot the dogs around the ring. Kate had known the judge, Abner Walsh, for about ten years and respected the quality of Samoyed he bred. He'd only gotten his judge's license four years ago and, since he lived in California, she'd not had a chance to show under him. The first thing she noticed was he was determined to wear out the handlers, having them move their dogs around the extra-large ring twice before lining up for examination.

Liam had stacked himself and was relaxed. Kate stood beside him, letting the royal-blue color of her skirt make a good background to show off the dog's head and neck carriage. Liam was totally focused on the judge with his ears alerting, watching his every move. Her friend Edna was behind Kate, and they respected each other's space. The man in front of her was baiting his dog so hard, she wondered if the poor dog would have an alert left in him by the time the judge went over him. Kate stepped forward and blocked the dog from leaping onto Liam with the guy's overhandling. He kneed the dog in the chest, forcing him to jump backward, slamming into Kate. Recovering her balance, she was about to tell him to back off, when the judge approached. Taking him by the arm, he pulled him to the corner of the ring and told him to wait there. Then the judging continued smoothly. Kate rubbed her hip still hurting from being slammed by the dog. When it was time, the judge signaled the man to come stack his dog. There were no more problems. Next, Kate and Liam stepped forward to be examined. Liam stacked perfectly on his own, and Kate moved to the end of his lead, giving the judge a chance to inspect the dog. Liam was a statue if you didn't count his tail which was wagging a mile a minute.

Kate stepped up to show the judge Liam's bite but then stepped aside knowing Liam would not move during the exam. The judge stepped back when done with the exam, and Liam ignored Kate, focusing his attention on Abner Walsh. When told, they moved down to the far corner of the ring and back. Kate gave Liam's lead a tiny flick when they reached the judge, and Liam became a statue of the perfect Samoyed, grinning at the judge with only his tail moving. At a nod from Walsh, they gaited around the entire ring to the end of the line. Kate made sure to leave extra space between herself and the dog in front of her.

When the last dog was examined, the judge made quick work of his choices. Liam was pulled out first, Joceline's male second, Edna's third, and a dog Kate didn't know fourth. He had them gait around the ring as he pointed one, two, three, and four. Kate reached down to hug Liam and gave him a treat from her pocket. She thanked the judge when he handed her the blue ribbon and headed for the crates to give Liam a chance to rest before going back into the ring.

Kate checked the catalog and saw Pavlik wasn't entered, so she pulled up a chair next to Maeve who leaned in and spoke quietly. "I assume this group of your fiancé's buddies are is not here for old time's sake."

"They call him Numbers. He was apparently well-liked when he was assigned to the DC office."

"You're not answering my question."

"I don't have the clearance to speak about anything. Talk to your friend Agent Brownridge."

Maeve gaped at her and seemed to lose her coloring. "Kate, the answer Krystyn said you had?"

Kate stared straight ahead as Malcolm Bullock pulled a chair over and got comfortable next to Maeve. "Tell me, Mrs. Donnelly, how many more times today does your great-niece have to run around the ring with a target painted on her back?"

Maeve stared at him for a few seconds. "Once, and you had better make sure nothing hits that target."

Bullock turned to Kate, who was sitting rigidly watching the ring. "Thank you for wearing your vest, Kate. I barely noticed it till Numbers told me you had it on."

Kate turned to him. "It's a pre-wedding present from Sadie. All the brides-to-be are wearing them this year."

"Ah, Sadie. An amazing woman. Numbers is lucky to have her."

"She is something. I think if we put her together with you, Maeve, we could solve the world's problems."

Maeve, at first stiffened but then relaxed and laughed.

Kate glanced back at the ring and stood. "Showtime. Maeve. We had better get the others ready. His judging is quick."

# Chapter Thirty-Six
*Thursday, afternoon*

Harry stood by Kate outside the ring with Jordy at his side. He took off the armband she'd forgotten she was wearing, and slid on Dillon's while Padraig took Liam's armband to slide onto Maeve's arm. She and Liam stepped forward, and Kate got behind her with Dillon. Cathy and Shelagh moved into place behind Dillon, and the Shannon Samoyeds were ready for the ring.

It seemed to be a cast of thousands. This year, unlike some others, there was no limit on the number of get, descendants of the stud dog, allowed in the ring. For Liam, there were two, Dillon and Shelagh, half brother and sister with Liam as dad. When their number was called, they filed in and joined the crowd. Kate glanced around as the ring filled almost to overflowing. There were probably close to a hundred people in the ring with dogs. The likelihood of someone shooting at her had to have dropped considerably. It would take a master shot with a clear view to hit her in this crush.

Slowly but surely, Abner Walsh worked his way

through his entries, managing the ring and the number of dogs. Kate checked those standing at ringside for the first time while the judge was examining dogs at the other side. Harry and his Bureau friends were working the crowd carefully, checking everyone.

Kate had been chatting with Cathy, Maeve, and two other handlers when she suddenly stopped and whipped around with an overwhelming feeling of being watched again. Her eyes scanned the crowd and finally went to the windowed room above them. She didn't see anyone, but the feeling didn't lessen. She felt a hand on her arm and jumped.

"Kate, what's wrong."

"I'm being watched. I don't see who's doing it, but I can feel it. The feeling just started."

Maeve turned her head and began scanning the crowd. Cathy joined in, looking around. The judge asked their group to step back so he could move the first group around the ring. As they stepped back, Maeve flicked her hand, and two seconds later, Agent Brownridge, Harry, and Bullock were right next to them on the other side of the ring fence. Maeve passed on the word Kate had begun to feel she was being watched. "Has anyone checked out the control room?" she asked.

Harry reached for his earpiece. "G, check in." He waited. "G, what's going on?" No answer. Bullock was instantly on the move, ordering Harry and Brownridge to stay on Kate. He was up the stairs with two men following before she could blink. She was watching him approach the control room when a hand grabbed her arm and she was jerked sideways by Cathy telling her they were ready to move. Kate wrenched her eyes back and glanced down with chagrin saying, "Sorry, Dillon." Kate moved into position with Maeve and Liam in front of her and Cathy with Shelagh behind. Their half of stud dogs class began to move out, circling the ring at a trot, and Kate forced herself to focus. She refused even to check on Bullock. The stud and get before them had four get with the stud dog. The judge worked quickly through each entry, examining each Samoyed and gaiting each individually then together as a family grouping. Finally, it was their turn.

Maeve moved Liam forward, followed by Dillon and Shelagh. The judge grinned when he saw his veteran dog, his gaze slid to Dillon and Shelagh, and an eyebrow lifted. He quickly examined Liam, and Maeve gaited him, letting him show himself. Then he moved to Dillon, who thought if his father liked this judge and could charm him, then so could he. Kate stepped back and let Dillon do his thing. It was obvious the gene for charm ran from father to son. Abner Walsh managed to keep a straight face as Dillon gave him the full treatment, especially after returning from gaiting. Then the flirt stepped up. Anything her father or brother could do, she could do better. Cathy stepped back and just let her flirt, and the charm gene burst forth. After examining Shelagh, he had her gait. Then the judge moved all three of them together, and Kate breathed a sigh of relief they'd been exposed in the ring and survived.

The judging continued for about ten more minutes, and then he made his cut, pulling out the eight family groups he would consider further and thanking everyone else for showing. He must have been tired, considering the vast number of dogs he'd already judged today, but he was still smiling. He had them spread out and move together and then each grouping individually. Then he rearranged the family groupings, had the them all move together again, and he pointed to his placings of first, second, third, and fourth. Abner Walsh celebrated the love of Shannon Samoyeds by putting up Liam, Dillon, and Shelagh for first place. Maeve hugged Kate and Cathy as she celebrated the win. The winners lined up for rosettes and trophies, and Judge Walsh laughed as he handed Maeve first place, saying he was used to seeing genetics pass down in heads, coat, or gait, but this was the first time he'd seen the gene for charm.

Together, they moved to the photographer's area to get the official photos. Kate turned her gaze on the booth, but though she saw several of the FBI people, she couldn't tell what was going on. She had only taken a few steps when she was surrounded by Harry, Rufus, Padraig, and two FBI agents. Harry hugged her and in a whisper asked if she was all right. She nodded and started to ask what happened only to have him shake his head. Padraig leaned in and kissed Maeve. "You were the most beautiful girls in the ring, ladies. You were all wonderful, and I got the whole thing recorded on my phone." Maeve stepped forward with Liam and Kate then Kate with Dillon and Cathy with Shelagh, and the photographer had them stack together. The judge held the rosette and trophy, and all three dogs focused on him in spite of the photographer trying to get them to turn toward the camera. Finally, Jordy saved the day by arriving with Liam's ribbon and Quinn. The dogs all turned to smile at their favorite boy, and the photographer got his shot then Maeve took Dillon, and Kate stepped into position to have Liam's Veteran win photo done. The judge told Kate how impressed he was with her breeding. And finally, it was done. Harry wrapped his arm around her, and the others surrounded her as they walked out to Charlie. Maeve said she'd take care of putting everything away and would talk to her later. Kate thanked Cathy and Jordy for their help. Rufus mentioned he'd filmed the stud dog class as well, and he'd send it to her. Kate scrutinized those around her. This wasn't a casual walk, this was a wall. Something had happened, and nobody wanted to tell her what.

In just a few minutes, Kate found herself in Charlie, the dogs crated, and two agents who knew Harry but she didn't know were riding in the back as Harry pulled the motor home out of the venue's parking lot. But, instead of heading for the hotel, Harry turned toward downtown Louisville.

Kate fought down the urge to pepper them with questions. Harry would tell her soon, but the tension coming off him kept her silent. One of the agents in the back said, "Next block. Parking lot is this side of the building." Harry pulled Charlie into the lot and swung around to park so it faced the exit. The men stood, and Kate jumped up, opened the roof vents, opened Dillon's crate for him to jump down, and gave each of the other dogs a treat, telling them she'd be right back. She grabbed her bag, not bothering with a lead, and watched as the first agent stepped out, scanned the area then signaled. His partner held out his hand, indicating she and Dillon could leave, and then followed.

Harry was waiting. He locked the door, moved her to his left side, away from his gun hand, and wrapped his arm around her waist as they headed for a doorway into the building that Kate learned from the small sign by the door was the Louisville office of the Federal Bureau of Investigation.

Assistant AIC Bullock was waiting for them after they'd worked their way through the building. He escorted them into an outer office where a female agent was waiting. He indicated Kate should sit and wait while the men headed into the office.

"No. Enough. I've put up with this silent treatment too long." Kate rounded on Harry. "If you don't want to be standing in the church next month by yourself, buster, you'll tell me what's going on. What happened to G? Someone had better start talking, or I'm out of here. And the first one who pats me on the head and tells me not to worry will lose an arm." She shook with anger. She was a take-charge person being treated like a helpless child. Kate stood nose to nose with Harry, Dillon plastered himself to her side, ignoring the others in the room.

Harry reached out, took her shoulders, and rested his head against hers for a minute. "I'm sorry, Kate. I got caught up in procedure from my days at the Bureau. You're right. I'll tell you everything. Let's go inside." A man standing beside Bullock started to say something but stopped as Kate and Dillon swept past. The conference room held a table and about a dozen chairs. Kate walked to the far end and took a seat on the right, putting Dillon on a down beside her chair, and Harry took the seat next to hers.

"I'll begin," Bullock said, "by saying thank you, Kate. Your instinct telling us something was wrong led to saving three lives, not counting your own and anyone else who might have been in the line of fire in the ring. When we got to the top of the stairs heading for the control room, we spotted two men leaving through a fire escape door. Since we had nobody outside the building, they managed to escape. What we found when we entered the room was the officer you call G had sustained a bullet wound to the shoulder, and both the men assigned to work in the booth lay unconscious. The other thing we spotted was the men leaving the building were wearing police uniforms."

"Like the fake cop who tried to kill me earlier," Kate answered.

"As far as we could tell, the fake cops entered the booth, knocked out the operators, and were getting ready to shoot you when your friend G arrived. They must have had a silencer on the gun they used to shoot him because nobody heard anything. If you hadn't warned us, they would have finished the job. As it is, there is a hunt for the men, and G and the others are being patched up at the hospital. Tell me how you knew something was going on."

"I was feeling fine then suddenly I felt watched, as though I were prey. Maybe because I've been surrounded by dogs all my life, I've come to respect my survival instincts. I didn't check Dillon, though I should have. He probably would have had his hackles up. All I knew was something nasty had me in its sites. I've had the feeling before, and it's always been right."

"I know when you and Numbers here decoded the information in the book, you acquired information about what's been going on. The men on the list want it kept secret. The men named all have unimpeachable reputations, which is why they've never been suspected when hints of these crimes leaked out. They are all being watched at the moment."

The door of the room opened, and Des stepped in, followed by Agent Brownridge. The younger agent walked first to Kate and placed a hand on her shoulder. "G sends his regards and thanks for sending the cavalry." Then he turned to Bullock. "Levasseur is now under surveillance."

Brownridge spoke up. "Considering the number of officials involved, the director has decided to keep this under wraps until everyone involved has been brought in. Since two of those named are foreign nationals with diplomatic immunity, it is going to involve some paperwork first."

"Is there a plan in place to wind this thing up and stop the threat?" Kate asked.

"Not yet. You wouldn't consider going into witness protection until this is over, Kate?"

"Not happening. I have a bitch to show tomorrow and Dillon to show on Saturday. Plus, if I suddenly disappear, they might figure something was up and make it harder for you to make your case and put them behind bars."

Kate glanced at her phone pulled from her pocket.

"I have to meet someone. A friend is bringing her daughter to visit in forty-five minutes, so I need to return to the hotel, plus I'm hungry since I've been running around a dog show ring all day. I need to leave now in order to have time to get my dogs settled. Let me know if you need my help bringing these men down. By the way, these people have access to tech equipment allowing them access to all your information. You may need to work this low tech."

Kate stood as did Harry, Des, and two other agents. Bullock stood as well to shake her hand. They left the room and returned through the building to Charlie.

Entering the hotel and crossing the lobby, Kate spotted her favorite waiter lurking near the entrance to the restaurant. She gave him a faint nod with an eye roll pointing up then said to Harry in a clear voice, "Why not order room service? I'm going to take a shower, so make it in about twenty minutes."

They entered the elevator, and when they reached the room, Kate had all the dogs go into their crates with treats, and Harry told Des he'd call if necessary. He called room service while Kate grabbed clean clothes and headed to the bathroom. She came out dressed in blue jeans, a T-shirt with the National logo on it, and sneakers. Then there was a knock. Harry checked the peephole then opened the door to a woman and a pretty young blonde girl.

# Chapter Thirty-Seven
*Thursday, late afternoon*

Kate stepped forward. "Hi, I'm Kate Killoy. You must be Jane, and this is Sasha. I'm so glad you're here." She showed them into the room and introduced Harry. Kate asked about their drive, what Sasha was learning in school and her favorite subject and what she did for fun.

The young girl was chattering away, though eyeing the dogs eagerly, when another knock came at the door and a voice said, "Room service."

Jane's gaze darted to the door as she jumped to her feet. Harry opened the door. The waiter had pushed the cart as far as the middle of the room, when he looked up and stopped. Jane reached out. "It's you, but you don't look like yourself."

"You are exactly the same, just as beautiful as the day I fell in love with you." He pulled Jane into his arms hugging her and kissing her hair and face.

"Mommy? Why are you kissing that man?" Sasha's uncertain voice caused the couple to look down. Kate watched the Coyote with tears streaming from his eyes squat down and reach out with a finger to touch his daughter's cheeks. Jane stooped down next to her and asked in a quiet voice, "What is the secret you and I share we don't tell anyone else?"

Sasha stared at her. "One day Daddy will come home."

Jane smiled and said, "Correct. And you know what? Today is the day we've been waiting for. Today is the day your daddy comes home. Sasha, this is your daddy."

The girl's saucer-like eyes took in her mother's smiling face with tears flowing down her cheeks and the smile on the face of the man who was crying as well and asked, "Are you sad to come home?"

"No, my Sacha, my Doch-ka. These are happy tears. I am so happy to come home to my beautiful little daughter. I've missed you so much." He stood and lifted the girl in his arms holding her tight while she reached out to wipe the tears from his cheeks.

Kate pulled the cart over to the desk and started unloading the tea things plus cups and plates of sandwiches. She poured tea in the cups and took the plates and asked Sacha if she was hungry. What the girl really wanted, was to play with the puppy. So Kate invited Jane and the Coyote to sit together on the bed. She handed Jane a plate of finger sandwiches and offered her a cup of tea the Coyote held for her. Then Kate put sandwiches on her plate, poured her tea,. and lifted the latch on Quinn's crate door. Quinn immediately ran to the girl and started to jump When Kate barked out, "No jump," the puppy's four feet hit the ground, but it didn't stop him from snuggling up to the girl and accepting her hugs and petting.

Kate watched the man for a minute while trying to decide something. Finally, she asked, "Roger, or do I use your real name?"

"Roger will do."

"I know you'll want to spend all your time with your family since you're reunited, but I was wondering if you planned to stay to the end of the show?"

"You said the shooter who killed Krystyn has been found, but what about his puppet master? The man I saw in the video was only a drone, carrying out orders. They have not caught the man behind Krystyn's murder. What are the chances he'll be found by the end of the show?"

"Chances are very good. We have an idea who he is, but just need the proof. We know why they wanted the book."

"I'll stay through Saturday then, though after I return this cart, I'll stop posing as a waiter."

"Terrific, because what I really need is a dog handler."

A look of astonishment came over his face as he turned to the dogs resting in their crates.

"No, not for my guys. I saw Krystyn entered Pavlik as a special. Maeve won't be able to show him since she'll need to take Liam. The major couldn't manage to show him. Pavlik is a magnificent dog, and he was Krystyn's pride and joy out of Liam's father and her bitch Darragh. The Best of Breed judge is Thomas Penneman. Would you handle Pavlik?"

He turned to Jane and asked, "Would you like to see what I use to do for a living? Could you stay until Saturday?"

"Yes, we'd love to see you show the dogs. You had to keep it secret before so I never saw it. I want to see you do this dog thing you love so much."

"There's your answer, Kate. If the major agrees, I'd be honored to take Pavlik into the ring."

The reunited family left about twenty minutes later, and Kate settled in with her laptop on the bed. Harry moved next to her and just sat for a minute. Finally, Kate said, "Penny for your thoughts."

"I think I fully understand what you meant by partners. But for the macho slip when I went back into Special Agent with Attitude mode, please accept my apology, I want to tell you the last two days, working beside you to figure this out have been wonderful. You don't realize how much talent you have for solving criminal puzzles."

"It's what Gramps used to tell me. He really wanted me to go into the business, but he finally accepted my choice."

"Well, I would love to having your input as I grow my business. But the question is how do we end this in two days so we can go home in peace."

"If Levasseur is confirmed as Secretary of State, he'll be free to make the deals outlined in the plan both harming this country financially and endangering us. The way it's set up, nobody will see it coming until it's too late. Did you recognize the names on the list?"

"Yes, they are all connected through large financial control systems like the World Bank, the International Fund for Agricultural Development, the European Investment Bank, and the CAF - Development Bank of Latin America. There may be more but those are the ones I can think of off the top of my head. Their plan is insidious, affecting them all, and I doubt anyone would spot it before it's too late to stop. Millions of people will be hurt. That the men involved are all 'above reproach,' will make it even harder. It does explain, if they assume you got the information from Krystyn and you're a Killoy, why you're their worst nightmare. Once they realized Krystyn had read the plan naming them and kept it secret, giving the information only to you, their targets were clear. They have murdered Krystyn. And now you are the only one who stands between them and success."

"Except I'm no longer the only one with the knowledge. The FBI and NSA have it. I hope they figure out how to stop this before I'm dead." She reached for Harry and snuggled, taking comfort from his closeness. A knock sounded at the door, and Des announced himself.

Harry opened the door to their protection unit."You've been invited to dinner by Captain Glasmann to thank you for saving G's life. We're all invited. Kate smiled and got her tote, gave small snacks to the dogs who'd be fed later, and joined them.

Everyone was waiting when Kate and Harry arrived in the lobby. A minute later, they headed out the main door and were ushered into a waiting town car. In barely five minutes, they were being shown into a private room of what appeared to be a very exclusive restaurant.

A man who resembled a slightly younger version of the captain, but could only be the chef, arrived and made suggestions for their meal. It all sounded wonderful, especially since an assortment of appetizers arrived before he'd even finished telling them what they'd be eating this evening. Harry began loading a plate for Kate with shrimp cocktail, stuffed mushroom caps, pâté de foie gras, mini quiches with asparagus, and mini zucchini with goat cheese tarts. When dinner arrived, it was filet mignon with a rich balsamic glaze, roasted baby potatoes, and fresh green beans lightly sautéed in butter with basil and garlic accompanied by an appropriate wine. As soon as it was served, all conversation ended, and the only sounds were small sighs. Dessert was a simple raspberry sorbet with candied mint leaves accompanied by delicate butter cookies.

"It would be a desecration to discuss what's been happening here after such a wonderful meal," Agent Brownridge said. "I've reserved the conference room for the evening, if everyone will join us. My people have come up with some new information." Everyone agreed, and the chef entered the room to ask how they'd enjoyed the meal and accepted their raves with a smile.

The captain finally introduced him as his "baby" brother who was the pride of the family." The captain went on to explain his brother owed him the dinner. Apparently, though his brother was a great chef and as tall as the captain, he also was a klutz, so Glasmann filled in coaching both the basketball and baseball teams where his nephews and nieces played. Plus, if for any reason he couldn't make a game, he could marshal a whole force to cover for him.

"My children prefer it that way," the chef said modestly with a shrug.

Back at the hotel and somewhat relaxed after the wonderful dinner, Kate and Harry, Glasmann, their protection detail, Brownridge, the major, and Maeve joined Bullock and the team from the FBI, plus a group of men who were introduced as being from FinCEN, the Financial Crimes Enforcement Network. They all gathered in the conference room. Kate recognized FinCEN as being the part of the Treasury Department, specializing in domestic and international financial crimes. Her father had told her they were like bloodhounds. Once they got the scent, nothing would stop them.

Kate, after listening to the money men, had to agree with her father's assessment. She was questioned up one side and down the other. They went over her background, her family, the fact she was a designer who showed dogs, her friendship with Krystyn, why Krystyn had trusted her with the information and more until she felt as though she'd been laundered with an extra spin cycle. What amazed them most was the fact Kate had been the one to find the code and figure out the key.

Harry spoke up, telling of Kate's friendship with Krystyn who knew of her special talent in seeing patterns. She had known, if push came to shove, Kate would figure it out. Maeve told the group Krystyn used to create puzzles Kate had to solve. She understood Kate's reasoning as well as her strong moral compass, and Maeve believed it was the reason Krystyn chose her.

When the round of questioning began for the fourth time, Kate couldn't hide a yawn. She'd had very little sleep last night, showed dogs all day, had the emotional family reunion, a dinner crying out for a siesta, and hours of questions being asked over and over again. All she wanted to do was feed her dogs and go to sleep. Saving the world's economy wasn't even on her top ten list. It was Bullock who stepped in and called a halt. "This lady is still a target for these men. She has to appear in the ring tomorrow in order to draw out the people behind this."

Everyone stood and began moving toward the door. Kate walked over to the major asking to speak to him for a minute. Harry watched them talk and as the major listened, a smile lit up his face. The major reached out and gave Kate a hug. Then both joined the exodus. When they reached the room, Harry and Kate quickly fed the dogs then Des and one agent stayed with Kate while Harry and the other took the dogs out. Kate cleaned the bowls and straightened up the room while the men spoke quietly. As soon as the dogs returned, the agents moved next door and Kate changed into pj's brushed her teeth, and slid into bed.

Harry tucked her in and bent to kiss her, only to find she was already asleep.

Harry stared at her a minute and then took out his phone and called Sadie. He gave her a rough outline of the game and the players and told her what he needed. He suggested, due to time constraints, she give Seamus and Satu a call and put them to work. They had the software. After chatting for a few more minutes, he said goodbye and headed to bed. It took a while for him to stop watching Kate and let sleep take him.

# Chapter Thirty-Eight
*Friday, morning*

Harry tried to be quiet bringing the dogs back from their walk, but Kate woke to not only the sound of dogs but a room full of agents. Quinn, seeing she was awake, bounded over, and with a jump and crawl made it up onto the bed to lick Kate's face all over. Of course, the rules then got tossed out, and soon Kate was diving under the covers as four Samoyeds tried to kiss her at the same time. When she stopped laughing, she ordered in a muffled voice from her blanket cave, "Everybody off." Liam and Shelagh bounded off immediately, but Quinn refused to budge until his dad, who was straddling Kate for her protection, knocked him to the floor and jumped after him. Kate peeked out and said, "Thanks, Dillon." Across the room she saw Harry, Des, three men, and two women whom she assumed by their similar demeanor were agents. "Good morning, everyone. Hope you enjoyed the show, but I've got to get dressed."

The woman agent standing by the open closet door reached up and took out a garment bag with a tag on it. "Friday, right?"

Kate bounded out of bed, took the bag, and said thanks as she slipped into the bathroom. The sound of the shower came two seconds after she closed the door.

Harry nodded to Des, and they all moved over to the desk where Harry filled them in on what he'd set in motion last night. He wanted Des to contact Glasmann and get him to keep his people out of sight until they were needed.

Kate came out, her curls still slightly wet, lipstick her only makeup, fiddling with the strap of her vest. "These vests were never meant to fit under normal clothes," she complained.

The woman agent closest to her reached for her shoulder. "It's twisted, hold on." She fiddled for a few seconds and then patted Kate on the shoulder. "Better?"

"Much, thanks." Kate inspected the group by the desk. "I hope you're coming up with a good plan to catch these people because I've probably lost ten pounds running around the dog show ring this week wearing this vest."

"We're doing our best, love," Harry said, walking over and giving her a hug.

"Fine. Let's get Charlie over to the site and heat up some of Gram's blueberry crumble for breakfast. I'm starving and need a cup of tea." She grabbed the leads off Harry's bed and released the dogs. The adult dogs came to sit in front of Kate, waiting for their leads. Quinn went to greet everyone, not knowing where to turn first, like a kid at Christmas. Des finally scooped up the puppy, took the fourth lead from Kate, and clipped it to his collar. "Okay, Quinn, time to go." When he set him down, the puppy moved quickly to the door and sat. Everyone laughed.

Harry's phone buzzed as they parked by the show building. Kate looked at him, and he signaled it was Sadie and answered. After making a few grunts, he smiled, said thanks, and told her he'd get back to her later. Kate defrosted two of the coffee cakes. Since they were eight in all with the two of them and the six agents, she figured there wouldn't be any leftovers. Harry and Des set up the outside exercise pen, giving the dogs some space to stretch their legs.

Kate had kept up a chatter with the other agents, telling them what a great cook her grandmother was and how she'd taught all of them, but her brother Will was the best. He was catering the wedding. Then she filled them in on the fact his career was to be part of Killoy and Killoy Forensic Accountants rather than a chef. She explained the rest of the family were mathematicians like Harry. "Good thing he found someone who understood all the mumbo-jumbo he talked."

Kate laughed and told them she was teaching Harry to speak dog.

When the last speck of the blueberry and peach crumbles had disappeared, they all headed inside. She put the dogs away then needed to use the restroom, so she and the two female agents whose names were Anna and Susan, headed out.

Harry's phone buzzed. The flights would land in

fifteen minutes. He checked the judging schedule posted at the ring entrance with the number of entries. The judging would start in ten minutes. With the three puppy classes and American Bred, it would be at least forty-five minutes before Kate was due in the ring. It would give the men time to find a taxi and get to the show. Harry crossed his fingers his plan would work.

Kate came back laughing with the female agents. Studying him, she grinned, and Harry had a feeling his former co-workers were telling tales out of school. Kate put on her lab coat and opened Shelagh's crate. The bitch quickly put her front feet on the grooming table, and Harry boosted her up. Maeve appeared at her side, picked up a second pin brush, and began working the opposite side from Kate. Shelagh switched from trying to snuggle Kate while she worked to snuggling Maeve. The bitch was a consummate flirt.

Harry watched the ring. The twelvemonth to eighteen-month-old puppy bitches were going into the ring, but there were only four of them. Harry pulled out his phone and once more reviewed the faces of the men. When he checked the ring again, he saw the puppies leaving and the three bitches entered in American Bred go in. Harry reached into Kate's tote bag and pulled out the armband with Shelagh's number and slipped it up her arm. She reached into a plastic bag and pulled out a few treats, hiding them from Shelagh, even though the bitch knew the "work first treat later" rule. Harry lifted the Sam off the table and, before he could tell her to shake, she had become a blur of hair, feet, and ears. When she stopped, she was magnificent.

He gave Kate a kiss for luck and walked with her to ringside. He caught the sight of three men in expensive business suits coming through the door and saw them spotting Secretary of State Nominee, Levasseur. Cathy and Jordy came to stand next to him, Cathy filming Kate in the ring. Harry was startled from his concentration quickly spotting Rufus approaching. Trying to watch three directions at once, he grabbed Rufus's arm and whispered instructions to him. He saw Kate had stepped into position for Shelagh to be examined, standing about three feet in front of her bitch. His eyes were distracted by movement above him where three agents were joking and laughing as they headed toward the control booth. Harry glanced at Kate moving Shelagh and then swung his glance to Levasseur, who was arguing with the three men at ringside. The judge was working quickly and, before Levasseur realized he'd been tricked, the judge was gaiting the class and pointing to Kate for first place.

Kate came out of the ring, and Jordy stepped up to take her ribbon and trophy while Anna, Susan, Maeve, and Cathy all hugged her. The open bitch class began, and Kate saw Joceline Levasseur enter. Her bitch was excellent and would be tough competition for the points. Kate swiftly surveyed the rest of the class and decided Joceline's bitch was definitely the best. She scanned the ring and spotted Mr. Levasseur watching his daughter. He wasn't smiling, in fact, he was furious. Suddenly she felt some sympathy for her nemesis. Her world was about to fall apart. The class had a dozen bitches, but the judge worked quickly. When he finished judging, he walked down the row, giving them one more inspection then put Joceline at the front of the line and pulled two other bitches in behind her. Next, he had them all move around the ring and pointed to Joceline's bitch for first.

"This is it," Kate said to herself as she stepped into the ring to stand behind Joceline, followed by the other class winners. The judge gaited them around the ring together. He then moved them up and back one at a time. Kate glimpsed Levasseur as Joceline moved her bitch. He was focused on Kate, and their eyes met. She stared into his furious eyes, squared her shoulders, and lifted her head. As Kate moved Shelagh, she noticed people crowded ing the edge of the ring by the man. She trotted around the ring, giving Shelagh the entire lead to do what she wanted.

The judge worked through the other bitches quickly. He then asked Kate and Joceline to move their bitches across the ring and back together. As they made the turn, Kate saw Levasseur reach into his pocket and pull something out. The judge returned them to the same order and pointed to Joceline for Winner's Bitch. He handed her the ribbon and trophy and the second place open bitch entered the ring. After moving the newcomer, he pointed to Kate for Reserve. She stepped to the judge's table. He handed her the ribbon and trophy, saying to her it was a hard choice between her bitch and the winner's bitch.

Joceline pushed her way back into the ring and stood in front of Kate. "Well, here I am, Kate. I thought I'd give you a chance to congratulate me for winning." Kate held out her hand to congratulate Joceline. The other girl grinned and gripped her hand, waving her ribbon over her head. It was then Kate saw Levasseur holding the gun. He raised his hand and pointed it at her just as Joceline stepped between them. Kate shoved the girl out of the way as he fired.

The world erupted with screams, shouts, and barking. Kate flew backward, shot. She hit the floor and didn't move. The FBI quickly grabbed Levasseur, his co-conspirators, and his thugs. Harry dashed into the ring and scooped up Kate.

Joceline screamed, "Kate's dead." She stared at her father in horror. Anna moved to the girl's side, spoke to her quietly, and then led her from the ring. Harry carried Kate out of the building, as the ring steward announced while taking the judge's arm and leading him away that there would be a thirty-minute delay in judging.

He carried Kate to Charlie, followed by an entourage of tearful followers. Rufus took the keys from Harry's pocket and opened the door then jumped lowered the table in the banquette and flipping pillows created a bed. Harry laid her gently down, and then Cathy eased him aside. She pulled open Kate's jacket and unbuttoned her blouse only to find the bulletproof vest with a deep dent in it.

Kate groaned. "Arggg, I hurt."

"Where do you hurt, Kate?" Cathy asked.

"My head and my chest ache, especially my chest. I feel like I've been kicked by a horse."

Cathy unhitched one side of the vest and lifted it

enough to check her patient. She glanced at Harry. "Could be a cracked rib, but I think from the position of the bruising, it's probably soft tissue. That being said, she's going to hurt for a while."

Jordy pushed in next to Kate, tears streaming down his face. "Don't be dead, Kate. Don't be dead."

Kate took his hand, and forced her eyes open. "I'm not dead, Jordy. I hurt but I'll be all right."

Maeve stepped away from Kate's side, took a breath, and stepped to the doorway to reassure everyone Kate would be okay. Then she turned to the tearful boy and said, "Jordy, I need your help. Padraig and I need to get the dogs and put everything away. Could you take care of Quinn? He might be frightened."

"Yes, I'll come. Quinn is good at recovering from Kate being shot at. It's happened before, and I played with him, and he felt better."

Maeve took the boy's hand and headed out.

Cathy sighed and said, "Bad timing. The annual meeting is tonight. The election. It was already messed up because of the hacking, and I don't know what this is going to do to it."

Kate sighed and groaned then frowned at Harry. "I've got to go to that meeting. I've got to talk to people."

"The FBI and NSA might not want details of this to get out before the charges are filed."

"Tell them they can come up with an acceptable statement by seven tonight, or I will. Leaving people afraid of going into the ring tomorrow, thinking they might be shot, would destroy the National. This is my club. I'm not going to let it happen."

Harry nodded and pulled out his phone. Then he stepped outside to talk to Des who told him apparently the powers that be had decided something had to be said. The club president had announced people would get answers at the annual meeting that night. Harry ended the call and saw Padraig, Maeve, and Jordy approaching. The boy was holding Kate's rosette and trophy above his head as Quinn tried to grab them. Harry opened the door to Charlie, and dogs, people, and paraphernalia were all loaded inside. He drove carefully to the hotel and then let the volunteers handle getting the dogs inside while he took care of Kate. Once everything was in the room, Harry chased everyone out and took Kate into the bathroom. He helped her get everything off down to her sports bra and panties. "If you need any help in there, just holler," he said, laughing and nodding at the shower.

Kate finished undressing and stepped into the shower, letting the water flow over her, taking away some of her pain. She stayed there until her skin wrinkled then dried herself, dressed in jeans and a sweatshirt, and went out to find Harry to help her with her shoes. Toweling dry her hair and finger combing it was the best she could achieve.

Images from the afternoon filled her mind. She remembered, as she flew backward from the force of the bul let, she'd hit something soft before her head met the concrete. She now realized she'd fallen against Shelagh. When she told Harry, he opened the bitch's crate, waking her. She bounced over to Kate, licking her face and snuggling. Kate ran her hands over her and asked Harry to move her up and back. Normal. She sighed and sent her back to her crate with a few kisses and a thank-you.

After a supper of sandwiches, tea, and pain pills in the room, they fed the dogs, and Des showed up to help exercise them and get them into Charlie. Brownridge had arrived and escorted Kate to the motor home. She explained the necessity of speaking to the group tonight. He agreed and said they'd decided Des should do the talking for the government.

# Chapter Thirty-Nine
*Friday, night and Saturday*

When they got to the venue, so many people had come, it required the meeting be moved to the main room beside the rings. Kate, Harry, the agents, Maeve, Padraig, the major, Cathy, Rufus, and Jordy all sat in the first row. People stopped to ask Kate if she was all right every other minute until the president called the meeting to order. He quickly worked through the Robert's Rules of Order requirements, and then he said, "A few hours ago we had something happen here, during the show, which needs to be explained. I am happy to see Kate Killoy alive and able to talk to you this evening."

Kate stood and slowly walked to the podium. She turned to the group filling all the available chairs and smiled. "Hello, everybody. As you might guess, I'm happy to be here tonight." Everyone laughed. "The past two weeks have been very unusual, especially for our Samoyed Club. You all received an email supposedly sent out from our friend Krystyn Machnicki. She did not send it. It was sent, using a hacking program, from a group of criminals who wanted to force her to become so upset she would change her plans to go out of state and evaluate a litter, and instead would remain in her house. The shooter then broke in, and she was murdered. Before I continue, I'd like for you all to stand and have a moment of silence where you think of all the wonderful things Krystyn has done for this club over the years." Kate bowed her head and, when she raised it, she turned to the major and said, "Major, we all want you to know how much we loved Krystyn."

Then, changing her tone, Kate got to what everyone wanted to know. "The reason Krystyn was killed involved the fact she was a former NSA agent who had information regarding the security of our country. The man who killed her has been captured and identified by her dogs. The people behind the killer, and the shooters who have gone after me this week knew if this information came to light, they and the plot they had created would be destroyed. Before Krystyn died, she told her husband if anything happened to her, I had the answer. Essentially saying, I could tell him the information. The problem was, I didn't know anything. However, during this week, we were able to figure out where the information was, were able to decode it, and were further able to capture all of the players involved in this, and they have been arrested. I have been working with some wonderful people from the NSA and FBI, who have been telling me all sorts of neat stories about my fiancé who was a former FBI agent. Because of my fiancé's former profession, one of my early wedding presents was a bulletproof vest." The crowd all laughed. "This kept me alive today—though I'll tell you, even with a vest, it hurts to get shot.

I don't want to extend this meeting so I will tell you

if you have questions regarding your safety, I have brought with me tonight Agent Wetherly Brownridge of the NSA who worked with Krystyn and Special Agent Deshi Xiang from the FBI. Stand up, gentlemen, so they can see you. These men will not be allowed to tell you anything about the crime, but they can reassure those of you who worry about competing for Best of Breed tomorrow. But, just think, you will all be able to brag you attended a National where a crime against America was thwarted. Now I'd like to thank our president for this time and return the meeting to him."

The rest of the meeting went quickly, and the vote went through with the original slate by acclamation. They spoke about judges' education and the breed standard, but people were more interested in wrapping it up and getting a chance to chat. Harry had wrapped his arm around Kate with her head resting on his shoulder. She was close to sleep when it ended. After the meeting, Des spoke to the group, stating there would still be a police presence as well as FBI until the end of the show for their peace of mind.

Kate slept fitfully due to her bruised ribs and nightmares. Harry ended up climbing in with her about three o'clock and holding her. Without waking, she relaxed, and they both slept until the pups told them it was time to get up. Kate reached to pull on her jeans as Harry did the same, but his hand stopped her. "We can't be sure they've rounded up all the shooters Levasseur hired. Stay here and get in your shower, I'll take out the pups." Kate decided not to argue when her body rebelled as she stood. As Harry left, Anna arrived. Kate asked for the latest news.

"They've got all the shooters and low level thugs in jail here. The foursome behind this is on their way to DC as we speak. They are being held on the commission of a federal crime, though Levasseur also has been charged with murder and attempted murder, and the others are being considered as accessories to murder."

"What happened to Joceline Levasseur? Nobody said anything at the meeting last night."

"She's left the show. The shock of seeing her father shoot you and almost shoot her by accident has her really messed up. She left her dogs with a handler and took a plane out. She'll probably call to thank you for saving her life."

Kate laughed. "Not in this lifetime. But I'm glad she's okay. She was gone by the time I was conscious."

Kate grabbed the final suit bag out of the closet and ducked into the bathroom. She was showered and dressed by the time Harry appeared with Des and G in tow, telling her the dogs were comfortable in Charlie. G's head wore a bandage, and his arm was in a sling, but otherwise he was fine. They all decided to meet over at the site for breakfast. Kate let them know there was plenty of food still in Charlie's freezer. "I hope there aren't any shooters left because my vest has a decided dent and I can't wear it."

After a delicious breakfast, of fruit and coffee cakes in Charlie, they all moved into the venue. Kate began brushing out Dillon, and Harry put Liam on the table, but after a few minutes, Maeve took over. The major walked in with an entourage featuring Cathy, Rufus, and Jordy with Cathy's bitch special Bliss and Yerik and Roger Krylov, aka the Coyote, along with his wife, Jane, and daughter Sasha with Pavlik. Roger and Jane came over to check Kate was okay. They'd heard last night she'd been shot. She smiled. "Kevlar is a wonderful thing."

Everyone pitched in with grooming. By the time the National Anthem was played for the start of the day's judging, they were ready. Kate slipped off her lab coat; Harry slid her armband over the sleeve of her royal-blue jacket and then lifted Dillon down to shake. They all headed for the ring, filing in as their numbers were called. Liam and Dillon had sequential numbers with Pavlik only four dogs away. There were so many Samoyeds entered, they wrapped around the huge ring, doubling up in some places. It took about fifteen minutes for the judge and steward to check everyone in and go over the rules for dividing the class. Then all but the first group of champion dogs paraded out to relax. It would be a long day. The steward's assistant, working quickly, listed the armband numbers beside each group designation. Dillon and Pavlik would be in group three, and Liam would be in the final group along with other Veteran class winners and the Working Samoyed winners and the Winner's Dog and Winner's Bitch. Roger came over and sat by her, quietly asking about the outcome of the capture yesterday.

"I never asked," Kate said turning to Harry who joined them. "Why did those three men show up and get in a fight with Levasseur right before he shot me?"

"Levasseur emailed them and told them they had to come. He just didn't know he did it." Harry's smile became infectious, and Kate grinned.

"Who sent the bogus emails?" Roger asked.

"Seamus and Satu. Kate's brother and his friend. They've got all the fancy software."

"So what began this crisis ended it. They were hoisted on their own petard."

Soon, it was their turn. Kate and Roger joined the others entering the ring. The judge was quick and thorough. Dillon managed to turn on the charm, but the one who startled Kate was Pavlik. She'd seen Roger handle dogs when she was a child, but he had taken his skill to a whole new level. People actually stopped talking as eyes turned to the ring. Then the buzz of voices started when they realized the connection to Krystyn. When he began his trip around the ring, following the up and back, applause broke out. Dillon and Pavlik both made the cut. As they moved from the ring to relax while the rest of the dogs got their first examination, Roger couldn't help grinning. "It has been ten years since I've been able to do that." He walked over to the major to tell him what a great dog Pavlik was.

The judging continued through all the bitch champions and then dog and bitch winners from the Veteran, Working classes, as well as the Winners Dog and Winners bitch. Maeve moved Liam, and it was a wonderful sight. Both Roger and Kate smiled noting Liam, of all the veterans, had made the cut. Then all the champions who had made the cut in their individual groups were invited back into the ring. This time, it was all about movement. Dogs and bitches competing against each other as the judge narrowed down his list. Finally, he stopped and took a microphone, complimenting all the entrants who'd shown under him and saying what a pleasure it was to be part of this National. Then, without further fuss, he pulled out twenty Samoyeds, had them circle the ring, and quickly made his selection. Best of Breed went to Pavlik, Cathy's bitch Bliss went Best Opposite, a dog who Kate didn't know was Best of Winners, Dillon was Select Dog, and Joyce's bitch Lexi was Select Bitch. Liam was Best Veteran and an Award of Merit winner, and Kate saw both Lily with Quinn's mother Katia and Ruthi Stern's Ziva were included in the Awards of Merit lineup. There was a standing ovation when the judge presented Pavlik the Best in Show ribbon.

Kate was gently hugged by Harry, and then they turned to congratulate the winners. The major was hugging Pavlik, tears streaming down his face while he shook Roger's hand. Roger was also being hugged by his wife and had lifted his daughter into his arms. Joyce, Lily, and Cathy were hugging each other, and Jordy was circling the group, whooping. The group finished with photographs and discussed celebrating at the annual banquet.

Kate buried her face in Harry's chest, giving way to tears for a few minutes. He pulled her away from the group, lifted her chin, and said, "Do you want to go home?"

Kate wiped her eyes, smiled, and nodded and said, "Yes, please."

Harry asked Padraig when they were flying home and was told they had a morning flight. Kate reached into her bag and pulled out their tickets for the banquet that night. "Harry and I want to head home. Would you two go to the banquet and represent the Killoys?" Padraig nodded and said he'd be at the hotel to help them pack in half an hour.

Kate and Harry loaded the gear from the show site, went back to the hotel, quickly packed their bags, and then loaded a luggage cart with suitcases, crates, and dog paraphernalia. While Harry and Padraig packed Charlie, Kate went to pay the bill. As she walked back toward Charlie, she saw a group of people gathered. Harry was standing with Des, Brownridge, G, and the agents who'd known Harry from the DC office, along with Roger and his family, Joyce, Lily, Cathy, Rufus, Jordy, Maeve, Padraig, and the major. Kate thanked each of them for all the help they'd been keeping her alive, getting her a laugh, and told them she looked forward to seeing them next month at the wedding. Then she walked over and gave the major a hug and a kiss on the cheek and repeated the hugs down the row, until her fiancé scooped her up into his arms and placed her on the seat in Charlie. Running around to his door, Harry climbed in, started the engine, and amid cheers and waves, and toots on Charlie's horn, they left the show and headed home.

*Dear Reader,*

*I hope you enjoyed reading this latest adventure with Kate and Harry as much as I enjoyed writing it. There is nothing quite like a National where you compete against so many excellent dogs in your breed. If you are lucky enough to have a dog that wins Best of Breed, it is the highest honor that can be achieved. It's not something that is ever forgotten, which I can tell you from personal experience, even many years later.*

*In the next book of the series, you'll be invited to a wedding. It's Thanksgiving weekend, Kate and Harry are getting married and all their friends will be attending. Unfortunately there is someone who is determined to crash the wedding with one goal in mind—to murder both the bride and the groom.*

*If you enjoyed National Security, I hope you will go online to the book's page on Amazon and leave a short comment in the review section. I read all the comments and often take the advice about characters which is given.*

*Until next time,*

*Peggy*

www.ingramcontent.com/pod-product-compliance
Lightning Source LLC
Chambersburg PA
CBHW020606310726
48979CB00008B/1372/J

*9780996453189*